Crestwood Falls

Emma-Louise Smith

ISBN: 978-1-0686533-4-6

DEDICATION

For those with magic in their veins.

PROLOGUE

A second knock echoed in the hallway and up the staircase as Freya ran down the two flights of stairs, from her attic room. Somebody was clearly impatient, and their frustration nagged at her.

"I'm coming, I'm coming," she shouted, hoping it would be loud enough for the persistent knocker to stop knocking. She reached the bottom of the stairs and looked through the frosted glass as she plucked the keys off their hanger. Great, just what she needed. Plastering a smile on her face she opened the door.

"Hello, Jacob, my parents aren't in." She smiled her sweet, sickly smile, the one reserved for whenever she spoke to Jacob Blackfriars, head of the Coven of the Crescent Moon, of which both she and her parents were members.

"Hello, Freya, I'm here to see you I'm afraid. This is Detective Peter Waite; I have asked him to join us. May we come in?"

Freya's smile dropped, and she opened the door wider to let them through. She wracked her brain, thinking back to the previous night. Had she done something stupid while she was drunk? She couldn't remember. She groaned internally.

They went through to the living room. Jacob was a tall, thin man with a gaunt face, dark eyes and a beak-like nose. His dark hair was thinning and styled in a way that made it look greasy and unwashed.

"Please, take a seat, Freya." He motioned to the armchair.

She sat down cautiously. He was being pleasant to her, which would have been odd in any circumstance but was even odder if she was in some sort of trouble. A nervous energy started to gnaw at her stomach. She could feel something was wrong.

"What's going on?" she asked, curiously.

"I'm afraid there is no easy way for me to tell you this, so I am just going to come straight out with it. While on duty last night, your parents and two other Guardians were attacked. One of them is recovering in hospital but unfortunately your parents and the other Coven member, were killed."

Freya's vision swam, and a cold, creeping sweat climbed her spine. Surely, she had misheard.

"What?" she croaked.

"I'm sorry, Freya, both your parents are dead."

Bile rose in her throat, and she vomited on the carpet in front of her. Embarrassed, she wiped her mouth on the sleeve of her jumper.

"Can I get you a glass of water or something?" the detective asked.

"No. Thank you. But I want to know how? How does that even happen? They are Guardians." Guardians rarely, if ever, died on the job, Freya thought to herself.

"I know and you are right, but Guardians are not invincible, Freya, and they walked into a trap. We don't have all the details yet, and we are still investigating. Peter here is a good friend of the Coven and is the one looking into it for us."

"I don't understand. They were here, sitting in this room last night."

"I know it is a shock. We are all saddened by this loss. I have asked Lillian to come over later to check on you. She was the one who identified them, and she has been desperate to see you, but we felt we should tell you first."

"Can I see them? Their bodies? I must know. For certain."

Jacob looked at Peter. "Of course. I can arrange for you to come in tomorrow morning before the autopsy is done," Peter responded.

"That's arranged then. I will send a car for you, Freya. You shouldn't be driving until you have a clear head. We don't want any accidents," Jacob said, his tone final. "I must get going now, but I hope we will see you at the Coven meeting this week. We will be hosting a memorial of sorts for all three lost members. If I get any more news I will call you, and I want to reiterate how sorry I am for your loss. Your parents were exceptional Witches and people." He stood to leave.

Numbly, Freya got up, barely registering her feet moving across the carpet as she saw Jacob and Peter out. She locked the door and slid down it, her back resting against it. Trying to calm the hammering of her heart against her ribcage, Freya felt the pressure building, almost suffocating as the edges of her vision dimmed and then she was swallowed by darkness.

CHAPTER ONE

"Balance and Harmony,
Peacefulness and Ease,
By the Power of Three,
Let all Turbulence Cease."

Freya scattered the cinnamon, thyme and rosemary onto the soil of the flowerpot. She let out a breath and relaxed as she completed her work. The new flat had been thoroughly cleansed. The black pentagram on her wall offered all the protection that was necessary for her place to be safe, secure and peaceful. After everything that had happened recently, this was a fresh start. A new town a million miles away from the place she had called home.

Freya unpacked the suitcase she had brought with her. She didn't own much, just a few changes of clothes, shoes, hairbrush and toiletries, herbs, crystals, runes, tarot cards and some essential oils and candles, she had enough cash for a few weeks' rent and her Grimoire. Each generation of the family wrote their own Grimoire, but they also included spells, incantations and recipes that had passed down through the generations.

The rain pounded the window, pulling Freya from her reverie. She got up and started to put away her things into the small chest of drawers. It was getting late, and she knew that she should head to bed. Tomorrow she would have to find a job; the money she had brought with her wouldn't last forever. Luckily, she had some master coffee making skills, and this town of less than nine hundred people had three cafes so she hoped it wouldn't be too hard to find a job.

Freya woke before her alarm, feeling refreshed after a peaceful night's sleep. The rain had stopped, but a heavy watery mist covered the sleepy town. Even the glorious mountains were hidden behind the clouds. After a cup of tea and some toast, Freya showered, as Fleetwood Mac played in the background - songs that reminded her of happier times. Dressed, and ready to take on the world, Freya headed out to the coffee shop feeling confident. This small town was the opposite of the big city she had left behind.

The wind blew a gust as Freya entered the street. She pulled up the hood of her coat to shield her face from the drizzle that splattered it. Scurrying past the storefronts she realised that there was not one person around; most of the shops were closed. Freya went into all the coffee shops to leave her resume, stopping at the last one to enjoy a hot caramel latte. She found a corner seat in the window and sat down. The remains of the cold damp clinging to her clothes soon dried as the coffee sent warmth through her body. She looked around. The place was small and cosy. There were about fifteen seats in the entire cafe and vintage furniture decorated the floor and walls. Two other people were sitting having a drink. An older man who looked to be in his forties with a kind face that had a sprinkling of white dusty beard along his jaw, and a younger female with bright pink hair who faced away from Freya. Freya assumed the young woman must be the man's daughter, as they seemed comfortable and at ease with each other.

She switched her attention to the street outside. The window was starting to steam up from the humidity and warmth, a stark contrast to the scene beyond the windowpane. A few people were now milling about, wandering in and out of shops. The mist was turning into a dense fog, and she could no longer see the end of the road. A small bookshop on the opposite corner took hold of her attention. The black storefront with faded gold lettering simply read, 'Moonlight Book Emporium'. Freya decided that she would have to go and have a wander over once she had finished her drink.

As Freya left the comfort of the coffee shop, she couldn't help but notice the eerie silence. There were no cars, no buskers, and no groups of people talking on the street. A far cry from the city she had come from, Crestwood Falls was turning out to be the perfect little place she needed; quiet, small, and hidden amongst the surrounding mountains. As Freya reached the bookshop, she noticed that there were no lights on - unusual given the dullness of the day. She tried to open the door, but it was locked. Looking around she found a sign that said, 'Shop Open 6pm Until Early'. Freya smiled to herself. *Such an odd time for a shop to be open.* She decided to come back later.

The rest of the day passed quite quickly. Enjoying the warmth of her apartment, Freya was reading on the sofa when the doorbell chimed. She opened the door to find the waitress that she had seen earlier in Marly's Café standing there.

"Hello. Marly has asked me to bring this around for you." The waitress passed Freya an envelope.

"Oh, thank you," Freya replied.

"No problem. Have a nice day," the waitress replied as she turned to leave.

Freya opened the note as she walked back up the stairs, it was a letter from Marly offering her a job for four days a week. Smiling, Freya placed the letter on her counter and went back to her book.

The rain had returned and as Freya headed out to the bookshop it was almost torrential. Hesitating in the doorway she pulled up her hood and headed out into the dark street. Moonlight Book

Emporium stood out against the black night like a shining beacon. The bookshop oozed old world charm. The window displays were made up of beautiful vintage novels, enhanced by the strings of fairy lights that looked like twinkling stars in the night sky.

As Freya opened the door, a little bell tinkled. In the background, Sinatra played in a hushed voice over a sound system. The walls were lined with dark wood shelves filled with books ranging from old to new, and mini displays were dotted about the main floor on little tables. The floor was covered in the most luxurious red carpet, and in the corner stood a glass display case. Intrigued as to what was inside, Freya made her way straight over. To her surprise, it contained a copy of Bram Stoker's 'Dracula', and other books on supernatural beings that looked very old.

"Nice wellies," said a voice from behind her. Freya jumped and turned around. Standing in front of her was a tall, well-built man with hair as white as snow which flopped down over his forehead, and eyes so blue they were almost transparent. He was utterly beautiful. Freya blushed, as she realised she was blatantly staring.

"Thank you. My inner child was also happy with the choice." She smiled at him. Freya was wearing a pair of bright pink wellies with little flowers - much to her embarrassment.

"I'm Valorian, I own this rather magical establishment." He held his hand to Freya to shake.

Valorian. Even the way he said his name was sexy.

"Hey, I'm Freya. I've just moved here. This is a great store, such an eclectic mix."

"Thank you, it's been in the family for generations." Valorian smiled.

"Wow, that's great. I love the vintage collection you have here. They must be incredibly old." Freya looked down at the books through the cabinet.

"It is one of the oldest books I have." He pointed towards the copy of Dracula. "It's a first edition, which was given to a member of my family in the 1800s and has survived all this time. The other books are almost as old. We have a thing about the supernatural and have researched it for many centuries." Valorian cast his eyes towards the other books in the display.

"That's really interesting, why the supernatural?" Freya looked at Valorian expectantly.

"Heh well, it's just something which interests us. Lore and legend tell us that there may be more than just humans around us - if you are to believe in the myth that is. Even if we can't yet prove anything else exists, yet." Valorian started walking towards the till, moving with a confident, charming swagger that made Freya's cheeks warm as she watched him.

What was it with this guy? She felt like a schoolgirl; her blood sang with his presence. Freya continued to look around - anything to avoid staring at Valorian - and found an Herbal Encyclopedia which she picked up. Hers hadn't managed to make the journey with her due to the rush in which she had left. Walking to the counter Freya placed the book down, said, "I'd like to buy this please," and pushed it towards Valorian.

"Great book choice; herbs are fascinating things," he replied.

"Yes, they are, and so much can be done with them." She gave him a quick smile hoping he wouldn't probe into her reasons for wanting the book.

Valorian placed the book into a black canvas bag with silver sparkly stars all over it and the shop logo on the front

It fit the store so well, Freya thought. She took the book and was heading towards the door, when suddenly Valorian appeared to her left. She hadn't seen him coming and it startled her.

"So, Freya, are you busy tomorrow evening?"

Hearing him say her name made her feel weak at the knees.

"I'm working at Marly's Cafe until eleven pm."

He let out a small laugh.

"They finally found someone to work the late shift. Marly has been looking for a while. If you fancy it, when your shift has finished, you could come over and I'll show you the rest of my vintage book collection." He raised an eyebrow at her as he awaited her response.

"I'd love that, thank you. It would be interesting to see what else you've got back there." She nodded towards the back door.

"Fantastic, it's a date!" He grabbed her hand and gave it a kiss.

Freya felt like her body had been set on fire and doused in ice water at the same time. She continued to walk out the door, trying to exude a calm demeanour - which was the opposite to how she was feeling inside. She had never felt anything like that before, such heat and coldness at the same time. It was as if her body was repelled by his touch, but her blood craved more.

Freya returned home and climbed into bed. Sleep came easily with thoughts of Valorian and their date tomorrow.

CHAPTER TWO

A beam of sunlight peeked through the curtains and stirred Freya awake. Checking the clock on the bedside table, she got a shock at how late it was as it blinked 11:16am. The sound of rain persisted against her window, but she made her way to it and pulled back the curtain. The rain was lighter than it had been the previous day and for the first time since her arrival she could see the mountains that looked on in the distance, masquerading as fierce protectors of the small town. Freya heard the mail drop through her box and stood to collect it. Not expecting anything for herself she was surprised to see a black envelope with her name written across the front in silver italics. Carefully opening it she found a card which simply read:

'Can you bring me a large black coffee and a jam doughnut when you come tonight, please? From V.'

The card made her smile, and she felt a rush of warmth flood her cheeks. She wondered how he had known where she lived - although she reasoned that Crestwood Falls was a small town, and everyone always knows everything in small towns.

The day passed quickly. Freya had already collected her uniform for her shift that night. As she put it on and applied the finishing touches to her make-up and hair, she realised she was nervous, not about her shift but about seeing Valorian afterwards. She blew out the candles and headed out the door. The last remnants of the weak sun were dipping behind the mountains as she made her way down the cobbled street. Even though it was only 3:40 pm, the dark evenings were still creeping in quickly, despite the winter solstice promising a return to lighter nights.

The coffee shop was quiet when she arrived, with one person sitting in the corner and a lady she didn't recognise standing behind the counter.

"Hello, I'm looking for Marly. I'm Freya, I'm due to start my shift tonight." Freya smiled at the lady.

"Well, hey there, Marly at your service. It's nice to finally meet you."

"Likewise, thank you."

Pop around darlin', there is a room back there to drop your stuff in, next to the office."

Freya ducked behind the counter, hung her coat up and put her bag on the floor out of the way before she headed back out front.

The afternoon turned to evening as Marly showed Freya everything that she would need to know. Freya was thankful that she was already accustomed to the machines, as it made things much easier. As the night steadily ticked over, Marly retreated to her office and left Freya to it. Customers dribbled in and the pace was nice and steady - not busy but with many more people in than she had seen during the day.

Marly came back out front to see how things were getting on.

"I have never seen as many people in a coffee shop this late at night as I have since I moved here. It seemed pretty quiet during the day," Freya remarked.

"That'll be about right. People here are much more active at night than during the day. Full of night owls in this town."

"Ah that explains why the bookshop opens late then I expect?" Freya asked.

"That would be it, Valorian is keeping up with the business hours." Marly smiled.

"He seems like a nice guy; he invited me over after my shift to look at some of his special collection books. He has some beautiful works there."

"He is one of the nice ones, Valorian. The shop is old, passed down through generations. Some of those books I imagine date back centuries. You're a lucky lady, he doesn't often invite people for a guided tour." Marly winked at Freya.

"Must be because I'm new. Maybe he is hoping to get another sale out of me." Freya tried to hide the blush in her voice.

"That's probably it, darlin'. Make sure he shows you his basement collection. I hear it's a marvel to behold."

"I will do. He asked me to take over a coffee and doughnut so I'm sure that should sweeten him up." Freya laughed.

"That will definitely help. Right, I'm back off to the office. Let me know if you need anything, hun."

"Will do," Freya replied.

To Freya's surprise, her shift only got busier after that, with a steady stream of customers until about 10:30pm. After putting a doughnut aside for Valorian, Freya set about cleaning up the seating areas ready to close. Thoughts of Valorian kept invading her head. There was something about him that made her feel strange, but in a good way. She couldn't pinpoint what it was, but she felt her stomach flutter with the prospect of seeing him soon. A couple of people came in to get takeout coffee and then she shut the door behind them, flipping over the closed sign. Freya made Valorian his coffee and cleaned out the machine. Once done, she popped to the office to say goodnight to Marly.

"Hi, Marly, I'm off now. I've cleaned everything up and switched the machines off."

"Great stuff, you've done well tonight, Freya, it's nice to have you onboard," Marly replied with a smile.

"Thanks, it's been fun finally getting to meet the townspeople."

"They will have been curious about you; they usually aren't that chatty, but we rarely get any new blood here."

"A couple of them mentioned the same thing. I'm glad I moved here, it's a lovely place."

"That it is, darlin', that it is. Well, you get that coffee over to the Dark Lord, he won't be happy if it goes cold," Marly said, sniggering a little as she spoke.

"See you tomorrow. Goodnight," Freya replied.

"Goodnight," Marly said as Freya shut the office door.

The night was bitter as Freya stepped into the street. The shop had kept her warm all night and the cold felt as though it had shocked her bones. Thankfully she didn't have far to walk to the bookshop, which twinkled in all its glory as she approached. The tinkle of the bell announced her entrance.

"Is that you, Freya? I thought I was about to pass out waiting for my sugary fix," a voice she recognised as Valorian's called out from somewhere out of sight.

"It certainly is. I've brought you the stuff you asked for. Nice touch with the note through the door. Not stalker-like behaviour at all." Freya smiled as she spoke.

"Ah, dear Freya, I have many talents. Stalking is just a side hobby," Valorian said as he walked towards her. He kissed her cheek and whispered, "Thank you" in her ear.

Freya felt like she would combust as his breath tickled her ear lobe. She took a step back, creating some distance between them.

"You're welcome," she croaked out. Sure that Valorian had noticed the blush in her cheeks she went over to the counter to put down the coffee and doughnut.

"How was your first shift? I bet the regulars ate you up for breakfast," Valorian asked while taking a bite of his doughnut.

"It went really well. I enjoyed getting to know everyone that came in. I've never been to a town so friendly. I'm glad I came here," Freya said.

"We are more than glad to have you," Valorian replied with a wink.

Freya rolled her eyes and smiled.

"Shall we head downstairs and look at these books then?" He motioned to the doorway.

"Oh absolutely, I'm really looking forward to it."

"Great, I'll just lock up while we are down there."

Valorian walked over and turned the closed sign and flicked the latch on the door.

The basement was not what ordinary people would call a basement. This was like a penthouse suite. The walls weren't dingy covered in mould and damp, these were a deep shade of burgundy. The fixtures and fittings were all gold. There were large bookcases along the left and right walls full of old leather-bound books, a chaise lounge just in front of one of them and a comfy brown leather sofa along the wall opposite the doorway with two end tables with big grand lamps on each of them. The room had an old world feel to it which made Freya instantly feel welcome and at home.

"Wow, this place! I think you just redefined the word 'basement' because this is not what I would call one," Freya commented and laughed.

"I guess you might be right. I had it converted properly a fair few years ago. I didn't want the books to get damaged in some damp place."

"That makes perfect sense. These look beautiful, Valorian, may I?" Freya nodded towards the books.

"Absolutely, feel free to have a good browse, that's what you are here for after all." Valorian took a seat on the sofa.

Freya walked over to the left bookcase and started scanning all the books. The majority were all supernatural based. Out of the corner of her eye Freya spotted a large black tome tucked onto the bottom shelf. There was only a sigil on the side that she recognised immediately. Protection. It was the same sigil she had tattooed on the bottom of her foot, which piqued her interest and caused a stir in her stomach.

Freya slid the book out; it was heavy and dusty. She walked over and sat next to Valorian with her legs crossed on the sofa as she looked at the front cover.

"That's an interesting book you've picked up. It is written in coded text. It has a very interesting history if you would like to hear about it?"

"I love a good mystery, please do tell." Freya turned and beamed at Valorian.

"The Book is a Grimoire that used to belong to a very powerful family of Witches. The Witches had always lived in Crestwood, generation upon generation. Speculation is that they helped keep this town hidden from non-supernatural folk. However, one night the family disappeared leaving behind all their belongings. The townsfolk tried to find them but there was no clue as to where they went or why they left. This Grimoire was given to my family for safekeeping in case the family should ever return."

"Do you think they will return one day? It's unusual for a family of Witches to leave behind their Grimoire, isn't it?"

"It is. From my research in this area, it seems the Grimoire is sacred, I can't imagine why it would be left - unless something more sinister happened and they didn't have a choice. None of the original Crestwood Witches would be alive now, so it would depend on what they passed down through the family. There was speculation as to why the family left but it is pure rumour."

"What was the rumour?" she asked, curiosity shining in her eyes.

"The youngest Witch of the family fell pregnant, which wouldn't have been bad. However, the father of the child was from a family of renowned dark Witches. Speculation is that they left the town to hide the baby from the boy's family."

"It really is fascinating and if true, very sad. To think there is so much history in one book. Something that must have been around for generations. I bet it holds so many secrets."

"Probably, though no one has been able to break the code, so we may never know. Whether you believe in supernatural beings or not, the tale is very interesting."

"Do you believe?" Freya asked, looking up at Valorian.

"I do, what about you?" he cocked his head to the side, watching her.

"I think that it would be a very narrow-minded view to think that only humans have ever existed. I would like to believe in magic, it's a nice thought." She smiled, resting her hands on top of the large Grimoire.

There was a brass lock on the side of the book. It looked worn and tarnished but had a small keyhole in the centre. Freya ran her thumb over it and wondered what secrets it held within.

"Do you have a key for this?" she asked.

"Yes, I do. I keep it up in the safe. Would you like me to get it for you?"

"No, no it's okay, thank you. I'm a little tired at the moment. Next time though?" she lifted her eyebrows in question.

"That's a deal. So does that mean you are coming back again?"

"I'm very difficult to get rid of, plus, I have no friends here, so this is the only place I have outside of work to hang out." She giggled.

"Well, their loss is my gain." he winked back at her.

Freya enjoyed Valarian's company. Growing tired she knew she should head home but it was hard to leave his allure. A yawn escaped her mouth and she realised Valorian was watching her.

"I guess I probably should be heading home, it seems I am more tired than I thought," she said sleepily.

"Well, you have had a night working, and it is getting late. Can I walk you home?" he offered.

"I would like that, thank you."

Freya and Valorian stepped out into the chilly night air. There were a few people milling about, much to Freya's surprise. Frost coated the path which sparkled in the moonlit rays. She looked up to the sky and noticed how clear it was. There was nothing but stars as far as she could see, as the milky way stretched out lazily in front of her.

"Wow, that view is amazing." She stopped walking.

Valorian looked up to see what Freya was looking at, standing beside her.

"It really is." A smile played in his voice.

Freya looked at him, noticing he was looking at her, not the sky above. She felt her cheeks flush and buried her chin into her scarf, hoping he wouldn't notice her smile.

They walked home in an easy silence. When they got to Freya's door, she stood on her tiptoes and gave him a peck on the cheek.

"Thank you for walking me home. It's been nice."

Valorian took her hand and gave it a gentle kiss.

"It has been my pleasure. Feel free to come over any time, won't you? I really enjoy the company."

"You say that now but may live to regret it when you cannot get rid of me." She smiled.

"I can't imagine that ever happening." He smiled back.

Freya unlocked her door and stepped inside saying good night. She closed the door and stood there for a few minutes smiling to herself before she headed upstairs.

CHAPTER THREE

Freya stretched out lazily and opened her eyes. The weak sun was trying to make itself known through a gap in her curtains. She rolled over smiling to herself about the night before, the spark she had felt around Valorian still warming her stomach. Glancing at the clock she saw it was a little later than she would normally wake up, but these new nighttime endeavours would switch it up a little anyway. Her stomach rumbled as she got out of bed and made her way to the kitchen to make eggs and toast with a large pot of tea. Looking out of the window she saw that the rain had let up. The mist still covered the mountains, but the sun was just rising behind them, giving off a warm glow that seemed to spread throughout her body. *Today is going to be a good day, I just know it.*

After eating breakfast, she showered and decided to go down to the local shop to pick up a newspaper and a few groceries. Stepping out the door in her blue winter dress and white jacket, the sun's milky rays warmed her shoulders. Despite the winter chill, the feel of spring was very much in the air, and this made her feel joyous and happy.

She entered the little shop and put what she needed in the

little basket, making her way to the counter. The man standing behind it was the same man that she had seen here before and who had greeted her warmly in the cafe the other night, introducing himself as Bert. He was a comforting sort of man, who looked to be in his sixties with a dash of salt and pepper in his hair, which replicated itself in his beard. He had kind, soft blue eyes and always wore a smile. He reminded her of the grandfathers you see in children's books that offer warmth and security.

"Good morning, Bert," she said as she placed the basket down.

"Good morning, Freya, lovely day today, isn't it?" he replied smiling.

"It really is. You can feel that spring air on its way now. It's glorious."

"Indeed, it is, still has a bite to it though. Crestwood is a lovely place to be whichever season you are in but every year the spring makes me feel hopeful. It's like the town starts to wake up after hibernating all winter."

"I look forward to seeing that. I am not planning on going anywhere for a couple of months at least, everything I need is right here and now I have the job with Marly it just feels like fate guided me to exactly where I needed to be."

"Aye, fate can do that to you."

Freya paid for her shopping and said her goodbyes, almost skipping out of the shop.

The street was a little busier than she had seen it before; Bert had not been wrong about the sleepy town waking after a long dark winter. She nodded and smiled at the people she passed as she made her way back to her apartment.

After putting all the groceries away Freya opened the windows to let in the breeze. Making a fresh pot of tea and grabbing the newspaper, she sat at the table near the large open window, which looked out across the town and mountains, and surveyed the town. The occasional person ambled along the street, enjoying the fresh warm air and bright sunshine. There had been nothing but rain since she had arrived four days ago, so having the sun was a welcome treat and it suited her mood. Her thoughts flitted back to Valorian; she wondered if he felt the same connection to her as she did to him. He seemed to enjoy her company well enough, and she had sensed something more between them when he had kissed her hand the night before. The butterflies in her stomach fluttered at the memory. *Would it be too much if I went to see him tonight after work again?* She wasn't sure. She really wanted to see him, but she didn't want to come across as needy, or to bother him when he might be busy. Admittedly it wasn't just Valorian she wanted to see, she really wanted to take a proper look at the Grimoire she had come across the previous night. There was something about it that pulled her in, and she was curious as to why any family of original Witches would just disappear like that without taking it with them. A Grimoire was sacred, it was the only thing that Freya would not have left behind. It held a wealth of information and while she had memorised many useful spells, the Grimoire contained many more spells she hadn't had the chance to see yet. She opened a page of the newspaper, alerting her to the moon phase. She had forgotten that the full moon was almost upon her with the move and excitement of getting a new job. When she had made her New Moon wishes a couple of weeks ago, she had never once anticipated that this would be the adventure she was seeking. This made her even happier. Working with moon phases was something Freya had enjoyed since she was a young child - she really believed that, if used correctly, the energy they produced could be harnessed and used to help shape her life, and every quarter she made a big deal about it, taking part in a ritual, basking in the moonlight and making the most of her offerings.

Not wanting to waste the glorious day, Freya put on her wellies and took off towards the forest. She hoped that there would be some great foragables that she could take for the ritual, and to make a start on restocking everything that she had left behind in the city.

At the end of the street where the road met the grassy field there was a muddy trail leading into the treeline. Pleased that she had thought to wear her wellies, Freya made her way down the mud-laden path. The giant pines reached high above her, instantly blocking out the light. Occasional rays broke through the thick canopy, bringing with it a much-welcome warmth through the sun-dappled leaves. Droplets still fell from the high branches following the previous day's rainfall. She stopped and took a deep breath, filling her lungs with the cool, fresh air that filled the forest. Looking around she could see a slight path continuing through the trees, and she noted that others must use this route regularly. Pulling a canvas tote from her pocket, she picked up some of the rough curls of bark on the floor and stored it in the bag. The first signs of spring were all around, with shoots of greenery starting to grow from the tree branches as she collected some of the pinecones which scattered the floor. Freya picked at the fungus she saw dotted along the base of trees and collected more bark and moss. Some of the trees were covered in a lichen, which looked almost golden in the soft sun. She could hear rushing water somewhere in the distance, but she decided to leave exploring the source of it for another time as she was growing tired and wanted to feel the sun on her skin again. The contrast of the red from the Winterberry Holly bushes looked vibrant against the dark browns and greens of rotting leaves and naked trees. Freya picked some of the berries and gave a prayer of thanks to mother nature before turning around and heading back home. As she came out of the forest, she welcomed the light, bright day and smiled up at the sun. Her wellies splodged along the path, and she did her best to wipe off the excess mud when she reached the road. The smell of coffee permeated the air alongside the smell of freshly baked goods, and she decided to stop at the coffee shop and enjoy a drink and a slice of cake at one of the outside tables. Grateful that she had put on matching socks that morning, Freya took off her wellies and left them just outside the door, not wanting to drag mud across the floor. The cafe was empty inside except for the person serving, who was not someone she had met yet.

"Hey. Could I get a black coffee and a slice of that wonderful looking cake there please?" she said and pointed to the large Victoria sponge which sat in the glass display.

"Of course. You must be Freya? Marly's new girl. I'm Anderson," he replied and held out his hand.

Freya shook his hand.

"Nice to meet you. I'm Freya.

Anderson smiled at her. "How are you liking Crestwood so far?"

"I love it here. The place is quiet and friendly, and the surrounding forest and mountains are beautiful. Everyone has been so welcoming," she said.

"I'm glad to hear it. We are a nice bunch. The community here is great. Pretty much everyone has been born and raised here for generations, so we all know each other very well."

"That is really something special. It is somewhere that will definitely stick in my mind after I have left."

Anderson gave Freya her drink and a box with the cake in and they said their goodbyes. Freya went back out and sat at one of the little tables. A breeze skimmed her shoulders, the chill of winter still in the air, she pulled her jacket around her snugly and sipped the hot, fresh coffee. She noticed a lot more of the shops were open, including the small clothing boutique, which had not been open since she arrived. Deciding this might be a good chance to go get some new clothes she picked up her coffee and cake and made her way to her apartment. She quickly changed her shoes and picked up some more money, leaving her cake and coffee on the kitchen countertop for when she got back.

The boutique was small but well packed. Light music floated through the air and the store smelled like jasmine. Freya made her way down the few aisles, adding clothes to the basket and picking up a pair of sandals ready for the warmer days. When she reached the counter there was no one there, but she noticed a bell placed on the counter next to a display of scented candles. Freya rang the bell and picked up one of the candles, Fall Festival, a deep orange coloured candle, which smelt like pumpkins, cinnamon and all things cosy. She added it to her basket as a lady came around from the back. Freya couldn't help but stare at her, she was beautiful, with long white hair which cascaded down her back over her bottom and the kindest soft hazel eyes. Freya guessed she must have been in her mid-fifties. Instantly a calmness washed over her, and the lady smiled.

"Hi, can I take that basket for you?" The lady spoke in a soft husky voice.

"Hi, yes, sorry." Freya put the basket down, realising she was still staring rudely.

"Beautiful day out, isn't it?" the lady said.

"It really is. It's the first day it hasn't rained since I moved here. I took a walk into the forest earlier; it was nice. You can see the signs of spring coming."

"The forest is nice once summer hits, and everything is in bloom. I'm Brigette, you must be Freya, if my sources are correct?" She was folding items up and placing them into a paper bag.

"It seems everyone knows me before I have had the pleasure of meeting them." Freya smiled.

"A new arrival here is so rare, you are unfortunately the current gossip," she said then let out a tinkling laugh.

Freya chuckled with her. She was totally taken with this woman, there was such a warmth about her that it made Freya feel totally at ease.

"Well, welcome to Crestwood Falls. I hope you love it here as much as we do." Brigette handed Freya her bag.

"Thank you, it's already growing on me quite rapidly. How much do I owe you?"

"That'll be £44."

Freya raised her eyebrows; she had expected the cost to be much higher. She gave Brigette the money and said goodbye. When she got back to her apartment, the coffee was still warm enough to drink. She took it, along with the cake, over to the table and sat down looking out over the street, smiling.

CHAPTER FOUR

Marly's was quiet when she arrived. One person sat near the window with an empty cup reading a book, and there was a couple sitting having an evening meal together. Freya smiled at them both as she walked past to hang up her coat. A sudden feeling of wooziness came over her as pins and needles made their way down her leg. She grabbed the counter to steady herself and the feeling left as quickly as it had arrived. *Strange*, she thought to herself. *It must have been sitting around for too long reading before I left for work.* Freya took a moment to centre herself, taking calm, deep breaths. The office door was open, and Marly sat behind the large cherry walnut desk.

"Evening, Marly."

"Hey, Freya. How was your day?"

"It's been good. I took the opportunity to go have a walk in the forest while the weather was nicer. I met Anderson and Brigette, I bought some clothes, and I may have even treated myself to a rather large slice of Victoria Sponge cake," she replied, not mentioning the wobbly episode.

"Well, that does sound like a good day. I am a little jealous about the cake though. Anderson's mum makes the cakes for the Spellbound Cafe, and they are very much out of this world. I must pop in and get myself some soon," Marly replied.

"I didn't know that. It must be nice to bake that well. My Gran tried to teach me to bake but I just don't have the skill for it. My cakes always come out like hard rocks."

"I don't either. But I am sure there are other skills we possess that others don't."

"That's what makes us all unique," Freya agreed.

"Talking of unique things, I have had your apron made for you, so tonight you won't have to wear the generic one." Marly handed Freya a light blue apron which had her name embroidered in silver across it.

"Oh, this is so very pretty," Freya said, putting it on.

"Each of my staff have their own, all assorted colours. I felt blue was very 'you' and I was not wrong. That colour really suits you."

"Thank you, it's actually my favourite colour so you picked a great one," she said.

The bell tinkled from out in the cafe and Freya made her way back to the counter. The evening passed much like the one before, but the sunny weather had brought more laughter with it. Everyone seemed to be in particularly high spirits. Anderson and his mum had come in and Freya had complimented her on her cake-making skills, vowing to return for a slice of the day's special. Marly had taken up a spot at the end of the counter for the evening, joining in the light-hearted banter, and Freya found herself disappointed when the last customer left, and she switched the sign to closed.

"What a great night. I really love working here," Freya said to Marly.

"You are a natural, and the townsfolk have really taken a shine to you. Some more than others it seems."

"What do you mean?" Freya blushed, wondering whether Valorian had said something about her.

"It's pretty clear Anderson has taken a very specific shine to you. He could not stop watching you the entire time he was here."

"No, really? I never noticed," Freya replied, taken aback. Anderson was lovely but Valorian had already caught her attention.

"Poor lad, he doesn't stand a chance when you only have eyes for Valorian."

Freya's mouth fell open, and she stared at Marly.

"I do not know what you mean," she said, colour filling her face.

"If it helps, he likes you too," Marly said, grinning

"Oh...he does?" Freya asked tentatively.

"It's obvious. I popped into the bookstore last night to see if you were still there so I could praise you on the wonderful cleaning job you did before you left, but you had already gone. When he talked about you his face lit up. The same way yours does when you mention him."

"Oh," Freya replied. Realising she was grinning like an idiot she got back to wiping down the tables. She was tempted to go over to the bookshop and see him - even more so now - but she also knew that she had to be careful, she couldn't let people see her true self. The risk was too great. After all, did she want to get involved with someone knowing she might not stick around? *It just wouldn't feel right to pull someone else into all my crap. I'll visit him tomorrow though; I know that for sure!* Freya finished cleaning up and said her goodbyes to Marly. She ambled along the street towards home, looking up to the sky. The moon was out in all her glory, stars scattered around her, and a splattering of goose pimples scattered Freya's skin from the cool air. She took a moment to just stop, close her eyes, and give thanks to the moon and all she brought with her. The last full moon of winter, ever watching.

Her apartment was cold. Closing the window that she had accidentally left open, she drew the curtains, lit the fire and filled the kettle, letting it heat up while she got dressed into the fluffiest pair of pyjamas she owned. With a mug of hot tea in hand she sat on the shaggy rug in front of the fire with her tarot cards, a white candle and her journal. Despite not using her innate magic she still appreciated mother nature and would continue to respect the practices she had been taught. As she shuffled the tarot cards she was thinking about her question to the universe. The last few weeks had changed her life completely, and this unsettled her. Her old life had been well organised and predictable, but now everything felt like it was up in the air. She focused on her question: *Will I be able to make a life for myself permanently here in Crestwood?* She had never intended to stay for longer than six months, but the pull of this town had firmly gripped her and the idea of leaving made her feel sick to her stomach. As she held the cards in her hand, she fanned them out in front of her and moved her hand slowly over them until she felt the familiar tingle of the card connecting to her inner consciousness. Pulling out the card she placed it face down next to her while she moved the rest back into the velvet bag. She turned over the card in front of her. Death. She smiled. A card that was often misunderstood, but one of her favourites. This card represented so much, and it told her everything she needed to know. The time to move on from her grief was here. Everything that had led her to this point was over, the end had passed and now she was living through a time of rebirth, of new beginnings. Relief poured over her. Pulling this card had been a sign that she was exactly where she was meant to be at this moment. Placing the card back into the velvet pouch she picked up her cup of tea and took a sip, cradling the large, hot mug in her hands. She took another sip, set it down on the rug, and picked up her journal. Tomorrow morning, she would wake and have a full moon bath to fully let go of these last few weeks but for now she wanted to write about everything that she hoped for in this coming moon cycle. Her mind couldn't help wandering to Valorian. Knowing that he might reciprocate her feelings had set off a group of butterflies in her stomach. Her mind went dreamy with the idea of it. She had planned to sit on the rug, finish her drink, and journal for a while longer, but she started to yawn and realised it was getting late. She put everything away, had a quick look at the moon out of her window and then took herself to bed, thinking about how much she was looking forward to seeing Valorian again.

Freya woke to the sound of pitter patter against her window, and she groaned. The rain had returned, and it sounded like it had done so with a vengeance. Pulling the covers around her, she snuggled back into the warmth of her bed. She heard the heating click on and decided she would wait for the apartment to warm up a little before she would leave the bed. She hoped that despite the weather that some of the shops would still be open. Aside from going to Spellbound Cafe for some more of the glorious cake, she really wanted to explore Odds and Ends Charity and Vintage Shop, and to get some fresh flowers from the small florist in the town. She climbed out of bed and made a cup of tea, scattering her full moon herbs of white sandalwood, lycopod, jasmine and gardenia in the bath, and letting it fill up as she drank. She lay in the bath thinking about her day ahead and decided to go get breakfast from the café. It had been such a long time since she had treated herself to a hot cooked breakfast and, while she had managed to resist the pull of the smell of the bacon yesterday, today her stomach yearned for it. She got out of her bath and put on the clothes she had picked out for the day. Grabbing her bag and coat she made for the door, where she noticed another one of Valorian's stylish cards had been slipped through her letterbox. She picked it up as she left, tearing it open on her way to Spellbound Café. In his typical way, Valorian was just asking her to pop over with a doughnut and coffee after her shift. It suddenly didn't matter that the rain was pouring because sunshine filled her heart. Placing the card in her bag, she smiled to herself.

Condensation filled the windows of the cafe as Freya tried to peek in. Pushing open the door she was met with a warm gust of air. The smell of fresh baked goods and bacon filled the air and instinctively her stomach rumbled. She made her way to the counter where a woman around her age with short blonde hair and a friendly face was on the till.

"Good morning, I'd like to order a cooked breakfast please," Freya said to the woman.

"Sure, no problem. Where will you be sitting?" the woman replied.

Freya looked around her and saw that there were only two unoccupied seats. She pointed to the one that was next to the window. "That one there please." She smiled.

Anderson came out from the back room.

"Hey, Freya, I thought I recognized the voice."

"Hi, Anderson. I thought I would treat myself to some breakfast."

"Well, we do cook the best breakfasts in town. Just don't tell Lena - she swears her bistro is the only place to go. I don't know about you, but I prefer bacon and eggs, not this continental stuff she serves up." He grimaced.

"I guess it depends on what you're in the mood for, I bet you are both equally good at what you do." Freya smiled.

"See, Anderson, you can't get anyone to agree with you on this. I'm Poppy by the way. I work here a few days a week. You are the new girl I take it?" Poppy said.

"Hi, Poppy, yes, I am. It's nice to meet you. I'm Freya."

Freya made small talk with Poppy and Anderson while she waited for her breakfast. When it arrived, she devoured it, groaning with pleasure. She saw Poppy heading towards her.

"That was so delicious," Freya said rubbing her belly.

"I will let the chef know. I was wondering if you were busy tomorrow evening?"

"I don't have any plans. It's my first night of two off work, so I was just going to read a book."

"Well, I am meeting a friend in Jackson's Inn just around the corner if you fancy it? Anderson will be there and most of the main townsfolk."

"I'd love that. Thank you. What time shall I be there?"

"We are meeting at seven thirty. I'll see you then," Poppy said, quickly returning to the counter to serve a customer.

Freya shouted her goodbyes, waved to Poppy and Anderson, and headed back out into the rain-filled street. As she walked towards the florist, she couldn't help but notice the way the cobbles sparkled with the rainwater, how they gave off a comforting glow reflecting the shop lights. She started thinking about all the people who would have walked over them, the stories they could tell and lives they may have lived. There was something about Crestwood that she just connected with. Freya could tell the florist was open, the smell of fresh florals greeted her as she crossed over and approached the shop. She was grateful that the owner had decided to open - because today was certainly a day to fill the house with bright colourful blooms. Freya entered the store and took it all in, smiling. It was like walking into a mystical garden. Plants and flowers greeted her from the walls, floor and ceilings. A lady stood at the back arranging some lilies in a large vase. Freya took her time looking around, picking up a selection of flowers that would fill two vases for her house, before taking them to the till.

"Hello, I'd like to buy these please, and two vases." Freya put the flowers down gently.

"A lovely selection you picked there," the lady replied as she bent down to take two of the vases from a shelf under the counter.

"I am feeling inspired by the brief sun we got yesterday, and my apartment needs some cheering up," Freya replied.

"Ah yes, you must be the new tenant who moved into the place above Bert's?" the lady asked.

"Yeah, I am. I didn't bring much with me so it's a little on the bare side for now. I am allowed to decorate it though, so it won't stay that way for long," Freya replied.

"I love bright colours as well. Nothing like a splash of yellow, pink or blue to lift anyone out of a dreary mood. My name is Alma, feel free to pop in anytime you like, even if it's just for a browse to lift your mood."

"Thank you. I'm Freya. It's lovely to meet you," Freya replied.

Taking her flowers and new vases, Freya returned to her apartment to set them up before they started to wilt. She placed one bunch on the little kitchenette table and one in her bedroom, immediately feeling her mood lift as she admired the vibrant colours. Grabbing her book, she curled up on the sofa, deciding to get a couple of hours reading in before she had to clean the apartment and get ready for work.

CHAPTER FIVE

Marly's was slow that night and Freya felt as if her shift had lasted twice as long as normal. A dull headache throbbed at the nape of her neck as she rubbed it trying to release the tension. Marly explained that Jackson's Inn only opened Thursday through to Monday, which was why she closed during the weekend, as business was a lot slower when he was open. They had made the arrangement many decades ago to ensure that both businesses easily stayed afloat. Tapping her fingers against the counter, Freya felt that nervous edge creep back over her. She shook her head trying to rid it of thoughts of Valorian, but she was too easily distracted with them. Finally, her shift finished, and she cleaned up. Grabbing the coffee and doughnut for Valorian, she made her way over to his store. She took a deep breath and walked in.

Valorian was standing behind the counter wrapping up some books for a customer. He looked up and gave her the largest grin, her stomach somersaulted, and she grinned back while walking over to him. Valorian said goodbye to the customer and gave Freya a kiss on the forehead.

"Thank you so much," he said, lifting the coffee to his mouth for a sip. Freya found herself watching his lips and she turned away.

"No problem."

"I'll go lock up and we can head down to the basement. I have something I want to ask your opinion on," he said in a serious tone.

"Oh, sounds ominous," she replied chuckling.

They made their way down the stairs and Valorian put his coffee and doughnut on the desk.

"So, I have been thinking. I want to redecorate down here. It has been like this for quite a while, and I want to change it up. What do you think?"

"Well, I mean, I like it like this, but a change is always good, especially if it has been quite some time since it was last done."

"It has. I like it, but I'm bored of it now."

"What are you thinking of changing?" she asked.

"Everything. Obviously, I will still need the floor to ceiling shelves, but I need more storage for the other items and perhaps assorted colours, something soothing."

"Sounds like a nice idea. Change of colour would be good. A dark teal would be nice in this space."

"I never thought of teal, but yes it would. I love the colour too. It would be soothing and not make the place too bright as I am not a particular fan of bright colours," he said.

"There you go then," she said, sitting down on the sofa.

"So, do you fancy helping me? I could use a second pair of eyes and hands." He smiled sweetly at her, fluttering his eyelashes.

"You know that doesn't work on women, right?" She laughed.

"It was worth a try." He pouted.

"Yes, I'd love to help. I've been invited to the Inn tomorrow by Poppy, but I am free any other day or after work."

"That will be nice, it's good you are making friends here. I will pop into Jackson's tomorrow so I may see you there. How about we make a start on Saturday night then? I could cook us something as well, as a way of saying thank you."

"That works for me, and the food would be great."

Valorian took a bite of the doughnut, wiping his sugar dusted fingers on his jeans, before pulling out a key and handing it to Freya.

She took hold of the key in her fingers and felt a flow of magic connect with hers, her brows knitted together with curiosity. Picking up the Grimoire she turned the cover over and a feeling of peace washed over her. She looked at the page and lifted her eyebrows. *Why can I understand what I'm seeing? How is that possible if it belonged to another witching family?*

"Valorian?"

"Yes," he replied with a mouth full of food.

"These symbols, you said no one has managed to read them yet, is that correct?"

"Yeah, not since the original owners left it. Why?"

"Well, I can." She looked up at him, concerned.

"What!" he said, jumping down from the desk he had been perched on, and sitting next to her. "You can read what it says? You're a Witch?"

"Yes. See here, it's an incantation to protect the Grimoire against anyone reading it who does not come from the same bloodline."

"But..." He looked at her, gobsmacked.

"I know. I can't explain it." She turned to the next page. "This one says that it is the Crestwood Original: Evermore Family Grimoire."

"Wow. Do you know much about your heritage?"

"All I know is that my grandmother said we didn't originate from the place where we settled. She never told anyone anything more, and I am not sure she even knew. She has passed away now," she said. They sat in silence for a few minutes, "I wonder if that is why I am here. I have never heard of Crestwood Falls, but I just kept driving until I was here. I let my intuition guide me."

"That's entirely possible. I can't believe it, this is fantastic," Valorian said, placing an arm around Freya's back and giving her a squeeze.

Freya continued to flick through the pages, checking whether she could read them, without paying much attention to what they contained. A sickly feeling pooled in her stomach. *I wish my mum was here to be able to talk about this.* Grief gnawed at her, and her eyes filled with salty tears. She tried to blink them away quickly - she couldn't cry in front of Valorian, that would be humiliating.

"Are you okay, Freya?" Valorian asked, concern lacing his voice.

"I'm fine, just shocked, and I wish I had someone I could ask about this too."

"Are you not able to ask your Mum?" he asked.

"I can't. She died a month ago with my dad, and all my grandparents have passed away."

"Oh, Freya, I had no idea. I am so sorry. Was your mum a Witch? You could ask her Coven."

Freya quickly told Valorian everything about her parent's death from what Jacob had told her. "I see. I can understand that. Nebula isn't exactly known for being forthcoming with the information they hold, but perhaps they are still investigating"

"Maybe. I haven't used my magic since then. I still practice some elements of Witchcraft, but I don't use my powers. I can't. My parents would be alive now if it wasn't for their magic. I wonder what happened to my ancestors."

"It must have been hard for you to lose your parents and your use of magic too."

"Losing my parents was the hardest thing I have ever experienced. That's why I came here. I couldn't stay near the Coven, and I couldn't be in the city. I always hated it there. Here feels different, there is something about Crestwood that feels like home. I guess I know why now though."

"I lost my original family a long time ago and the pain is still present, even now."

"Your original family?" Freya asked; she had suspected there was more to Valorian than met the eye.

"My birth family. I am not human either, Freya. My family are not my biological family, but they are my blood family."

"You're a Vampire? That's what you mean, isn't it?"

"Yes, I am. This town has many supernatural beings, and those who aren't know what we are and help keep our secrets. We don't usually accept outsiders, but we all felt a connection to you, an openness we don't usually share."

"My heritage. That's why, isn't it? It's like the town itself is alive and can feel it."

"I suspect it is, yes."

"This is a lot to take in. I thought I was heading for a fresh start, somewhere completely mundane and without magic, and I have inadvertently ended up in a place quite the opposite. I'm not sure what that means for me - for what I want - especially now I know there are so many forms of magic here."

"Does that change how you feel about being here? Will you leave?"

"Honestly, I'm not sure. Crestwood feels like home. I love it here. But at the same time, I don't know if I can stand to be around a place where my blood, my magic, feels more active. It's harder to resist the pull to use it."

"Well, there is a lot to consider for you. I am getting quite fond of having you around, and I will still need help with this redecorating, so if you can hold off any big decisions until after, that would be great," he said, a cheeky grin on his face.

Freya laughed. "I'm sure I can hold off for now."

"You can take that with you," Valorian said, indicating the Grimoire.

"Are you sure? I would like to read through it all properly."

"You are the only one who can read it, so it makes sense for you to have it. Besides, it belongs to your family. I was just its guardian. Now I know why you picked that up out of all those books."

"Fate has definitely got its hand in here."

"It really does."

Freya and Valorian talked for what felt like hours about the town and its inhabitants, gossiping about who among them was human and who was supernatural. Freya couldn't believe it; Marly was a Werewolf. She would never have guessed. She marvelled at the way that all of them had come together with humans, and how they had formed such a wonderful community. Outside of this town she had never seen that happen. Usually, Werewolves and Vampires kept to their clans - but not here. She felt warm throughout her body as she realised how safe and secure she felt surrounded by all these supernaturals. Freya tried to stifle a yawn, as she realised the time.

"I'm so sorry, I didn't realise how late it was. I should get going, you probably have lots to do," she said,

"I don't, it's fine. But it is late. Can I walk you home?"

"You don't need to do that. I am sure I'll be fine," she said reluctantly.

"I would really like to," Valorian replied hopefully.

"Okay then it would be great. Thank you," she replied.

The cool air sent a chill through Freya as they stepped out into the night. Valorian put his arm around her and pulled her close.

"Thanks, it's a bit nippy out here."

"It's that cool air coming down from the mountains, wonderfully fresh but very bitter."

"It's lovely though. Beats the smog from the city air I am used to, that's for sure." She laughed.

"I was thinking. Perhaps tomorrow after Jackson's closes, or if you get done before that, I could take you to the old church yard. The Evermore Mausoleum is there, if you want to see it that is? You may learn more about your family there."

"I would love that. Thank you."

It didn't take long for them to arrive at Freya's apartment.

"Thank you for walking me home and keeping my arms from freezing off."

"They are good arms, I need them to help me paint," he said, smiling at her.

Freya laughed, before reaching up to kiss Valorian on his cheek. He kissed hers in return as they both lingered just those extra few seconds, long enough to make Freya's head go dizzy and her throat to dry. She took a step back and unlocked the door, wishing him goodnight. She kicked her shoes off and climbed the stairs, a grin still plastered to her face. She was looking forward to helping Valorian redecorate – it would be a good excuse to spend more time with him. She was sure he didn't need her help - not with his super vampire speed - but she was glad he had asked, nonetheless. She felt like she floated to the bed, sitting down on it, pulling off her clothes and putting on her nightie. Her eyes closed as soon as her head hit the pillow.

CHAPTER SIX

The next morning arrived too quickly. She felt like cobwebs had invaded her head while she slept. Dreams had plagued her sleep - the same dream she had had numerous times since arriving in Crestwood. A purple butterfly trapped in a room, tapping against the window, trying to get out. Freya could feel it's emotions: the fear it felt of not being able to escape, scared it would be stuck there forever. She felt as if she hadn't had any rest - the dream had set her on edge and she felt like there was a meaning she was missing in it - yet the clock told her it was almost lunchtime. She groaned loudly before sliding her legs out into the cold air, and quickly grabbing the bathrobe, pulling it over her arms and securing it tightly. She peered out of the window. The rain had stopped but a thick fog had descended in its place. Freya wrinkled her nose and opened the window a little to let in some air. Once she had made a cup of tea and lit the fire she crawled back into bed. *Surely there's no harm in having a lazy day,* she told herself to ease the guilt she felt. She reached for the journal she kept on her bedside table. Having been too tired to write in it the previous night she had a lot to say this morning. Stopping occasionally to stroke the cover of the Grimoire, she mulled over the idea that it had once belonged to her family. *Why would they leave it behind when they left? Even if the speculation was true, it would be rare - unheard of, in fact - for a Witch to leave their Grimoire behind. It would have been everything to them.* Even though she wasn't using her full magical ability she would never have left her Grimoire behind. She wondered whether Marly would know anything about her family. After all, she had been born into a Crestwood original family too. *In fact, given how werewolves age, there is a possibility that she was even around when Everlyn lived here.* Freya wondered who the boy may have been - if the story was true of course. *Does his family still live in the area, and if so, would they come for me?* She had a lot of questions and very few answers. She knew if she just used her magic at the mausoleum, she could probably find out a lot more about her family's history here - if her ancestors would communicate with her - but she couldn't bring herself to do it. Not even for this. She was grateful that Valorian had offered to take her, and that she had him to talk to about her family. He was someone that she trusted, and she hoped that their conversations would bring them closer together. Her stomach rumbled and she put the journal and Grimoire back on the bedside table and climbed out of bed, making her way to the kitchen. The rest of her apartment had warmed up now. She pulled open all the curtains and smiled at the fresh flowers, which looked even more vibrant against the swirl of grey outside her window. The fog was so thick she could barely see the lights of the cars as they drove past, and she hoped it would clear up before nightfall.

The day dragged past. Freya couldn't wait to get out of the house to meet Poppy at Jackson's. She was glad that she had made the decision to buy some new clothes so she wouldn't have to wear her old worn jeans and holey jumper. She sat at the small mirror, applying a little blush and mascara, to accentuate her features. The floral dress she had picked matched her white canvas shoes well. *This will have to do.* She hoped that she wouldn't look too out of place there. She grabbed her bag and left the apartment. Her denim jacket did nothing to protect her against the cold fog, so she quickened her pace almost to a run to get to Jackson's. She pushed open the solid wood door and was greeted with raucous laughter. The Inn was busy, with patrons sitting at the bar and at tables around the room. There was a cosy and homely feel to the place. She scanned around trying to find Poppy, but couldn't see her.

"Freya, you made it." Poppy appeared behind her.

"Hey, yeah. I just arrived."

"You look great. Shall we go to the bar and get you a drink?"

"Thanks, and yes, let's."

Poppy grabbed Freya's arm, pulling her through the crowd. She wore her short blonde hair in loose curls and was dressed casually in jeans and a t-shirt. Freya was glad she blended in with everyone. They got to the bar and a tall stocky man came straight over to them.

"Can I have a glass of white wine and... what would you like, Freya?"

"I'll just have the same, thank you."

"And another glass of white wine then please."

The man went off and brought back the two glasses.

"Thanks, Jackson. This is Freya, she is new here."

"Howdy," he said in a deep husky voice. "Nice to meet ya." He held out his hand.

"Hey, nice to meet you too," Freya replied.

"So, you are the new one working at Marly's then?" he asked.

"I am, yes. It's great," Freya replied.

"Aye, Marly is a good one. I best get off and serve some other customers. Was nice to meet ya, lass."

"Bye," she said.

She turned to Poppy.

"He was nice. In fact, everyone is nice here." She sipped her cold wine, enjoying the feel of it sliding down the back of her throat. The crisp sweetness of the apple made her smile.

"He is great. Everyone here is nice and friendly. You fit in just fine," Poppy said, linking her arm through Freya's.

"Let's get back to the others, we saved you a seat."

"That was kind of you, thank you," Freya said, as Poppy pulled her towards what looked like a back room.

They stepped through a narrow opening and into a quieter

room. Freya recognised Anderson sitting at the table Poppy was walking towards, along with three other people.

"Hey, everyone, this is Freya, she is new in town and works with Marly. This is Rusha," she said pointing towards a tall thin girl with long brunette hair and a warm face. "Silas," she pointed towards a guy sitting with a baseball cap on and foam across his top lip from his beer, "and lastly Eric." She nodded towards a guy sitting next to Anderson with long, dirty blond hair and a deep scar across his cheek.

"Hey, everyone," Freya said.

A chorus of 'hellos' came from the group and Freya and Poppy sat down. Freya was seated between Poppy and Rusha and the three of them talked casually about Freya's life in the city and how it compared to life in Crestwood. As the evening passed, Freya found herself increasingly relaxed in their company. She learnt that Eric was back home for the winter holidays from university where he was studying marine biology, Silas was in a band, and he played the drums and bass guitar, and that Rusha worked at her father's doctors practice - but that she really wanted to leave Crestwood and live in the city. Freya felt a tickle of cool air behind her, and she instinctively knew that Valorian must have come into the bar. She tucked her hair behind her ear and realised she had stopped listening to the conversation. She saw Eric look up and smile.

"Hey, Val, come to join us?" he said.

Freya turned around and saw Valorian walking towards them.

"Hey, guys," he said. He pulled a stool over to where Freya was seated, squeezing himself between her stool and Rusha's. Sitting, he leaned over and kissed her cheek.

Freya blushed and Poppy giggled. Nudging her with her elbow, she whispered to her, "I didn't realise you knew Valorian so well."

Freya turned and smiled at Poppy.

"Yeah, he was the first person I really spoke to here. His bookshop is amazing."

"I'm sure that's not the only great thing about him." Poppy smirked.

Freya chuckled, trying to hide the heat rising in her cheeks.

Valorian was deep in conversation with Silas, but he kept glancing over to her.

"Twenty minutes, ladies and gents," Jackson called from the other room.

Freya hadn't realised how late it was. The night had gone well; she liked all the people she had met, and she felt like her friendship with Poppy was blossoming.

"So, Freya," Poppy said. "Fancy meeting for breakfast tomorrow at the café? I don't start work until eleven, so I was going to grab some food before I started my shift."

"Oh yes, that would be nice. I am dying to try the pancakes!" she exclaimed.

"Great, I will see you there about ten-ish?"

"Sounds perfect," Freya replied, and with that Poppy, Rusha and Silas said their goodbyes and left.

Eric finished his drink and said goodbye too, leaving Freya and Valorian alone.

"Did you have a good night?" he asked her.

"I did. They're such a lovely group of people. Time went a little too quickly," she said letting out a small laugh.

"Yeah, they are a great bunch. Shall we finish our drinks and head over to the Churchyard? If you still want to, that is?"

"I do, I've been looking forward to it. Seeing where my ancestors are buried. Plus, I have some great company to be my tour guide."

Valorian laughed. "I hope that I am more than just a tour guide." He winked.

"Of course, You are my friend too." She grinned.

"For now," he said, standing, and offering her his hand. "Let's get going."

Freya took his hand. A tingle of electricity buzzed through her body. She liked how her hand felt in his. He didn't let go - and she was not about to make him.

Chapter Seven

Stepping outside, Freya noticed the fog still hadn't cleared and in the dark of the night it seemed thicker and more menacing. She was glad that Valorian was with her; even walking home alone in this would have set her senses tingling, there was something about the fog that made her wonder what might be hidden within it. Wrapping her arms around herself, she silently scolded herself for wearing such a light jacket.

Valorian took off his jacket, placing it around her shoulders.

"Thanks. This fog is something else. Does it get like this often?" she asked.

"Only at this time of year. As the earth is heating up and the cool mountain air comes down, we usually get a week or so of thick fog."

"It's kind of creepy." She laughed.

"Yeah, I guess it is. You'll soon get used to it though."

He took hold of her hand again and she felt those butterflies start to flutter in the pit of her stomach. They walked towards the meadow, which bordered the forest and turned up towards the mountains. Freya couldn't see a thing and was glad that

Valorian knew the way. It only took a few minutes to get to the Church, and Freya could see the dark spire outlined through the wisps of fog as they passed through a wrought iron gate. Gravestones were scattered around the yard, large old ones, some of which could barely be read, as time and weather had worn away the writing that once covered them. They continued to walk around the side of the building until Valorian turned off onto a small gravel path. He stopped in front of an old stone mausoleum with the name 'Evermore' etched into the stonework at the top. Valorian handed her an ornate black key which felt oddly familiar in her hand. She took a few steps forwards and ran her hand across the imposing black iron door. There were runes etched all around the frame, and Freya recognised them as protection runes, designed to keep the sleeping out of harm's way and prevent evil from disturbing them. The lock was surprisingly easy to open considering how long it must have been since someone was last here. She turned and looked at Valorian quizzically.

"I have been coming monthly to keep the place tidy and bring fresh flowers. I do it to all the Crestwood original families' graves. My father did it before me, and his father did it before him. It's our way of showing respect for those who have passed," he told her.

"That was nice of you," she replied, pushing open the door, grateful that he had cared for her ancestors when no-one else had.

A blast of cold, stale air rushed out from the stone tomb, leaving a scattering of goosebumps across her flesh. She stepped over the threshold and immediately the sound of breathless, whispering voices assaulted her mind. Her legs felt like jelly, and she wobbled on her feet. Valorian wrapped his arm around her waist to steady her.

"Are you okay?" he asked, his brows knitted with concern.

"I can hear them, feel their presence," she replied croakily.

Different conversations swam around her, but she couldn't quite make out the shape of the words. As she took a few more steps forward, the sound of her name became distinguishable from the rest of the noise. Soft, echoing words gently cascaded over her; she could almost feel their breath skimming her skin.

"Freya Evermore," a whispered voice spoke, standing out from the jumble of sounds.

Freya stilled. The ancestors knew who she was, recognised her as family, and a chill of unknown fear climbed her spine.

"You don't have anything to fear here, child," a female voice whispered to her knowingly.

The voice was that of an older female, which reminded her of her grandmother, sending a trickle of warmth through her blood.

"Hello," Freya replied tentatively.

"Hello, dear," the voice replied.

Freya turned and smiled at Valorian.

"I'll give you some privacy and I will be just outside the door if you need me." He squeezed her hand and left.

"I am glad you came," the voice said.

"I'm sorry I didn't come sooner. I didn't know about the place."

"We know. It isn't your fault, child. We are just happy you have found your way here now."

"How many are you?" Freya asked, her warm breath visible against the frigid air.

"There are several of your ancestors occupying this space."

"Who are you?" Freya asked. Taking a step further in, she looked around. There were black iron sconces on the walls that looked as though they had once held candles. The walls were dark and damp and there was a feeling of abandonment here, but it was clear that the mausoleum was a place that had once been well looked after.

"My name is Agnes. My grandmother was one of the first Witch settlers to make up what you know as Crestwood Falls," the soft voice replied.

"It's lovely to meet you. I have not been in Crestwood long. I had no idea this was where my family had originated from until I found an old family grimoire."

"That must have been a shock for you. We were told about the family leaving the village, but we had hoped that one day our legacy would be passed down and someone would return. It saddens me it has taken this long and that your visit to Crestwood was not planned with this in mind."

"It was a shock, and I wish I had known about our history here, but I do not know much about what happened to my family, no-one ever mentioned Crestwood." Freya wrapped her arms around herself, bracing herself against the chilly air.

"Dark magic can be a dangerous thing, but of course, it is not the magic that is at fault but the person who uses it. Chaos magic is hard to control. Over generations those who could use and access it became fewer and fewer - unless the practice was kept within generational families. It could be used for many good things, but that magic has a hold on people. It is more powerful than any other magic and it becomes seductive, it brings out the worst in people with low self-control."

"So, it wasn't necessarily the magic they ought to have feared but the people wielding it? I had no idea there was such a magic."

"That is correct, dear. Unfortunately, in our time we had yet to see a Witch able to resist that pull towards it, and every time it was used in excess, the consequences were dire. All we know is that the youngest Evermore was in love with a Witch from a chaos magic family."

"It sounds as though the Evermores made the right decision to leave."

"It was a sorry situation. They both clearly loved each other deeply and I hope, wherever their lives took them, it was full of love and light."

"I know on the Evermore side that things were okay after, but nothing more than that."

"Whatever happened, it has now brought you back here. Fate is at work, showing its hand in letting you know where you belong."

"Maybe. Though my reason for being here may just be coincidence."

"How so, child?"

"My parents were killed, and I couldn't bear to be in the city any longer, so I packed my car up and drove. I had no idea where I was going, and for days I just slept in the car until I ended up here and decided to take a break. I liked how peaceful it was away from any big towns and cities. It was quiet, private and best of all, no-one knew who I was."

"I was sorry to learn of your parents' passing. Even in the ether, word has a way of travelling. You may feel that it is coincidence, but you know, Witches never believe in that, we know that whatever happens is destined, so you being here now has a purpose even if you do not know what it is yet."

"I'm not sure if I will stay yet, but I will make sure to come and see you more while I am here. I would love to get to know about my heritage."

"We would love that. Take care, Freya and I hope you decide to stay with us all long term. Now, you go get back to that gorgeous Vampire of yours before he paces a hole in the ground." There was the hint of a smile in Agnes' voice as she spoke.

"I will. See you soon."

Freya left and heaved the heavy iron door shut behind her.

"Everything okay?" Valorian stood leaning against the wall of the church in front of her.

"Yeah. It was strange experiencing that, but I am glad we came. I want to visit more while I am here. I also found out a little more about why my family left."

"That sounds wonderful, it will give them some peace if you spend time with them."

"I hope so. I just wish I could get the full story of what happened with my family. All I have are bits and pieces."

"I can revisit the topic with my father if you would like me to? Knowing you are here might trigger some memory he had forgotten."

"Would you do that for me? It would be helpful if he did know something."

"I will call him before tomorrow night."

"Thank you."

Valorian smiled at her and took hold of her hand again as they started walking back towards the main street.

"I'm looking forward to tomorrow," he said casually.

"Me too."

"Is there anything you are allergic to? I don't want to poison you the first time I cook for you."

"Nope, I'm good. Though I should warn you, I don't like

shellfish," she replied grimacing.

Valorian laughed. "Okay, noted. No shellfish."

The streets were quiet, any noise subdued by the heavy-set fog. They approached Freya's door.

"What time would you like me tomorrow?" she asked.

"Is six okay?"

"Absolutely."

"Great, I shall have dinner ready for m'lady at six p.m. sharp."

Freya chuckled.

"Why thank you m'lord," she said with a curtsey.

They both laughed. She reached over and kissed his cheek, and he bent and kissed hers in return., As they pulled away, he kept hold of her hand just a few seconds longer.

"See you tomorrow," he said as he started to walk away.

"See you tomorrow," she replied unlocking her door

Freya woke abruptly. It was still dark, and her heart was racing. There had been a nightmare, she thought. Spirits seemed to have invaded her dreams, angry, shouting, and impossible to escape. She sat up and took some calming breaths, grateful it was just a dream. She got up to get a fresh glass of water. The dream hung over her oppressively, it felt ominous, as if it were trying to tell her something, but she had no idea what. Looking outside she saw some of the fog had started to clear. It was still the early hours of the morning and there was no way she wanted to stay up now, otherwise she would be stupidly tired tonight and would have to leave Valorian's early, which she didn't want. She got back into bed and thought about the night ahead, hoping the good thoughts would push out the bad dreams hanging on at the edge of her sleep.

An alarm bleeped, cutting through her sleepy haze. She reached over, trying to find the alarm and turn it off, accidentally knocking her journal onto the floor.

"Crap," she said out loud.

She turned off her alarm and then opened her arms and dangled herself over the bed to pick up her fallen journal. She had enough time to get a nice cup of tea while reading the rest of yesterday's newspaper, before taking a hot shower. She couldn't wait to head down to meet Poppy for breakfast; she was starving this morning. The idea of pancakes made her mouth water. Once she was ready, she grabbed her tote bag, carefully placing the grimoire in there along with a notepad and pen, and left. She was glad to see that all that remained of the fog was a fine mist, which turned out to be wetter than it looked. She arrived at the cafe and found Poppy already there, talking to Anderson.

"Hey, guys," Freya said, taking off her coat to hang on the peg near the door.

"Morning," replied Anderson.

"Hey, bit wet this morning, isn't it?" Poppy replied.

"Wetter than I thought it would be." She laughed.

"Let's order, I'm so hungry."

"Me too, I woke up feeling like I haven't eaten for days," she said as her stomach rumbled.

They put their orders in with Anderson and took a table seat near the window.

"Sooooo..." said Poppy.

"What?" Freya looked up at her new friend.

"You and Valorian? There is definitely some chemistry there," she said wiggling her eyebrows.

Freya laughed.

"Maybe. Honestly, I can't tell. I thought he might like me, but I have been wrong about this sort of thing before."

"Oh, girl, he likes you. Valorian has never been like that with any of us - not like he was last night with you. The kiss on the cheek, the way he watches you, that expression on his face."

"Oh, behave." Freya chuckled.

"Seriously though, there is something there. I could feel it. And you like him too, right?"

"Right, I do. I'm going over there tonight. I am helping him redecorate and he is cooking for me as a thank you."

"Oh, see? A date!"

"Not a date! A favour! I'm helping him out," Freya protested.

"Sure, if that's what you want to call it." Poppy laughed.

"What about you then? Do you have a boyfriend?"

"No, I don't. My heart is taken with someone who doesn't have a clue I think of him like that." Poppy looked sorrowful.

"Oh, have you told Mr Mysterious how you feel?"

"No! Absolutely not. I couldn't, it would ruin everything. At least this way I still get to see him, and it isn't awkward."

"Who is it? Someone I have met?"

Poppy nodded and glanced over towards Anderson. Freya looked over, realising who the object of Poppy's desire was.

"I get why you haven't said anything, but he might feel the same, you never know."

"Surely he would have said something if he liked me though?"

"Like you have, you mean?"

"Yeah, I get your point," Poppy said.

"I saw a poster in one of the shops advertising the midnight outdoor movie next weekend. Why not invite him?"

"You aren't going to drop this, are you?"

"I think that if you like him then you should try. It must be better than seeing him every single day and never knowing how he feels about you".

"Okay, if I ask him to come to the midnight movie with me, will you ask Valorian to go with you?"

Freya considered it for a minute.

"Deal. I will ask Valorian tonight."

"I'll ask Anderson today then. What time are you going over there tonight?"

"About six-ish is when he is doing dinner. Why?"

"I finish at four, can I pop around to yours? Let you know how it went with Anderson?"

"Yes! I want to know aaaalll the details," she replied.

They both laughed. Anderson brought over their breakfasts, Freya tucked into the pancake and groaned as she ate them. She had never tasted anything so delicious. Saying goodbye to Poppy and Anderson, Freya left and headed towards the Churchyard pulling up the hood on her jacket. Looking up towards the mountains as she walked, she thought about how she loved the way they looked, the tops of them buried beneath the misty clouds. It made her feel comforted surrounded by such giant protectors. She wondered what it would be like to live in Hawthorne Hollow, the small village which sat on the edge of the mountain line. *I bet waking up to those views is magnificent.* She pushed open the wrought-iron gate to the churchyard, shutting it carefully behind her. The gravel crunched under her feet and a crow cawed in the distance as she approached the mausoleum. The idea of spending some time here with her ancestors made her feel calm, a peace washing over her. She realised that this was the only family she had, and even in death they were there. She unlocked the door, pushing it open. Pulling some candles from her bag she set them into the torch holders around the stone walls, lighting the place up in a warm glow. She was greeted by two of the voices she had heard the previous night, and she greeted them back. She placed the small blanket she had in her tote on the stone bench, wanting to be as warm and comfortable as possible. The spirits were quiet, but she could feel them. She began decoding the Grimoire.

"Hmm," she said querying to no-one in particular. "I wonder what Devil's Cherries are?"

"The common name for that is belladonna," a spirit responded in a voice she did not recognise.

"Ah, thank you."

Spells from the olden days sound much more interesting with the old names, she thought, smiling to herself as she imagined throwing Bat's Wool into a cauldron. She noticed that the longer she sat there, the more spirits came to visit. Some would communicate with her; others would just make their presence felt. Eventually, she felt herself tiring. De-coding the grimoire was harder work than she had anticipated, but it was fascinating. Checking her watch, she realised that it was almost two p.m. and she wanted to get home and shower before Poppy came over. Packing up the blanket and Grimoire, she started blowing out the candles. Her heart sank as she left the spirits alone in the darkness of the mausoleum - not that they really noticed the dark. Letting them know she would be back in a couple of days, she locked the door behind her and walked back to her apartment.

CHAPTER EIGHT

Freya sat at the table near the window, her hair wrapped in a towel. She picked up the sandwich she had made and opened her book. She had just enough time to grab a small bite to eat and dry her hair before Poppy was due to arrive. She hoped that Poppy would help her pick the perfect outfit for tonight, as she wanted to find something cute but practical for decorating. The butterflies in her stomach had started about an hour ago and had only increased as the time drew closer. At this rate she would be a nervous wreck once six p.m. arrived. Tonight, she felt could be the start of something, she could sense a shift in the air - but she didn't know whether that would be for better or for worse. Freya finished her food, cleared away the plate and made her way to the bedroom to dry off her long brown hair the best she could with a towel, plaiting it to keep it out of the way.

Poppy arrived just after four p.m., bringing with her cake and hot chocolate.

"So, how did it go then?" Freya asked, putting another forkful of cake in her mouth.

"Well, it took me ages to pluck up the courage to ask, but he said yes."

"Ahhhh that's fantastic!"

"I was ready to add in that everyone else was going, to make it appear less like a date, but I didn't need to. He said he was looking forward to it." Poppy's face had lit up with excitement.

"I'm really happy for you," Freya replied.

"I wouldn't have done it if you hadn't pushed me to, so thank you."

"I really didn't do anything; it was all you. I am nervous about asking Valorian tonight though. I may have read the situation so wrong."

"Nah, I mean, he wanted to spend time with you badly enough that he even asked you to help him decorate, *and* he's cooking you a meal. Who knows what else he'll offer you," Poppy said with a wink

"Oh my god, haha, behave." Freya blushed the colour of a mailbox.

They both giggled.

"Do you have any plans tomorrow?" Poppy asked.

"Nope, it's my last day off. I might be helping Valorian late on but that's it."

"I have to go to Hawthorne Hollow to pick up some baked goods for the café. Would you like to come with me?"

"I would really like to. I've never been and was wondering this morning what it was like there so close to the mountains," Freya replied. *There goes that pesky fate again*, she thought.

"It's a spectacular little place. There are a few quirky little shops as well, so we can have a browse around while we are there. I could do with picking up some new herbal candles and the lady who makes them there does really nice ones."

"Sounds good. I can fill you in on my evening with Valorian as well then."

"Well, I will need all the gossip of course!"

After Poppy left, Freya tried to distract herself from her rising nerves by sitting down with her book, but she found that she kept reading the same paragraph over and over again. Fed up with her restless energy, she cleaned up the dishes in the sink and closed all the curtains, so she wouldn't have to do it when she got home later.

The crisp air chilled Freya as she walked over to Valorian's. The lights from his bookshop reflected on the wet pavement in front of the shop, making her smile. She opened the door, and the bell tinkled, signalling her arrival.

Valorian, who was standing behind the counter, looked up and smiled. "Hey."

"Hey," she said.

He walked up to her, giving her a kiss on the cheek, before flipping the sign on the door to 'closed' and letting down the latch on the door lock.

"Let's go upstairs and eat. I don't know about you, but I am seriously hungry."

"Me too. I have to ask though: you're eating too?"

"I am. I need blood to survive but I can eat normal human food, though it doesn't offer me the same benefits as it does for you."

"I had no idea. I've only ever met one Vampire before, and we weren't exactly on friendly terms."

"There is a lot of myth around my kind but only a fraction of it is true." He gestured to the doorway at the back of the room.

Freya followed him up the stairs and was greeted by a huge room with a kitchen at one side and a dining table at the other. The dining table was set with lit candles and a red rose in a vase. The room smelt delicious.

"Mmm, it smells so good up here," Freya said.

"I made lasagna for dinner, with garlic bread."

Freya looked at him, one eyebrow raised.

"Garlic is just another myth, it actually does nothing at all to us," he said, smiling.

"I feel like I am getting an education on Vampires this evening. It is fascinating," she replied.

"I bet there are plenty of things about Witches that are pure myth too," he said.

"I would think so, but it's hard to know because each one of us is unique, so what may be true for one of us won't be for another. All our magic differs from family to family."

He pulled out a chair for her. "Would you like a glass of wine?"

"Yes, please," she replied.

"White, red or rosé? I bought all three as I didn't know your preference".

"That was a sweet thing for you to do. White or rosé please. I don't drink red wine. Haven't since I accidentally got drunk on it one Yule and was sick all over my parents freshly made dinner."

Valorian let out a loud belly laugh.

"That is brilliant. I bet they never let you forget it either."

"They thought it was hilarious, even when I woke up the next morning with a very bad hangover, wishing my life was over. Safe to say, I have never touched the stuff since." She smiled.

"You are a very naughty Witch it seems."

"Oh yes, I was the biggest rebel you have ever seen." She smirked.

Valorian poured them each a glass of rosé wine and they both headed back to the kitchen.

"It's much bigger up here than I imagined," Freya said.

"It is deceptively large. There are two master bedrooms up here and a big bathroom as well as a living room through there." He nodded towards a closed door.

"It's nice."

Valorian brought over the food and dished it up onto Freya's plate.

"This looks really good," she said, waiting for him to sit down before eating.

"I hope it tastes as good as it looks," he said.

They made conversation as they ate, and Freya felt the nervous energy dissipate the longer she was around him. He made her feel relaxed and she relished how easy it was to be around him, even if it was becoming more and more difficult not to kiss him or touch him.

"We should probably make a start in the basement," he said, when they finished eating. "That reminds me. I have some spare overalls if you want them? I would hate for you to ruin your clothes."

"That might be a good idea actually. I am quite partial to this sweater."

Valorian went through to the living room and brought her back the overalls.

"The bathroom is through there if you want to get changed. You can leave your stuff up here for when you want to change again."

"Thanks."

Valorian hadn't been joking when he'd said the bathroom was large. There was a corner bath, which reminded Freya of the 80s tv shows she had seen, a large double shower, matching his and hers sinks, and a toilet. She ran her hand over the black and white tiles, which had a delicate floral bordered edge. She changed quickly, folding her clothes into a pile, and putting on the overalls, which fit her surprisingly well. She left the clothes on a little table in the corner of the room and went back out to Valorian, who had also changed into a matching pair.

"I left my clothes on the little table in there if that's okay?"

"Yeah, that's not a problem. You look totally adorable in those by the way."

Freya looked down at herself and pulled a face.

"I'm sure I do," she said sarcastically.

Valorian chuckled and led the way back down the stairs, through the shop and to the basement, which he had already cleared of all the books and furniture.

"Wow, it looks strange in here without any of the shelves in," Freya said.

"Yeah, it's quite a spacious room. It will look nice with a more modern look," he said, popping open the tin of paint.

Freya picked up one of the rolling trays and a brush.

"I'll make a start doing all the cutting in," she said.

"Perfect, I will crack on with the roller and do the walls."

They began painting, making easy conversation as they worked, and enjoying the lull of the occasional comfortable silences.

After a while, Valorian stopped to ask whether she wanted a drink, and she saw he had paint across his nose and cheek, as well as flecks of grey in his stark white hair. She couldn't help but burst out laughing.

"What are you laughing at?" he asked.

"Nothing. Nothing at all," she tried to reply through her laughter.

"I refuse to believe you are laughing at nothing." He retrieved a mirror that had been hanging on the wall and checked his reflection.

"Oh, so *that*'s what's so funny."

"I mean, well…" She laughed again.

"You look far too clean to call yourself a decorator. I think we need to change that," he said picking up his roller.

Freya looked at him. *Surely, he wouldn't dare.* But he did, he shook his roller over near her and coated her with paint sprinkles.

"Oh my god!" she said, blobs of paint dripping from her hair.

"Now that is funny," he said.

"You just wait," she said getting to her feet.

Dipping her paintbrush in the paint tin beside her she walked up to him and ran it along his cheek, smiling at him smugly. He grabbed her arm with one hand and removed the brush with the other and ran the brush over her the same way. They both laughed as, trying to fight over the brush, they tumbled into a heap on the floor. They lay there laughing, for several long minutes.

"Oh, my belly aches from laughing," Freya said.

"We look ridiculous," Valorian replied laughing again.

He stood, offering Freya his hand, and pulling her up.

"Perhaps it's time we got cleaned up and left the rest for tomorrow."

"I think you are right, but we can't go back up there like this, we will get paint everywhere."

"I have jeans on under these overalls. I'll go up and get something for you to put on until you get cleaned up."

"Okay," she said.

Valorian took off his overalls. Freya did her best to avoid looking at his naked chest but found herself peering at him from under her eyelashes, as he headed upstairs. It didn't take long for him to return, and when he did, he had a bathrobe and face cloth for her.

"Here, let me clean that off your face and then you can pop this on until we get upstairs."

She stood in front of him while he gently wiped the paint from her face. His thumb grazed her lip, and she felt herself exhale with a sigh. That was all it took, and she felt his lips on hers, his tongue probing her mouth as he held her face in his hands. Her hands found his chest and shoulders, pulling him closer. Time and space melted away around them and she felt as if she was floating. He slowly pulled away, keeping her head in his hands, resting his nose against hers

"I've been wanting to do that since the day we met," he said breathlessly.

"I'm glad you didn't wait any longer then." Her voice trembled. He ran his hands down her side and took her hand in his.

"Let's go get cleaned up."

They returned to the flat above the shop, and Freya made her way to the bathroom to clean up and get changed. When she left the bathroom, Valorian was sitting on the sofa in his living room.

"Where shall I put this robe?"

He got up and walked towards her.

"I'll hang it here for tomorrow," he said, grazing her finger with his as he took it from her.

"Do you want a drink? Tea, coffee, hot chocolate or another glass of wine?"

"I would, but I should head home. Poppy is coming to pick me up tomorrow morning. I'm going with her to Hawthorne Hollow."

"It's a nice place. Me and Eric often go through there when we go mountain hiking."

"She said they have some quirky little shops I am interested to see."

"Well, if I can't persuade you to stay a little longer, can I at least walk you home?"

"I would like that very much," she replied.

Valorian locked the door behind him then took hold of her hand.

"Would it be wrong of me to take you the longer way so I can spend more time with you?"

She glanced up at him, as he flashed her that smile that made her insides turn to jelly.

"No, the scenic route works for me," she replied, moving herself closer to him.

He removed his hand from hers and wrapped his arm around her shoulders, pulling her in closer. Freya took a breath, taking in his scent. Oakmoss and cedarwood. It made her head swim a little, so she gripped his waist tighter. They walked in silence holding each other. To anyone who saw them, they would have looked like lovers taking a late-night stroll. The thought made Freya feel special, and incredibly happy. They arrived at Freya's apartment, and she felt the disappointment that the night was about to be over creep through her muscles. Valorian stood close in front of her and lifted her chin with his hand. He looked her in the eyes before moving in to kiss her again. Her arms felt like they belonged to someone else as they wove their way around his neck, her hand running through the back of his hair. He groaned into her mouth and her knees weakened, almost buckling under her. Even after they parted, they remained standing close together.

"Same again tomorrow?" he asked, twirling a loose hair of hers around his finger.

"Absolutely," she replied, unable to make use of her thoughts.

He gave her a last kiss on the lips, turned, and walked away. Freya unlocked the door and practically floated up her stairs. Her head span, she felt giddy and alive as she wondered how on earth she would sleep now. She licked her lips and could still taste him on her. She couldn't believe how good the evening had been. Stripping off her clothes, she climbed into bed and grabbed her journal from the bedside cabinet. Tonight, she had so much to say that her wrist ached from writing so fast, but pouring her heart onto the pages was the only way she knew to make sense of what was happening. Her cheeks were starting to hurt from smiling so much. She put the journal back and lay down, letting out a wistful sigh. She wondered what Valorian was doing now, whether he would be thinking of her the way she was thinking of him. *He kissed me a second time so it can't have been something that he regretted the first time.* She closed her eyes, drifting off as she replayed the feeling of his lips against hers.

CHAPTER NINE

Freya woke early the next morning after having the best night's sleep she could remember having in ages. She was excited to see Poppy, and to tell her about what had happened between her and Valorian, and she couldn't wait for night to fall so she could go see him. As if it sensed her happiness, the sun was trying desperately to burn its way through the milky clouds that hung over the mountains.

The beeping of Poppy's horn pulled Freya from her thoughts. Grabbing her bag and purse she ran down the stairs, locking the door behind her.

"Morning," Freya said as she got in the car.

"Good morning, you look chirpy today."

"Well, I had a good night." Freya beamed.

"Oh, do tell. Did you ask him to the movie?"

"Ah, dammit, I forgot. I will tonight."

"Ah, okay. Come on then, don't leave a girl waiting," Poppy said, setting off down the road.

"He cooked a wonderful meal, there were candles, a fresh rose, it was really romantic. We got a lot of painting done and it was such a laugh. But when he was cleaning paint off my face, he kissed me."

"What? Oh, wow, that is fantastic! Was it good?" Poppy glanced at her, smiling.

"It was...amazing," she said letting out a sigh.

"So, then what happened?"

"He walked me home with his arm wrapped around me and then he kissed me again. It's like he didn't want to leave, but I am going around tonight as well."

"For more painting, yeah?" Poppy laughed.

Freya laughed too. They talked about Valorian and Anderson until they got to Hawthorne Hollow.

The mountains had looked big from Crestwood but that was nothing compared to the view from Hawthorne Hollow. Freya stood staring at them, open mouthed. Standing so close, she could smell the pine and fresh snow in the air. When she managed to pull her attention from the mountains, she could see that Hawthorne Hollow was smaller than Crestwood. Looking around her, she saw a small main street, consisting of various shops situated in a horseshoe shape, with a main tourist information booth sitting in the centre of them all. The ground was covered in a fine mud, clearly brought down through the trails leading down from the mountains. Poppy told her she would be a few minutes to get what she needed, so Freya went over to the tourist information to have a look at the brochures while she waited.

It didn't take long for Poppy to return, and they both went straight to Lunar Nox, a shop full of witchy items. The scent of sage and lavender wafted through the air, the shelves were full of items for altars, statues, tarot card decks, crystals and various other items. Freya noticed that the shop also sold fresh herbs. Walking over, she picked up some of the small hessian bags. It was the perfect opportunity to start stocking up, especially with Imbolc on the way. As she made her way to the counter, she passed some boxes full of crystals. Freya usually didn't use them in her practice, but she was drawn to a lovely piece of rose quartz and hematite, so she picked those up, as well as some candles. After she had paid for everything, she found Poppy browsing the tarot card selection.

"I can't decide between these two decks. Mine are so worn I thought I would treat myself to a new deck." She looked at them, frowning.

"Put them down and just hold a hand over each deck without touching them. See if the energy connects to you. If not, buy both," Freya said, offering a smile.

Poppy put them down, did as Freya had suggested, and then put one of the decks back.

"This one had a much bigger pull than the other. Thanks for that tip."

"No problem," Freya replied.

Poppy paid for her tarot cards and they both visited the small clothes shop. Freya desperately needed some new jeans and was lucky enough to find a pair in her size.

"Poppy, have you seen these? How cute!" Freya said, picking up some socks with stags and foxes on them.

"Oh, those are adorable. You should treat yourself," Poppy replied.

Freya agreed, plucking them out of a box laden with socks.

They grabbed a hot croissant from the bakery and sat in the car to eat before setting off home.

"That was delicious," Freya said, wiping crumbs from her coat.

"They do some amazing food here, considering how small the place is."

"I will definitely be back for more of those," she said, swooning.

Poppy dropped Freya off at home.

Freya took some jars and placed all the herbs in them, writing out some little labels and sticking them down with Sellotape. She placed them all on one of the empty shelves on the built-in bookcase which sat opposite the fire in the living room, and then she turned her attention to the crystals, holding them in her hand. It was unlike her to pick out crystals, but she knew better than to ignore her intuition when it called to her. After some thought, she walked to the bedroom and placed them on the bedside cabinet next to her journal.

Freya was just about to sit down to read, when the doorbell rang. She rushed down the stairs, expecting to see Poppy, but to her surprise, Marly stood on the doorstep. "Hey," Freya said.

"Hey, Freya, just thought I would pop around and see if you fancied joining me for lunch at Jackson's. I am just heading over now."

"That would be great, come in a minute while I grab my stuff," she said, opening the door for Marly.

Jacksons was fairly quiet compared to how busy it had been on Thursday night. They both sat near the cosy fire, and Marly ordered food from the bar.

"So, how are you finding Crestwood? I wasn't sure if you really knew anyone other than me and Valorian. I had images of you sitting alone for days," Marly said, taking a sip from her glass.

"Honestly, I'm loving it. I have been spending time with Poppy and I met some of the others. I've been helping Valorian decorate as well."

"Sounds like you have been busy."

"There is actually something I wanted to talk to you about, but I was going to wait until tomorrow when I was back at work."

"Oh?" Marly said.

"I found an old grimoire at Valarion's. It was written in code and Valorian said that no one had been able to read it."

"Ah yes, I know the book you mean. It belonged to the Evermores before they disappeared."

"Well, I can read it. It turns out that my family are the Evermores, but it was hidden from me as I grew up. I guess this is why my intuition brought me here." Freya replied. She felt confident trusting Marly with the information about her heritage.

"No way! That is crazy," Marly said, sounding astonished.

"I know. I can hardly believe it myself."

"This is great though."

"I was wondering if you knew anything about my family? Maybe why they left?"

"Unfortunately, all I know is the rumour, which I am sure Valorian has told you about himself. I was born not long after that time." Marly said, taking a moment to think. "There is an old Witch called Holden who was around when your family lived here. He is a recluse and rarely comes out of his house, and with his age he is very grumpy, but it might be worth asking him. If he does know something though, he has never talked about it before."

"It would be worth a try. At this point I would give it a go. I need to know what happened. Plus, it is keeping me distracted, and I need as much distraction as I can get. It stops me from overthinking things."

"Yes, I can imagine. Your parents' death wasn't that long ago, was it?"

"No. It was at the beginning of December. But I would rather not discuss that if that's okay."

"Of course. Just so you know, I am here if you ever want to talk about it."

"Thank you."

"So, I take it you are a Witch too then?"

"I am but I haven't practiced magic since… well, since my parents. I keep up other traditions though, but I just don't want to use my powers. Valorian told me about himself and some of the others in the town. I had no idea it was such a varied place.

"Yeah, there are plenty of us oddbods around." Marly smiled.

"It's great. Back in the city, different supernatural beings kept to their own kind; there was a lot of rivalry between them. Especially the Vampires and the Shifters."

"As is the way, old arguments are hard to let go of for many. Here though we all strive to work together to keep the town a wonderful place to live."

"And it works so well," Freya replied as Jackson placed their plates on the table.

"Thanks, Jackson," they both said.

Freya tucked into her meal of salad with jacket potato. It was delicious. The warmth of the fire made her feel sleepy, so when she left Marly, armed with Holden's address, she decided to go home to have a nap first. The last thing she wanted to do was fall asleep later, or be too tired to help Valorian. Or worse yet, be too tired to stay there for long. She was desperate to spend as much time with him as possible - if she had it her way, she wouldn't be leaving him at all. She smiled, imagining being wrapped in his arms all night long, kissing his soft lips.

Freya awoke with a jump; confusion muddling her thoughts for a moment. Clarity came into focus when she realised that she had overslept. Groaning, she got up off the sofa and poured herself a cold water from the fridge. Knitting her eyebrows together, she sighed, disappointed with herself. There wouldn't be enough time to go visit Holden now. A smile stretched across her face when she reminded herself that at least she was closer to seeing Valorian. She walked to the bathroom, grabbing a towel and bathrobe on the way. There was enough time for a quick shower before heading over. Freya stood, letting the shower fire out bullets of water that hit her shoulders. As much as she wanted to find out about her family heritage, she was worried about visiting Holden, given what Marly had said. *He may not even speak to me and then I would have to wait for Valorian to speak to his father. There's always the chance Holden knows what happened, what if when I find out, I wish that I hadn't? There was a reason why it was all done so secretively.* Freya hated the idea that she could be related to dark Witches. Her entire life, she had been taught about respect for magic, using it only with balance, the karmic effect. She couldn't imagine ever using magic to harm or hurt someone, or for greed and wealth. *Everlyn must have really been in love to accept that sort of magic in her life.* She stepped out of the shower and dried off. Pulling on jeans and a plaid shirt she looked at herself in the mirror. Her brown hair fell in waves, and she patted off any excess moisture with a towel, ran the comb through it, and applied a little mascara. She didn't want to look like she had made a big effort for Valorian, but she didn't want to look like she had made no effort either. She shoved a hairband in her pocket ready for painting. Looking at the clock she saw it was time to leave.

The town was a little busier than usual as she walked through, and a couple of people waved hello to her as she passed. As usual, Valorian was waiting for her in the book shop. He rushed straight over to her when she walked in, planting a kiss on her lips. Her head spun as she slid her arms around his waist.

"I missed you," he said, pulling back slightly to look at her.

"I missed you too," she said looking up into his eyes.

Freya was caught in the warmth in his eyes as he looked at her, setting off the butterflies in her stomach again. Valorian locked the door and took her hand, guiding her upstairs.

They ate their meal talking about Freya's trip to Hawthorne Hollow.

"I had lunch with Marly today. She told me someone I can contact who might know more about Everlyn and why my family left town," she said, putting down her wine glass.

"Oh yeah?"

"Someone called Holden? Marly said he was a recluse and could be quite grumpy, so I am not exactly jumping at the idea of visiting him tomorrow."

"Ah, I completely forgot that Holden will have been around back then. He's quite a character but is harmless enough. He is a particular fan of the cake from Spellbound Cafe so you could take some to butter him up. He never goes out, so I am sure he will appreciate it."

"I'll definitely get some before I go over there then. Thanks for the tip."

"I would come with you, but it will be too late to go over after you have finished work, and it is too light for me before then."

"It's fine. I can manage on my own, but I appreciate the offer."

They finished their drinks and sat together on the sofa. Valorian sat with his arm around her as she snuggled into his chest, and she couldn't help to think how strange it was not hearing his heartbeat.

He ran his fingers down her side, leaving a trail of fire in their wake. She needed a distraction before things escalated to a point she wasn't ready for yet.

"We should make a start downstairs. We only have a second coat to do and then it will be ready for all the furniture," she said, sitting up.

"Yeah, we should, before it gets too late for you. And I would really like to see how cute you look in those overalls again." He winked.

"Me? Nah, it was you who looked cute with paint all over your face." She chuckled.

Freya got changed in the bathroom and made her way downstairs. Valorian had already made a start. The room looked completely different with the new paint - clean and crisp compared to its previous traditional Victorian style décor. She noticed he had already painted all the shelving units in a deep teal paint, and there was a pile of honey-coloured cushions, and a blanket folded in the corner to accent the teal. She was impressed at his style; they were colours she would have picked herself.

"I love the teal and honey colours. They'll look great together."

"When you suggested the teal, I knew I would have to use it. I didn't want a bright yellow though, and when I was making honey on toast the other day, it struck me that the colour would be perfect."

"Ah, food inspiration! Always the best type." She started laughing.

"They do say the way to a man's heart is through his stomach. Apparently, it is also the way to his colour palette."

They both laughed. Valorian put on some music, and they got on with the painting. The second coat went on much quicker than the first, and Freya found herself still wide awake when they'd finished.

"Do you fancy going for a walk?" she asked.

"Are you not tired?"

"Nope, not yet, and I feel like going outside. I love the dark and the night sky here is amazing. It was pretty clear when I was walking over, so hopefully it still will be."

"Then yes, I would love to walk with you. I actually know a great place to get a good view of the sky if you would like me to show you?"

She smiled. "I would like that very much."

CHAPTER TEN

Freya got changed and cleaned herself up. Luckily, there were only a few spots of paint on her arms this time. She came out of the bathroom as Valorian was folding a blanket up and putting it in a backpack.

He looked at her. "I'm bringing a blanket because where I am taking you, the view is best seen lying down."

"Ah, saves us getting damp and cold."

"Exactly." He picked up the bag, smiling at her.

They made their way towards the meadow that bordered the forest. The path was wet and slippery, and Freya kept a tight hold of Valorian's hand, following just behind him into the forest. She was glad he could see in the dark because she couldn't see a thing. It was pitch black – except for the occasional glint of moonlight which poked through the thick canopy and highlighted the trees around her. It was silent, other than the sound of an occasional twig snapping under their feet. Once or twice, Freya could have sworn she saw white eyes watching them from the trees. She would have to remember to ask him about the creatures that dwelt within this forest. *I wouldn't be surprised if there were fae folk here, given the supernaturals in the town. Usually, they all stick close together. Safety in numbers.* Valorian led them through a part of the forest which didn't have a trail. Freya caught her leg on fallen branches and almost fell on a couple of occasions. Eventually, they came to a clearing. A large moss-covered rock stood in the centre; moonlight bathing it in a cool white glow.

"Wow, this is pretty," Freya said, surprise evident in her voice; she hadn't expected to see such a beautiful place within the forest.

"I thought you'd like it. Come on, let's get on top of that rock," he said.

She followed Valorian, watching where he put his feet to climb to the top. Thankfully, the rock was only about twice her height, and the moss wasn't slippery, so it didn't take much effort. Taking his backpack off, Valorian unzipped it, pulling out the blanket he had packed. He laid it on the rock, gesturing for Freya to take a seat. She sat down, grateful for the material between her and the cold rock. Valorian sat beside her and then lay back. Doing the same, Freya looked at the sky above her. The outline of trees on the edge of her vision gave her a tunnel view of the night sky as the stars blinked at her, flashing colours of blue, red and white.

"You were right, this is a great view," she said.

"I like to come out here sometimes to think. I love just looking up at the universe. It's good to remind myself sometimes that everything isn't everlasting."

"I get that. It's quite humbling to think about it all really."

"When I was first turned, I hated it. I couldn't think of anything worse than living, let alone living for eternity."

"It wasn't something you wanted then?"

"No, not at all." He hesitated. "In fact, quite the opposite. I had tried to take my own life when my blood father found me. I was almost dead - and would have been - but he saved me. Back then I called it a curse. I didn't want to live. My life was a mess, and I couldn't bear it any longer. But in time, with my new powers and a different insight into things, especially with my heightened responses, I learned to be happy again. To find new joy in life. It wasn't easy though." His voice sounded pained.

"I'm sorry. It sounds as if your life before death - and during – wasn't the easiest."

"It's good now, that's what matters."

"Well, I'm glad you are here." She moved her hand over his, giving it a squeeze.

"I am as well." He turned towards her.

They lay together under the stars, holding each other, mouth against mouth for what felt like hours.

"I should get going," Freya mumbled into Valorian's neck as she placed butterfly kisses along it.

"You should. It's cold out here and I don't want you to get ill. I have an idea though."

"Oh, what's your idea?"

"If you want, I can come back to yours and stay with you for a bit while you sleep. If you want me to, that is? Truth be told, I don't really want to let you go."

"I think that is your best idea yet. I don't really want to have to leave you either, so I feel like that's definitely a winning solution."

They got up and headed back towards town. Freya was excited to have Valorian stay with her. He brought her a special sort of comfort that made her feel safe and secure - something she hadn't felt since her parents' death. Freya was grateful she had tidied up, as she put her bag down on the small dining table.

"I'm going to make a cup of tea. Would you like one?"

"Sure, thank you," Valorian replied, looking at her bookcase. "It's pretty cosy in here," he said.

"I like it. It isn't much but it's home. I like the vibe I get from it."

"You've made it your own, with just the small touches. Like the Pentagram on the wall, the herbs on the bookshelf, the very colourful rug…" he said looking down under his feet.

"Well, I can take credit for it all except the rug. Bert bought me it when I moved in. He said the place needed brightening up if someone as young as me was going to live here." She chuckled.

"Well, he wasn't wrong. It suits you and this apartment."

They sat together on the sofa, drinking their tea. Freya yawned.

"We should get you to bed," Valorian said.

"You are probably right. The fresh air must have worn me out." She stretched lazily, standing up.

Valorian lay on the bed, while Freya grabbed a pair of pyjamas from the drawer and headed into the bathroom, to get changed and brush her teeth. She looked in the mirror and took some deep breaths. *I've never spent the night with a Vampire before.* Her excitement mingled with nervous energy.

She walked back into her room. Seeing him lying there made her pulse quicken and she cursed herself, knowing it was likely he could hear her heartrate increase and would sense the change in her. She climbed into bed and shuffled close to him. He put his arm around her so she could lay her head on his chest. She ran her fingers across his abdomen, and she felt him shift slightly. She smiled to herself; she liked the idea that she got under his skin as much as he got under hers. The struggle to resist him was hard; the pull she felt to him was stronger than any she had ever experienced. She felt as if she had known him her entire life. As she thought about the depth of connection she didn't understand, comfort took hold and lulled her into a deep, dreamless sleep.

Freya woke, reaching out but finding nothing but a cold, empty bed. She groaned, opening her eyes. Warm yellow stripes decorated the wall in front of her, and she smiled. Finally, the sun was out again. She rolled over to check the clock on the bedside cabinet and saw a note had been placed there. Picking it up she saw it was from Valorian, wishing her a good day and luck with Holden, along with a reminder about the cake. He said he would meet her at work later. She climbed out of bed, pulled open the curtains and surveyed the town, surprised to see the scene in front of her. The street was full of people, and she noticed a cart had been set up selling what looked like toffee apples, roast chestnuts and other wintery goodness. She couldn't wait to go get some, she hadn't had a toffee apple since she was a child at a Halloween fayre. She dressed and made her way to Spellbound Cafe, making sure she got a slice of cake before they sold out. Poppy wasn't at work, so she didn't stop to chat. Instead, she made her way to the cart and purchased a toffee apple, a bag of roasted chestnuts and a small bag of candy floss and then set off in the direction of Holden's house. Marly had said he lived just behind the first trees of the forest behind Mystique's Boutique and that she would instantly know which cabin belonged to him.

There was no path to guide her, but there were small cabins dotted around the edge of the forest. She saw smoke before she saw the chimney it belonged to. Marly was right, Holden's cabin stood out. *You wouldn't think it was winter looking at it.* Wild meadow flowers were jammed into the tiny garden, ivy covered the walls and roof. It looked as though it was mid-summer in the garden where it was winter everywhere else. A small window next to the door was wedged open slightly. She opened the gate, shutting it behind her. Immediately the smell of heather, lavender, bluebell, daisy and foxglove assaulted her. She noted the lack of butterflies or bees that would normally be present in this type of garden during summer as she walked up the cobbled path and knocked on the small wooden door.

"I'm not buying whatever you're selling," a voice boomed from the window.

Freya jumped. "I'm not selling anything. I'm a friend of Marly and Valorian, they advised I come and speak to you about my ancestors."

"I don't know you, go away."

"I brought some cake for you, a Spellbound special," she replied, hoping it would entice the man to speak to her.

Slowly, the door creaked open, and a voice from within told her to come inside. She entered a small kitchen. It reminded her of something from a children's fairytale book. There was a gurgling cauldron in the corner and a hunchback man standing at a counter with his back to her. Spoons stirred themselves in strange looking pots and a sweeping brush worked its way across the room. The room was dripping with magic, making Freya smile.

"Don't just stand there making the place look messy. Take a seat."

"Freya sat on one of the uneven stools at the cluttered table to her right, putting the cake down on top of it. The man turned around and eyed her curiously.

"Ah yes, I see. You are an Evermore child."

Freya looked at him in confusion.

"How did you know that? Not even I knew that."

"You all have that same look. Just like Everlyn and her mother, the same face."

"I don't know much about them. My mother didn't speak about them, and my grandmother passed away when I was a teenager. I had no idea that we were from Crestwood; I just ended up here."

"Instinct and intuition is a big part of our kind's blood. It knows where you needed to be, and it brought you here."

"Marly told me that you were living here when Everlyn was, that you might know why my family left."

"I was very close to your family. Our parents had hoped that Everlyn and I would marry one day and produce the perfect offspring. However, Everlyn only had eyes for one man. I never got to say goodbye to her, but I was left something when they went."

Holden walked over to a locked cabinet, waved his arms around and muttered an incantation under his breath. The cabinet door popped open, he reached in and took out a small box. He walked over and passed it to her.

Freya took it and instantly felt a connection: this belonged to her family. The small trinket box was ornately carved with tiny forest animals and pine trees. She opened the latch. Inside was a brass key sitting on top of some paper. She took out the key, removing the papers. The first was a letter to Holden. An apology for leaving, explaining that Everlyn was with child and her family were leaving to protect the child from Carrington Emery and his family. The letter stated that they would not return, and begged Holden not to utter a word about their disappearance until 'the time was right'. The second piece of paper was a deed to a shop with an apartment above it. It belonged to the Evermore family.

"They must have known one day someone would come back here. The shop and the apartment have not been touched since the day they left. It has remained the only empty shop in the town, but everyone knows who it belonged to - who it still belongs to - so it has been protected. The Evermores were a fine family. Upstanding, respected, friendly, and warm. The town has missed them greatly. Perhaps, now is the time for the Evermore name to make its way back into the town and the shop to reopen."

He looked at her, sitting opposite her.

"I... I am not sure that I am the one to do that. I don't even know if I plan to stay here indefinitely yet."

"And why not?"

"My parents were killed a few weeks before Yule. I left the city and just ended up here by chance. I want nothing to do with magic."

"What utter nonsense. Who gives up their power because of something like That? Witches are killed by magic all the time - do you think we all haven't suffered some loss?"

Freya was taken aback by the lack of empathy; she had never met anyone who didn't understand. She was lost for words.

"Look, I don't mean to upset you, but life goes on. Your power is within you. You might think you can hide from it, but it will come out, it has to. You cannot keep that much energy locked up and when it does come out, you might hurt someone. You might hurt yourself. What would your parents have thought of that?"

"My parents...well, they would have supported me no matter my decision." She couldn't keep the anger from her voice. *How dare this man come at me like this!*

"Your parents would likely have told you it was unnecessary, that you will cause more harm than good trying to pretend your magic doesn't exist."

"You have no idea what they would say, you didn't know them!"

"Your mother was the same blood as Everlyn, as the rest of them. They would never have turned their back on their magic."

"No, they turned their back on their town, their birthright, the people they cared for. My mother wouldn't have done that either."

"To protect you, I can bet she would."

Freya sat, her rage simmering. *He has no idea what he's talking about.*

"Nevertheless," he continued, "the shop, the apartment. It is yours. What you do with them is your choice."

"What happened to Carrington Emery?" Freya asked, trying to diffuse the tension.

"His family never lived in Crestwood. They were from Hawthorne Hollow. Once Everlyn left, they never came around anymore. I have no idea what happened to them. I heard that Carrington's father was angry and tried to hunt Everlyn down but never succeeded. As far as I know the family still live there, what they know of the situation though...I have no idea."

"Were they that bad?"

"They used magic in a way most other Witches would never dream of. To gain wealth, success, reputation. They hurt people. All magic has a balance, as you know, so whenever they took something for themselves, something bad happened - and they didn't care. They enjoyed the darkness so much it consumed them. Carrington always seemed different to the others, but ultimately, with a family like that, association was enough."

"I see." Freya said pensively, her eyebrows furrowing.

"My advice is not to look for them. While I may not know how they live now, that sort of magic use doesn't dwindle easily. It's addictive, and you don't want to find yourself in amongst all that."

"I had no intention of looking for them. My family hid from them for a reason."

"And you would do well to remember that."

Freya found her eyes narrowing as she glared at the old Witch. She had been warned he was grumpy, but the way he spoke was unnecessary. He didn't even know her. He certainly shouldn't be making assumptions about her.

"As I have already said, I have no intention of looking for them. I was more interested in trying to understand why my family would leave this place when it clearly meant a lot to them."

"Well, now you know, and you have the keys and deeds to the building, so if there was nothing else?"

"No, there wasn't." She stood, walking towards the door. "Thank you for your help."

Holden nodded at her, and the door creaked open to let her

out, shutting with a bang the moment she was over its threshold.

Freya hurried down the path and out through the gate. The box was still in her hand, and she placed it carefully into her bag. She had no idea what to do with the key. *If Crestwood is somewhere I decided to stay, it would at least give me a permanent home, and I wouldn't need to worry about rent again. The alternative would be to lease the entire building, with the shop, to someone else.* A headache started to build at the front of her head. She didn't like having to make such big decisions, perhaps she could talk it out with Poppy, Marly and Valorian - see what they thought. Crestwood wouldn't be a bad place to build a life for herself. She had made friends here and she had a job. Plus, her ancestors were here, and she wouldn't feel right abandoning them the way the others had - even if they'd had a reason. Intrigue gnawed at her. If the shop and apartment had just been left, she wondered what was still in there. The family had left in a hurry so they must have left things behind. She decided to ask Valorian if he would go with her to have a look when she finished work.

CHAPTER ELEVEN

Freya sat cross-legged on the sofa, the old grimoire in her lap. She flicked over the page and began to decode the writing. She laughed as she deciphered the name of the spell. *Remedy for Stink Throat.* The names they had for things back then were so different to now. Looking at the ingredients, it was a basic tonic to remedy a sore throat. She looked up at her bookcase. It had been a long time since she had made any tinctures or tonics. Her mother had kept a cupboard full of all sorts of things for various ailments. It didn't matter what Freya came home to complain about, or how she had hurt herself, her mother always had a fix. She smiled as a memory floated into her head. She had been around six years old and had been in the large open park in the middle of the city. Her mother had been sitting on a bench with a book in her hand enjoying the lazy summer sun and she had been lying out on a yellow blanket drawing with her new favourite pens. A curious bee had come and taken a seat on her pencil case and as she tried to shoo it off, it had stung her on the arm. Her mother had taken her home and applied a poultice to the sting, wrapping it in a bandage. Her arm had recovered within an hour, leaving just a small red mark where the sting had been. Freya ran her finger over her arm, tears pooling in her eyes. She wondered what her parents would have thought about all this, sure that they would have loved a town like Crestwood. They had never liked the city, and she couldn't understand why they had stayed there, even with the Coven. *They would probably be alive now if they had moved away instead of becoming Guardians.*

Freya looked back at the grimoire. Deciding that she couldn't allow herself to get distracted by her thoughts, she carried on reading until she had to get ready for her shift at Marly's.

Making sure she put the key in her bag, she decided to leave early and get a coffee before starting work to catch up with Marly about the day's events.

The Cafe was busier than she had expected, as she slid onto one of the stools at the counter and ordered a strong black coffee. Marly brought it over to her with a smile on her face.

"How did it go with Holden?"

"Well, you weren't wrong about him, he is quite grumpy. But he was helpful."

"So, what did you find out?" Marly asked, taking a seat next to her.

"Well, everyone was right about the rumour. The Evermores left because Everlyn was pregnant, and the father of the baby was Carrington Emery. Apparently, his family were dark Witches, and my family wanted to protect the baby from them."

"It sounds like they did what they thought was right. It's been a while since I have heard of the Emerys," Marly said.

"Holden gave me a key and deeds to the property they left behind. It's the shop on the corner opposite Valorian's and the apartment above."

"Oh, wow, that place has been empty for as long as I can remember. That must have been quite a shock."

"It was. I have no idea what to do with it yet. I haven't faced selling my parents' house yet either. I just didn't know where I would end up or whether I would go back, so I didn't want to rush it in case I needed somewhere to stay."

"Understandable, it's hard to let go and there is no rush to do anything with either. The shop has been empty for over 130 years, it doesn't need dealing with immediately. And as for your parents' house, that will be hard to say goodbye to, but there will come a time when you feel ready to part with it or do something with it. It won't go anywhere in the meantime.

"That's true. I really can't see myself going back to the city though, not to live. I guess things will resolve themselves, they always do." Freya sighed.

Marly gave Freya's hand a squeeze.

"Life is never easy, but sometimes the best things come out of the worst situations."

Freya nodded.

"Well, I better go put my stuff away and get ready for my shift," she said, finishing the last of her coffee.

"It's been a little busier than usual tonight, hopefully it will stay like this," Marly said.

Freya stacked the coffee cups on the tray and sighed, as she walked over and placed it on the counter. She took the cloth and cleaning spray back to the table she had just cleared; coffee stains and crumbs scattered the surface. Her feet ached, and the evening had been so busy she hadn't given a second thought to Valorian or the old property. The bell tinkled behind her, and she turned her head to see Valorian walk in. He looked at her and she smiled, the ache in her feet no longer relevant. She hadn't realised that it was almost the end of her shift.

"Hey," he said, sitting at the counter.

Freya walked around to the opposite side.

"Hey."

"How was your visit to Holden?"

"Enlightening," she said with a smirk.

She told Valorian about her visit and what she had found out. Valorian hadn't known about the shop, and he was excited to go and look around with her.

"My father is planning a visit here for the Imbolc festival in a couple of weeks. It should be a good opportunity to find out more about your family," he said.

"That would be nice. Does he often come to celebrate Witches Sabbats?"

"He does. They have become part of the town's traditions,

and now most residents celebrate them with the Witches. It's a good way to remind everyone that the dark of winter is almost over, and spring is beginning. Even our town needs that hope sometimes."

"It sounds lovely. I'm looking forward to the festival and to meeting your father," she said.

"He was very intrigued to hear you were here, he is looking forward to meeting you too."

The pair talked while Freya cleaned up and prepared to close the cafe. Marly had come out from the office to join them.

Collecting her bag and coat, Freya and Valorian left the cafe and went over to the old property. The windows were covered in grime and Freya couldn't see through them. She took out the key and asked Valorian if they could use the torch on his phone.

"You really do need to get a new one of these," he said wiggling it at her.

"I don't need one."

"You say that, but we could have two torches now *and* it would allow me to talk to you more often. I am sure Poppy would agree too."

"I'll think about it," she said.

Freya put the key in the lock and turned it. She felt a magical barrier, which dissipated as she entered. *I should have known there would have been some magical protection around the shop.* Valorian entered behind her, using his phone for light.

"You know, this would be easier if you'd conjure a little Witchlight," he said as he looked around.

"Funny," Freya replied, rolling her eyes.

She realised that whether she decided to stay and live here or rent it out that she would need to get some modern electrics and plumbing put in the building. They walked around, scanning the room. There was a long counter which ran the full length of the back wall, and behind it was row upon row of shelves which still held all sorts of potion bottles and other items. There was a door tucked in the corner of the room next to a row of shelves. A thick layer of dust covered everything.

"It's like going through a time warp," Valorian said.

"Yeah, everything is exactly how it was left all those years ago."

In the back room, was a staircase leading to a larger room. Inside, Freya spotted a large black cauldron in the middle of the room, and various cupboards, shelves and work surfaces, along with a fireplace against the walls.

"This must have been the mixing room, or where they made all the potions and things."

"We're going to have to get some electricity through here. You should go speak to Jackson; he's the town's Electrician."

"I didn't know that. I'll see if I can get in touch with him. I bet it'll cost a fortune to get everything fixed."

"Possibly, but Jackson will give you a great deal. I can talk to Silas as well; he is a plumber."

"I'd appreciate that, thank you."

The stairs going up to the apartment had a thick, black carpet. Valorian led the way, Freya following close behind him. The door at the top was slightly ajar, and Freya stopped abruptly as they reached it. Vivid images flashed through her mind of people scurrying out of here with whatever they could carry. She could almost taste their fear.

Pushing open the door, Valorian shone his light around, breaking the connection between Freya and the memories of the past. Freya gasped. She had known that the apartment would still have a lot of furniture inside, but she hadn't expected it to look like it did. Cups still sat on the table next to the fireplace. What looked like some sort of old print newspaper was placed clumsily on the chair. Clearly, they hadn't planned to leave so quickly.

"I can't decide if I think this is amazing or really eerie," Valorian said, almost in a whisper.

"I'm going with eerie, though I am sure it looks totally different in the light. I wonder if Poppy is working tomorrow. Maybe I can get her to come with me. I don't much feel like coming here alone."

"Poppy works day shifts usually. I could drop in at Marly's tonight if you want? I am sure she would come with you. She isn't usually at the café until the afternoon."

"If you wouldn't mind that would be helpful. If you can ask her to meet me at about ten?"

"Sure, I can do that."

Freya and Valorian continued looking around at the main room. There were old paintings and black and white photographs adorning the walls. The air gave off a damp musty smell and it felt noticeably cooler in the apartment than it did outside. Freya knew she would need to spend some time here airing it out and warming the place up. *Perhaps I could bring some firewood with me tomorrow, I'm sure I saw some at the DIY store.*

"I'm done here tonight. I'll come back tomorrow when it's light," she told Valorian.

"You sure? You haven't checked the back rooms or kitchen yet."

"I'm sure. It's just depressing being here in the cold, dark night. It saddens me they just left like that. They clearly loved this home."

"They must have been really scared to leave it all behind."

"Yup," she said, sorrowfully.

They made their way to Freya's apartment, where Freya made some tea while Valorian added logs to the fire. She watched him stoking the flames and smiled to herself. It didn't matter how much time she spent with him, it never felt like it was enough. She wished he could have stayed the night and wondered whether she should perhaps invest in some blackout curtains for the bedroom so he could stay over without worrying about the light. She had noticed all the windows in his apartment were tinted.

She placed the mugs of tea on the table in front of the sofa and took a seat. Valorian joined her, and she snuggled into him as he stroked her hair.

"I should probably think about getting a TV," she said.

"Why? If you don't watch it, then it would be pointless."

"I usually just read but it might be nice to watch a film when you are here."

"Well, I have a solution for that without buying a TV."

"I don't think watching something on your tiny phone screen

will cut it," she replied.

Valorian laughed.

"Not that. I have a projector and screen at home I don't use. I can come and fit it if you'd like. Then we can just hook my phone up to show it on the screen through the projector."

"Oh," Freya said, feeling silly. "That makes more sense."

Freya found herself dozing off. She felt Valorian pull a blanket from the back of the sofa and lay it across her. He softly stroked the side of her face, occasionally pulling his fingers through her hair. Her body tingled as if it was static, but she couldn't help falling asleep. The last thing she felt was him placing a kiss on her head.

CHAPTER TWELVE

Freya saw Marly standing on the corner and gave her a wave. "Morning," she said.

"Morning," Marly said, offering a smile.

"Thanks for coming, I wasn't sure how I would feel being alone here. Me and Valorian didn't get to see much last night, it was just too dark."

"I don't mind. I'm quite intrigued to see the place if I am honest."

Unlocking the door, Freya pushed it open. In the daylight the shop was much brighter than she had anticipated. White walls, stained with time, framed the dark wooden counter and shelves.

"This is incredible, they left everything as it was," Marly said.

"You should see upstairs, there are cups on the table. Clearly, they left in a hurry. It reminds me of those films you see where a family disappears, and the police are trying to figure out what happened to them."

Freya showed Marly the back room, and then they made their way up the stairs and into the main living room of the house. Freya could see so much more today. Books lined the shelves, alongside trinkets and ornaments. Thick grey dust coated every surface, making her nose tingle. She walked over to the windows and gave them a push to open them. She looked at the photos on the wall, the black and white images were more detailed than she had thought they would be.

"That must be Everlyn," Marly said, standing behind her.

"It must be. And those must be her parents," she said, looking at the family portrait.

Freya opened the door to her left and found a small kitchen area. A black stove dominated the wall at the back of the room, and a large worn wooden table and two benches sat in the centre. A sink of sorts still held unclean dishes, and dead flies lay across the counter tops. Freya pulled a face.

"This place needs a good clean up," Marly said.

"Yeah, it's pretty gross," Freya agreed.

They moved around the apartment, finding a room with a single bed, dresser, a small mirror and a desk. *This must have belonged to Everlyn,* Freya thought. As they approached the next door, Freya could hear a tapping coming from inside the room.

"Can you hear that?" she asked.

"I can, I wonder what it is. It's coming from in there." Marly replied.

Freya pushed open the door, and found it was the main bedroom. It was grand in comparison to the rest of the house. A dark, wooden four-poster bed stood dominating the space, with a dresser on either side and an old fancy dressing table along one wall, still adorned with perfume bottles. Freya moved towards the window, which she was pretty sure was the source of the tapping sound. The curtain was closed, and she pulled it back, almost falling over in her surprise. She startled at a large purple butterfly knocking against the window.

"Is that a butterfly?" Marly said.

"It is," she replied. "This is really weird."

"Well, I have never seen one like that before," Marly said.

"I have, but never in real life," Freya whispered.

"You have?"

"In my dreams. Since I moved here, I have had a recurring dream about a butterfly trapped in a room unable to escape."

"So, this," Marly said, pointing at the butterfly, "is not a coincidence."

"I don't think so. But I don't know what it is."

"Maybe Holden will know, you said he was close to the family?"

"From what he told me, I think he and Everlyn were paired to marry. Before she fell in love with that Carrington guy."

"Might be best to pay him another visit then."

"I think I will, I could take him one of these photographs of Everlyn too, he might like one to keep."

"Good idea."

Freya moved closer towards the butterfly. It stopped moving, almost as if it was anticipating what she would do next. She pushed open the window, allowing it the opportunity to fly away, but instead it flew over to her and rested on her hand. She peered down at it curiously. The markings on it were incredible, she had never seen anything like it. It had deep rich purple wings with white spots, with two marks, one on each wing giving it the appearance of a pair of orange rimmed eyes. She didn't dare touch it, worried the delicate wings would fall apart if she did. She smiled at it as it watched her before flying off to sit on the ledge of the open window.

"How strange," said Marly.

"Mhm," was all Freya could reply.

They carried on looking around, and Freya decided to go over to the DIY store to get some firewood and boxes while Marly checked to make sure the chimneys weren't blocked.

As Freya returned, she could hear voices. Jackson was standing in the hall, talking to Marly as she came up the stairs.

"Hey, Freya, Marly gave me a call and asked me to come have a look at the place. You need some electrics sorted in here?"

"Hi, Jackson, yes, I do. I was going to come see you, but this will save me the trip. Is it going to be possible?"

"Yeah, it won't be a problem. The rest of the street has them so I can just hook you up to them and put in a meter here, then we just run them through the house. If I can get Poppy to help, her magic will have this done in no time and save a lot of destruction and cost with the walls."

"Poppy's magic?"

"She's a Witch, just like you," Marly replied.

"Huh, I had no idea."

"We could have this done in about five-ish hours," Jackson said.

"Wow, that's fantastic, I thought it would take days."

"The chimneys are fine as well. Someone had put grates up top so there was nothing stuck in them, the bottom just needs a clear out and they should be fine," Marly said.

"Thanks, that will really help until the electrics are sorted. This place needs heating up."

As the three of them discussed the plans, Freya found that the longer she was there, the more connected she felt to the familial energy in the place. She started to imagine what it would be like to live there. *Fresh paint on the walls, new carpets, clean up the furniture, and a nice new mattress on the four-poster bed.* It made a warmth spread through her and brought her comfort. She didn't know what to do about the shop below though. If she did move in here, would someone rent the shop if they didn't have the apartment above? She wasn't sure how she felt about that either. It felt wrong, the idea of someone else living here - almost like an invasion. She went over to the window and looked out at the street below. She could still see the mountains in the distance, even if the view of them wasn't as clear as it had been from her apartment. The forest was closer, and she liked looking out at the trees. *Summer would be lovely; the smell of the meadow would come in through the windows.* It was then that she realised that she had come to love it here. *Perhaps I could convince Valorian to help me renovate, since he owes me for helping with the basement?*

Marly left to go get the cafe ready to open, and Jackson left not long after to go speak to Poppy. Freya had offered to get a key cut and drop it off with Poppy so that they could make a start on the electrics while she was at work. She hoped that Valorian had managed to speak to Silas about the plumbing. *The sooner I get this place sorted, the better.* She picked up the portrait of Everlyn that sat on the fireplace and put it in her bag to give to Holden the next day. Before leaving, she walked around closing some of the windows, making sure she left one on the latch in each room. The purple butterfly was still perched on the ledge of the window, and she could feel it watching her as she pulled the curtain across the other window. She left the window open where it sat, she didn't want it to be trapped in here if it wanted to leave.

Being back in her apartment felt strange, she could still feel the energy of the other place over her body. She took a quick shower and got changed for work, making a sandwich and salad before she left. Dusk was arriving later as each day passed, and she felt hope swell inside her. She loved all the seasons; the crisp leaves falling in autumn, the snowfall in winter, the fresh blooms of spring, but most of all, she loved the lazy, sunshine-filled days of summer. They always made her feel like anything was possible, the way the sun poured into people's skin, and brightened their very soul. It made everyone happier and less stressed. She had often felt that the city could be claustrophobic during summer, but she knew Crestwood would be different, the town oozed calm and everyone here was relaxed and open.

The evening shift at Marly's was going well, a steady number of customers kept Freya busy – although she still had time to daydream about the old apartment and the work she wanted to do with it. It was the first time in a while that she had felt passionate about something.

I wish my parents could have been part of it, she thought.

The reality that if they hadn't died, she would never know about this place sat heavily in her stomach. Happiness and sadness were linked hand in hand, and she went through waves of excitement and guilt.

I know my parents would be happy that I feel so at home here and that I'm making new friends, but it hurts to think about them that way as well.

She was sweeping the floor when the door opened, and she looked up to see Silas. She put the broom down and went over to serve him.

"Hey, what can I get you?" she said.

"Hiya. Just a coffee please. I'm here to see you."

"Oh?"

"I spoke to Valorian, he said you might need some assistance with some plumbing issues in the old shop and flat."

"Ah yes, I do. It's not had any updating since about 1850 so I suspect the plumbing isn't up to code now."

"I can almost guarantee it won't be." He smiled.

Freya laughed.

"If it's okay with you, I can look in the morning about nine? I'm about then for a quick job at the florist."

"That would be perfect, thank you. I'll meet you there," she said, handing him a coffee to go.

Silas left and she felt her excitement start to build. Things were moving quickly, but she loved the community here. It would have taken weeks to get work done in the city and she certainly wouldn't have had friends offer to help. She would have to thank Valorian with a coffee and doughnut tonight when she finished work.

"Are you thinking about Valorian again?" Marly asked.

"What? No," Freya answered, a blush creeping over her cheeks.

"There's no use in denying it. Your eyes go all dreamy when you're thinking about him." Marly walked away, smiling.

Freya finished cleaning up, moved the sign to closed and collected her jacket, and the coffee and doughnut for Valorian. She shouted goodbye to Marly and left the café, feeling an arm wrap around her as she shut the door.

"I was just coming to get you," Valorian whispered in her ear.

Lust ran through her like a fire.

"I was just going to bring you these to say thank you for coming with me last night." She turned to face him.

"There was no need to thank me for that, but I won't say no," he said, taking the coffee and doughnut from her. "Let's go to mine?"

"Okay." She looped her arm through his and they set off walking to the bookshop.

CHAPTER THIRTEEN

Freya met Silas outside the shop. She showed him around, pointing out what she thought needed doing, and then she left him to get on with things. Jackson and Poppy arrived a few minutes later. They were going to make a start on the electrics, as Poppy had a day off.

"I am so excited!" Freya said.

"Me too. I am really looking forward to seeing this place full of life. It's going to be a great place to have our girly nights," Poppy said.

Freya could sense how excited Poppy was. "Yes. I can't wait. Lots of wine, snacks and movies." She smiled.

"Exactly. It's going to be great," Poppy said, hugging Freya.

While Poppy, Jackson, and Silas worked, Freya started clearing off some of the shelves in the main room and boxing up all the books and ornaments. She took everything that needed washing to the kitchen sink ready for when the water was sorted. Freya was amazed at all the old items there. *They must be worth a fortune, still in pristine condition.* She was worried she would break something, so she wrapped each item in an old newspaper before she placed it carefully in the box. In the main bedroom, the purple butterfly was still sitting on the window ledge looking out across the town. The apartment felt good with all the windows open, and her friends working inside. A warmth flowed through her and she felt it slowly filling a gap that had been left wide open by the death of her parents. She could hear the faint music coming from another room, where Poppy had her phone on, playing some album that Freya didn't recognise. It felt good to be here, and it felt even better to be among people. She had never had this back in the city. The friends she'd had there had all been drawn to her parents' reputation, and she didn't feel any of them were genuine. It had always felt like they were trying to benefit from their friendship with her, the daughter of two revered Guardians. She hadn't heard from any of them when her parents had died, so she'd had no problem leaving them all behind when she left.

Freya decided now would be a good time to go see Holden, take him the portrait of Everlyn, and see what he knew about the butterfly. She shouted through to the others to let them know she would be back, and left the apartment. As she walked past the shops, she decided to get him a piece of the cake he liked. *It wouldn't hurt to butter him up, he might be a little less grumpy that way.* She walked through the trees and made her way to his house. The sight of the flowers still took her breath away. She knocked on his door, it creaked open as he shouted to her to come inside. She went in, shutting the door behind her.

Holden stared at her. "You again. What is it this time? he asked.

"I brought you something I thought you might like."

"What is it?" he said, gesturing for her to sit down.

"Well, I brought you some more cake but also a gift, of sorts."

"Hmm. Tea?"

"No thank you, I won't be stopping long."

"Good," he said, reaching for the cake as she put it on the table.

"I found this in the old Evermore apartment. I thought you might like it - given your history with Everlyn." She put down the portrait on the table.

Holden picked it up, running his finger along Everlyn's face.

"Thank you," he whispered.

"No problem. It must have been hard when they left."

"It was, very hard. I appreciate you bringing me this. It feels like a lifetime since I last saw that sweet face," he said. His demeanour and tone had changed, and he sounded so sorrowful that Freya found herself feeling bad for him.

"I was wondering something. Do you know much about a purple butterfly at all? There is one in the apartment, and it seems reluctant to leave."

"Yes. He was their familiar. I assumed they took him with them, but perhaps they left him as a guardian to the property. It wasn't unheard of, not back then. Familiars were often left to protect people's homes when they went out or left for long periods of time."

"That could explain why I've been dreaming about him since I got here. He was trying to send me a message."

"He will have sensed your blood the moment you entered town. He belongs to you now. He is a fantastic creature. He has been with your family for many generations and his loyalty clearly knows no bounds," Holden said, before shoving a forkful of cake in his mouth.

"To sit there all this time." Freya shook her head. "I'll have to seek guidance from the spirits to see what I can do for him by way of thanks."

"That would be a good idea, they will know what he likes."

"Thanks, Holden. I'll let you get back to things now. Sorry to have bothered you again."

"I know I come across as someone who doesn't want people here, but if you ever feel like dropping in again, please do. It is nice to have an Evermore around again." He turned to look out of the window,

"I would like that," Freya said as she made her way to the door, "Goodbye, Holden," she said letting herself out.

By the time Freya got back to the apartment, Silas was almost finished with the plumbing. Poppy had been helping him install new pipes through the walls at a quicker pace, and the unfamiliar scent of her magic still lingered in the air.

Freya left Silas and Poppy and headed into the bedroom, where the butterfly still rested on the window ledge. She looked down at it.

"Thank you for looking after this place. No-one would have expected you to still be here after all this time," she said out loud.

The butterfly spread its wings and flew towards her, landing on her hand. She lifted it so they were eye to eye.

"Now your time here is over, little one. I want you to be free. If you wish to stay here as my familiar, then I would be honoured, but after all this time if you want to fly freely and enjoy your life, then please do."

The butterfly flew and landed on her nose, flapping its wings. Peace engulfed her, as she realised that the butterfly was communicating with her. He wanted to stay; this was his job, and the Evermores were his family.

"I am grateful you are here. What is your name?"

A male voice whispered through her mind: *Mael.*

"Mael, It's nice to meet you. I'm Freya," she said as she ran her finger down his soft furry body. Mael fluttered his wings enjoying the attention.

"I must get back to cleaning up now before I have to go to work. I will see you later, little friend."

Back in the kitchen, Jackson was deep in concentration fitting a plug socket. Not wanting to disturb him, Freya went down to the shop front and picked up the remaining mail off the floor, tidying it into a pile. She would need to go through it all and see if there was anything important, she decided. One by one she took the jars of old herbs and mixtures off the shelves and started emptying them into the bin. She left all the jars on the counter, planning to clean and reuse them. She cleaned a spot on one of the windows, allowing the sunlight to shine through.

The shop is a lovely open space. It would be great to get it opened again.

She thought about making a 'to lease' sign to put up in the window, and her stomach ached at the thought. She decided that she needed to get back to her apartment, to get ready for work and have something to eat.

Freya arrived at work to find Marly standing behind the counter, deep in conversation with a man she had never seen before.

"Evening," Marly said to her.

"Hey. Been busy?" Freya asked.

"Steady, people are enjoying the sun, so I put the tables out there for them."

"Good idea. I was surprised how warm it was when I left the apartment earlier. It was still chilly when I got back from seeing Holden."

"Yeah, it's nice. I hope it stays like this for this weekend's outdoor movie night, and for Imbolc next week."

"Me too. I don't fancy sitting with an umbrella watching films in the rain," Freya said.

"If it rains, people usually pop up some gazebos to sit under, but it isn't the same."

"Well, I will keep my fingers crossed for good weather," she replied.

Freya unpacked stock and tidied the shelves, until she noticed that the man who had been talking to Marly earlier was watching her.

She turned to look at him, forcing a smile. "Can I get you anything else?"

"Black coffee please," he replied.

There was something about him that set off Freya's defences. She didn't like the way he watched her; it was as if there was a negative vibe coming off him. She took him the coffee and when he left, she spoke to Marly

"That man, do you know who he is? she asked.

"The one who I was talking to when you came in?" Marly replied.

"Yeah. That's the guy."

"I don't know him well. He is from Hawthorne Hollow. I don't know his name though. He was asking about the movie and where he could buy tickets from. He also asked me about your family's place. Said he walked past and saw that people had been in. He was curious if it had been sold."

"Ah, right," Freya said, fighting a growing sense of unease.

"I told him that I had no idea but assumed it must have been. There was no way I was going to give him any information. You can't always trust the Witches of Hawthorne Hollow."

"He was a Witch?"

"Yes, I could smell his blood a mile off."

Freya had forgotten that werewolves had a keen sense of smell, and that they were often able to distinguish species by their scent.

"There was something about him that gave me the heebie-jeebies," Freya said with a shiver.

"I felt it too. He made my hackles go up. It won't be a surprise if people come and ask questions though. It has been a long time since someone occupied that place - but I don't trust people I don't know."

"Considering why my family left, neither do I. Thanks, Marly, I'm glad I have you around." Freya smiled.

"You're part of this town now, Freya, and we protect our own," Marly said, patting Freya on the back.

CHAPTER FOURTEEN

Freya was glad to close the café for the evening. She really wanted to get back to see the shop and apartment now that all the lights were working. Jackson had popped over with the key earlier to let her know that he, Silas, and Poppy were all finished. She had a flushing toilet, hot water, lights and an electric hook up for the oven. She was sweeping the café floor when she heard a tap on the window. Looking over, she saw Valorian peering in, and she laughed.

Opening the door, she ushered him through, and then kissed him.

"Good evening to you too," he said, pulling away to look at her.

"Hey," she said.

"How did it go today?"

"It's been brilliant. I spoke to Holden and found out the butterfly is my family's familiar. I spoke to him, his name is Mael. I got some clearing up done, and Jackson, Poppy and Silas have sorted all the electrics and plumbing out for me while I was at work."

"Oh, I can't wait to see that tonight."

"Maybe you can help me pick out some colours for the walls?

I am going with sage in the kitchen, but I need to figure out the rest."

"I would love to help. I have something for you actually, but I'll give you it when we get over there."

Freya finished cleaning up, and she and Valorian headed over to the new place. Freya opened the shop door and flicked on the light switch, illuminating the entire area. As she walked through, she checked all the lights. She couldn't wait to see the back room. There were no windows in there, so she hadn't been able to get a proper look at it. It was much bigger than she had expected.

"This is such a good space," Valorian said.

"It is. I have been thinking about trying to rent it out, to let someone use the shop. It seems a waste to just let it stand empty."

"Have you not considered opening a shop yourself?"

"I wouldn't know what on earth to sell, so no, I hadn't thought about it actually."

"You could open an Apothecary or something. As a Witch, even one who isn't using her magic, your tinctures, salves and such would be valued in the town."

"Hmm," she said. "I'll give it some thought while I sort out upstairs."

"There is no rush. At least you can sort the rest out and move in before you decide. I bet it's going to look amazing when it's all done."

"I have thought about it all day. It's given me something to focus on at work until I could see you this evening." She blushed.

"As long as you are still excited to see me, that's what counts." He winked.

They made their way upstairs and Valorian had a look around while Freya started the fire and made a start packing boxes.

"We are going to need to get some radiators hooked up. They will be more effective than the fireplaces," he said, coming back through the kitchen.

"Yeah, I spoke to Silas. He said once I bought some to let him know and he would fit them. No-one has given me their bill yet though, so I have no idea how much this will all cost."

"Don't worry about it. I tried to pay them, but no one would accept the money. They just want the place lived in again. They said it was a welcome home present."

"That was very generous of them. I will have to host a dinner when it is all sorted and invite them all as a thank you."

"That sounds ideal. Make it a late one though so I can come."

"Of course!"

"I almost forgot. Here," he said, handing her a small box.

She opened it and inside was a new mobile phone. She looked at him and raised her eyebrows.

"I know you didn't necessarily want one, but I thought it would be a fresh start, and with all the work you will need to do and stuff you will have to order, having a mobile will be useful. Plus, I already programmed mine, Marly's, Poppy's, Jackson's and Silas' number in here, along with the number for the local doctor."

"It's very kind of you, thank you. Perhaps it is time to jump back on the telecommunications train," she said.

Valorian started helping Freya with the packing.

"What's life like here?" Freya asked.

"Honestly, it's great. I've lived a few places and none of them have ever felt more like home than Crestwood. I don't know if it's because of the magic, the creatures that dwell here or the fresh mountain air, but there is something uniquely special about the place."

"It feels so much more open here. Back in the city you wouldn't ever find a Vampire and Witch talking to each other, never mind anything more."

"Creatures have always interspecies dated; they just don't advertise it. There are too many old-fashioned rules because those in power feared what would happen to them if they didn't hold all the power for themselves".

"It's always those who are hungry for power who ruin it for others." She sighed.

"You can say no if you want, but can I ask about what happened to your parents?" Valorian asked.

"My parents were Guardians, employed by the Witches Council to protect Witches against other supernatural folk. Each faction had their own council, and they often worked together.

They had been on a case for around three months. Witches were turning up dead with their magical essence having been drained from them. They found out it was another Witch who was doing this, and they managed to catch him, but in the struggle, they were both killed. The Council destroyed him, ensuring he couldn't do it again, but there was nothing they could do to bring my parents back."

"I'm so sorry, Freya, that's just awful."

"It was a risky job to have, but that's why I refuse to use my magic. What happened to my parents just shows how damaging it can be, how destructive it is. Even the Evermores had to run to hide from the dark magic. It's like poison."

"I can see why you have made the decision you have. I will never push you on it. I will support you no matter what you decide to do, whether that is to use magic, never use magic, or even paint these walls neon pink." He smirked.

Freya pulled a face. "I was actually thinking neon yellow, if you must know," she replied.

It was starting to get late, so they finished up. Valorian had to go back to the shop and do some work, so he walked her home and left her with a soft kiss.

Freya woke with a start, her heart hammering in her chest. She couldn't recall what she had been dreaming about, but something had forced her to wake up. Her hands were clammy and sweat beaded her forehead. She got up and padded to the kitchen and filled a glass with cold water, gulping it down. The clock read 5:30 and Freya decided that there was no point in trying to get back to sleep, so she lit the log fire, curled up on the sofa under a warm blanket and picked up her book. She must have drifted off as the next thing she knew, her new phone was ringing from inside her bag. Her stomach rolled with a feeling of nausea as she scrambled for it. The phone abruptly stopped ringing. She pulled it out of her bag and checked the screen, seeing that the call had been from Poppy. She hit the 'redial' button to call her back.

"Hello?"

"Hey, Poppy, it's me. Sorry I missed your call. I just woke up."

"Oh, it's not a problem. I was just going to ask if you were heading to the apartment today? I'm free if you would like a hand packing stuff up?"

"I am going over there, and I would love the company. I can be dressed and there in about thirty minutes if that works for you?"

"That's perfect. I'll meet you there."

Freya hung up and made breakfast, hoping to settle the sickly feeling in her stomach. When she had finished eating, she felt much better, and she dressed quickly before heading out.

Freya was relieved to find that it was another warm day. This was her last night at work and the outdoor midnight movie was only two nights away. Despite the sun, Freya felt a chill, and she looked around her. A feeling of being watched settled over her but she couldn't see anyone around. She pulled her jacket tightly around her and picked up her pace. *I know I'm probably being paranoid, but I'll feel much better once I'm back indoors.* She saw Poppy walking towards her and gave her a wave, unlocking the shop door as she waited for Poppy to join her.

"Morning," Freya said.

"Morning. Everything okay? You look kinda pale."

"Yeah, I'm fine, just had a weird chill walking over here, that's all."

"Ah, you're probably tired. Doing this place up and working must be quite tiring."

"It is, but so much fun too. I am so excited to get all this done and move in here. It feels like home."

"It's that strong Witch energy. I couldn't imagine living anywhere other than my family home."

"Yeah," Freya said, sorrowfully.

"Sorry, I didn't think. I know you must miss your parents and the home you all shared together." Poppy pulled Freya into a hug, before releasing her, her cheeks red with embarrassment.

"I do, but we moved a few times. I don't think they ever felt like our houses were homes. I bet they would have loved this place though."

"It's gorgeous, and when you have it all done up it is going to be so nice."

"Talking of, I need to pop over to the DIY store when they open in an hour, to pick up the paint. There is still a lot of clearing up to do first though, and I can't settle on a colour for the main bedroom."

"We'll get it done. What about a nice pale yellow for the main bedroom?"

"Hmm, I hadn't considered yellow, but it would brighten that large room, especially in the winter. I'll grab some tester pots while I am there, and we can see which might be better. Thanks," she said, offering a smile.

"You're very welcome. Have you picked a colour for my room? Aka the spare bedroom?"

Freya laughed.

"Yup, lilac. I had every room sorted except the main bedroom. Light sage in the kitchen and living room. I want them tied together - plus that colour goes so well with the dark wood. Light blue in the bathroom, lilac in the small bedroom, and then I guess yellow in mine. The hallways I was just going to repaint white."

"Oh, that sounds nice. I can't wait to see it finished. I'm off over the next three days as well if you want the help. Obviously, I have my date tomorrow night though."

"I'd love the help. I'm looking forward to tomorrow too, it'll be mine and Valorian's first outing as a couple. Are you nervous about your date?"

"Not nervous really. Just excited. Since I asked him out, we've been getting closer. He has been texting me a lot and he keeps touching my hand and stuff at work. It makes my body tingle all over," Poppy said, blushing.

"It seems Anderson just needed a push in the right direction," Freya said, smiling.

Freya and Poppy got to work clearing out the rest of the kitchen as they chatted about the upcoming movie night and the picnics they were going to pack.

Freya felt wistful. *I wish all my dates with Valorian weren't all centred around the night. With the summer approaching, we might not get to spend much time together outside, enjoying the weather. By the time the sun is setting and Valorian is able to come outside, I'll be going to bed.* For the first time, she wished that there was some kind of magical solution that would allow Vampires to be outside in the sunlight.

Freya looked out of the window and noticed the DIY shop was open, so she grabbed her purse and went over to collect the paint and supplies she needed. Making her way back up the stairs, she could hear Poppy talking to herself and she smiled. *She is a very interesting person, and I'm glad we're becoming such good friends.*

"I'm back," Freya said, putting the heavy bags down.

"That means it's time to paint. Mael here was saying he likes the idea of a yellow bedroom."

"Oh, Mael spoke to you?"

"He needed some water, so I set him up a small bowl. It got us both chatting."

"Well, I am glad you approve," Freya said, turning to Mael.

Poppy picked up the large sage paint tin and set up the roller trays for her and Freya, while Freya placed masking tape around all the edges of the walls. Music blasted from Poppy's phone, and they both sang as they painted.

With both of them working, it didn't take long for them to finish giving the room its first coat of paint.

"It looks so much better already," Poppy said.

"A second coat should be all that's needed. Shall we have a lunch break while we wait for it to dry? My treat."

"Sure, what were you thinking?"

"We can either go to Jackson's or Spellbound. Any preference?"

"Jackson's. I think we deserve a glass of wine on our break."

"Now I can agree with that, one hundred percent," Freya replied.

CHAPTER FIFTEEN

Jackson's was fairly empty. Freya and Poppy sat at a table near the bar. A young man behind the bar waved at Poppy as they picked up the menus.

"That's Seamus, he's Jackson's nephew. Comes over to stay for Imbolc. He's quiet but is nice enough," Poppy said.

"Ah right. Is he a Shifter too then?"

"Yes, he is. Only males in their family carry the Shifter gene. It obviously skipped his sister and niece. It's why Seamus likes to spend time here; more freedom to be within nature. He's from the city, there's not much to do out there."

"Yeah, it isn't an easy life living in the city for anyone non-human, especially not Shifters. Only the Vamps have it easy out there."

"It's a large killing ground for them, that's why."

"That and the city is more alive at night."

Freya and Poppy ate while they continued to gossip pleasantly about Crestwood and the upcoming Imbolc festival. When they were finished, they headed back to the shop.

Poppy gently touched the last place that they had painted, checking her finger to make sure it was dry.

"It's all good for another coat now. If we start where we started the first time it will just give this a little more time to settle before we get to it."

"Good idea," Freya said, pouring more paint into the trays.

"I really like this colour; it was a good choice for these rooms."

"For some reason I just saw it in my mind and had to do it," Freya replied.

"Witches' intuition is rarely wrong." Poppy said.

"No, you are right there."

Freya thought back to that feeling she had earlier. Her intuition had told her that she was being watched, was she being stupid to ignore it? *Even if I was right, why would somebody be watching me? It doesn't make any sense.* She decided to speak to Valorian about it, he might know whether there were any creatures who would have a reason to watch her.

Freya and Poppy were making good progress when the doorbell rang. Freya shrugged at Poppy and went down to see who was at the door.

Marly stood outside with a large carrier bag.

"I've brought you something. Well, I've brought that butterfly of yours something," she said.

"Hey, come on in. Me and Poppy are just finishing the painting upstairs."

"Oh lovely, I get to be one of the first to see it then," she said, making her way through the shop before going upstairs.

"This looks good. Amazing what a different paint and a clean-up can make. It will look fantastic when it's all done."

"I'm really pleased with it too. The colour against the dark wood just makes all that detail stand out in the carvings," Freya said.

Marly walked back over to the table and pulled the carrier off the item she had brought. It looked like a large ornately sculpted bird cage. It was made with bronze and was beautiful.

"Wow, that is gorgeous," Freya said, admiring the cage.

"But...what is it? A birdcage?" Poppy asked.

"Close, but no, it's for butterflies. This one has no door, but it has a place to put food and water, and it has a perch. I thought your butterfly friend might like it," Marly said.

"That is incredibly thoughtful of you, let me go get Mael."

Freya left and returned with Mael on her hand as she stroked his long, furry body.

"Marly brought this for you, Mael, what do you think?"

Maels voice echoed around her head: *I think it is a fine place for me to sleep, please give her my thanks.*

"Mael said thank you and that it will make a good place to sleep. We could keep it in the bedroom; perhaps I can get Valorian to hang it for me near the window," Freya said.

"A bedroom within a bedroom," Poppy said.

"I'm glad he likes it. He deserves only the best after protecting this place for so long." Marly nodded at the purple butterfly.

Mael flew from Freya's hand and rested on Marly's shoulder. Freya knew it was his way of thanking her.

"Right, I best get going. I am doing a lot of baking and cooking ready for tomorrow's movie. They decided a hot and cold buffet would be put on for all the attendee's as well. As if we don't have enough to do with Imbolc four days away!" Marly said, heading to the stairs.

"Okay, Marly, thanks again and if you need a hand with anything tomorrow just send me a text," Freya said.

"Me too," added Poppy.

"Thanks, girls. Will do."

"And thanks again for the cage," Freya shouted, as Marly closed the door behind her

Freya left Poppy finishing off the main room. She went through to the main bedroom and pulled all the furniture to the centre of the room, putting any items in boxes and sweeping up the dust from the wooden floor. She wanted to work on this room next, since the bathroom only needed a quick coat of paint - thanks to Silas sorting out and installing a new bathroom suite for her.

Poppy finished painting and made her way to the spare bedroom to do the same. Once all the rooms were prepared for painting, the girls pulled out a couple of stools in the kitchen and opened two cans of pop.

"Thank you for your help today, Poppy. I know it would have

been easier for you to use your magic."

"I've really enjoyed it. I think we would have been a lot quicker if I had used it, but it wouldn't have been as much fun."

Freya and Poppy stepped out into the cool evening air. Locking the door behind her, Freya waved to Poppy as they set off walking in opposite directions.

She was just about to head home when she bumped into Valorian, who was coming from the direction of her apartment.

"Hello, beautiful," he said, before kissing her lips.

Freya caught him up on her day and on how the decoration was going. Valorian offered to take her key and finish the rooms overnight for her as he wasn't opening the shop. They decided to go to Valorian's to watch a movie together first. As Freya sat on his sofa and snuggled into him, it didn't take long for sleep to claim her.

Freya woke realising that she had fallen asleep at Valorian's. She sat up and looked around, the room was pitch black and she was in a bed. Valorian must have put her in it when she fell asleep rather than waking her. The other side of the bed was empty. She got out and made her way for the door, feeling against the wall carefully. Opening the door, she saw that there was a little light in the living room from a couple of candles and Valorian was fast asleep on the sofa. On the table was her bag, phone, and keys for the flat. She picked them up and quietly crept out of the front door and fired off a text to Valorian to let him know she would see him later for the movie and to thank him for a lovely night.

She made her way over to the new apartment first to check whether Valorian had finished the rooms while she slept. She opened the door and was greeted by the smell of fresh paint.

The bedrooms and bathroom had been finished. Mael was asleep in his new cage, so Freya carefully put out fresh water for him before leaving to go back to her old apartment for a shower and fresh clothes. She walked past Spellbound Café and could smell the coffee and bacon coming from inside, and her stomach rumbled loudly. Picking up the pace she started walking faster, determined to go down for breakfast once she had got ready.

Freya sat in the café, feeling refreshed after her shower. She pushed away the empty plate in front of her as she saw her phone light up with Marly's name.

"Hey, Marly," she said, as she answered.

"Hey. I was just wondering if you had some free time this morning. I have loads of food to take over to the meadow ready for tonight and wondered if you could lend a hand?"

"I've just finished having some breakfast at Spellbound. I'll finish this coffee and head over to you. I have no plans until tonight so I can help."

"Thanks, you're a star. See you soon," Marly replied and ended the call.

Freya spent the day helping Marly and the other organisers setting up all the food and drinks tables. She enjoyed the hustle and bustle of getting involved - setting up stalls, hanging lanterns - it made her feel more like one of them with every passing day. As the sun started to set, it brought a chilly night air. Freya made her way home to get changed into something warmer, and to wait for Valorian to come and pick her up.

The doorbell rang and Freya grabbed her jacket and phone and ran downstairs to answer it. Valorian stood on the doorstep, with a picnic basket in his hands.

"Good evening, beautiful," he said to her, reaching over to kiss her.

"Good evening," she replied.

They walked hand-in-hand to the meadows, which were alive with sparkling lanterns and the chatter of people. Valorian found a spot slightly out of the way but with a perfect view of the screen, and he laid down a blanket he had brought with him. Freya looked around and spotted Poppy and Anderson sitting cosily together a little further away. She smiled. The way they were looking adoringly at each other made Freya happy they had finally come together. She took a seat on the blanket next to Valorian as he unpacked the rest of the picnic basket.

"I thought it would be nice if I brought some popcorn and

wine to have during the movie. I figure we can get something more substantial and warmer from the tents."

"Sounds lovely. It's the perfect night for a hot dog or chips. It reminds me of going on holiday when I was a child, when we would go to bonfires."

"Shall I go get something now before the movie starts?"

"Sure, makes sense. Then you won't miss any of the film later."

Valorian left to get them both some food while Freya opened the wine and poured them a glass each. She felt a coldness creep over her, and as she turned to look around, she noticed that the creepy man from the cafe was walking towards her. *Dammit* she thought, *he must know I own the building he was asking Marly about.* She looked around, hoping that Valorian was on his way back, but there was no sign of him yet.

"Hello," the man said as he stopped in front of her.

Freya stood up. "Hi," she replied cautiously.

"Are you the lady who owns the empty shop on the corner?"

"I am." She couldn't help the coolness in her tone; something about this guy seemed off.

"I was wondering what your plans were for it. I have been interested in buying it for many years, but no one seemed to know who to contact."

"It was a family property, and I have no plans to sell."

She saw Valorian heading towards them and felt a sigh of relief leave her body.

"That's a shame. I can make you a good offer."

"Thanks for the offer, but it's a no all the same," she replied.

"Hey," Valorian said, passing Freya a hot dog and nodding at the stranger.

"Thanks for your time. I'll be off now. Enjoy the movie." The man left, glancing behind him towards Valorian.

"Who was that?" he asked.

"It was someone who wanted to buy the shop and apartment. He came into the café while I was working the other day and spoke to Marly. He said he has been wanting it for ages - but there is something off about him."

"Yeah, I feel it too. I don't like the look of him."

"Me either. Hopefully now he knows I won't sell we won't see him around anymore."

Freya and Valorian enjoyed the movie. There was no further sign of the stranger, but Freya did catch Poppy and Anderson sharing a tender kiss, which made her heart happy for her friend.

Valorian had asked Freya if she would like to spend the night at his house with him. The romance in the air seemed to be catching and she found herself saying yes, excited at the prospect of being wrapped in his arms all night.

Valorian went around lighting candle lanterns in his bedroom. The warm light gave off a soft glow, and Freya looked at him, lust burning through her body. Valorian pulled off his t-shirt, and Freya found her eyes fixing on his perfect abs, as she sat on the bed and started taking her shoes off.

Valorian made his way around to her. "I thought you might like this to change into." He handed her one of his t-shirts.

"Thanks," she said, blushing.

"I'll go make some tea and give you some privacy. I'll be back in a minute."

Freya quickly slipped off her clothes and put his t-shirt on before making her way to the ensuite bathroom. She shut the door, her heart pounding in her chest. She stood in front of the sink and splashed water on her face to cool her down before taking a deep breath, letting it out slowly. She gave herself a shake, went back out to the bedroom and slipped under the covers.

Valorian came back in with the tea, wearing only shorts. Everything about him raised her temperature, and she knew he could sense it. Vampire senses were better than anything else in this world, he would sense her lust, hear her increasing heartbeat - and he would know she wanted him. She wished she could do the same and know what he was thinking and feeling. As he slid into the bed next to her, his leg brushed against hers and she felt static buzz through her body. He looked at her and licked his lips. He knew exactly what he was doing, and she was enjoying every moment. She rested against his chest, the teacup in her hands, but no words were exchanged between them - just a soft, expectant silence. She put the cup down on the bedside table and lay down next to him. He did the same, wrapping an arm across her waist and pulling her closer. His lips found hers and she opened her mouth to let in his tongue, pushing herself closer to him. She could feel every part of him against her as her temperature rose rapidly. All her thoughts melted away until the only thing she knew was that she wanted him right there. Sensing her need, Valorian ran his hand up her back tracing fingers across her neck and into her hair, gripping her closer.

All of a sudden, every lantern in the room shattered.

Valorian jumped off the bed in a blur of speed, putting out the candles on the floor before a fire had chance to spread.

Freya pulled up the cover around her, her face pale.

"What was that?" she asked.

"I suspect it was your magic," he said.

"But…I didn't do anything."

"It was probably because you weren't in control of how you felt, it was probably an extension of your passion." He winked.

"Shit, I'm so sorry, Valorian."

"Why? Don't be sorry. It couldn't be helped," he said, getting back under the cover and pulling her close. "There's no rush for us to do anything you're not ready for. I am falling in love with you, and we have all the time in the world," he said.

Her heart stopped. She hadn't realised how much she had wanted to hear those words from him until he said them. She smiled up at him, her heart swelling fit to burst.

"I am already totally in love with you," she confessed. He kissed her lips softly; she snuggled closer to him and together they fell asleep.

CHAPTER SIXTEEN

Freya woke surrounded by darkness, to find Valorian snoring softly beside her. Shame over the night before tugged at her. *I can't believe I let my magic escape like that. It could have really hurt both of us! I'll have to be careful in the future; this can't happen again.* She got up from the bed, grabbing her phone and going to the bathroom. She turned on the light and checked the time on her phone, realising that she had slept for most of the day and it was much later than she had thought. It would start getting dark in a couple of hours and she had no idea what time Valorian usually woke. She finished on the toilet and was washing her hands when she heard a tap on the door.

"You okay in there?" he said through the door.

She opened the door and looked at him, she was still naked, and his eyes lit up with appreciation.

"I'm great," she replied.

"I was going to ask if you wanted some breakfast, or in your case dinner, but I think we might need to shower first." He smirked at her.

She bit her lip, as the previous night's heat returned with gusto.

"I think we really should shower first," she responded,

looking up at him through her lashes.

That was all he needed; he swooped her up and took her to the shower, keeping hold of her with one arm as he turned on the water with the other. He held her against the tiles, their coolness conflicted with the heat she felt as the water ran over them. The fear that she would lose control again was at the front of her mind as she grabbed some shower gel and smiled at Valorian.

"Time to clean up then," she said, trying to laugh off the unease she felt. *I want him so much, but I just can't risk it. Not until I've learnt how to get a handle on my emotions.*

The irony wasn't lost on her. She was dating the most predatory species in existence, and yet it was her magic that was causing the danger between them.

The next couple of days went by quickly. Between spending time with Valorian, finishing the renovations on the new apartment, work, and helping the town prepare for Imbolc, Freya felt she hadn't had a second to catch her breath. She flopped down onto the sofa, exhausted. The morning had been spent putting in the new carpets that had arrived - with a little help from Jackson. The apartment was now ready to move into - which she was doing the following morning before work. The next day would be the New Moon and then Imbolc, and she was determined to get moved in ready for it. Freya was looking forward to the sabbat; a fresh start and new beginnings, and she really hoped it would help to push away the trauma of December once and for all. She groaned as she pulled herself off the sofa and plodded her way to the kitchen. Her head throbbed and her body ached. She wasn't used to feeling unwell. Trying to do things without magic, as humans would, was hard - harder than she had anticipated - but she was certain that eventually things would get easier. *It's just an adjustment. Before, I would have used my magic to do everything. It would have been easy and quick. Oh well. At least it'll be character building.* It was times like this she missed her mother's extensive medicinal cabinet, full of tinctures and salves. She was sure there would have been something in there to help her feel better. She would have to ask Poppy if she knew of any good Herbalists in the area. In the meantime, she decided to take a painkiller before making her way to Marly's for her shift.

As the painkillers kicked in, Freya began to feel a little better. Work was a nice distraction, she decided. Thankfully the night had been going slow and customers were few and far between, giving her plenty of chance to rest. Marly had spent the night in her office doing paperwork, and Freya found she had missed her company, but a part of her was relieved that she didn't have to make conversation. She heard the door open and looked up. Valorian walked in and her heart fluttered. She had avoided getting up close and personal with him since that first time, and she was sure he had noticed, he looked dejected with his shoulders hunched. She wanted nothing more than to keep the intimacy between them, especially after they had both admitted the depth of their feelings, but she was afraid that she wouldn't be able to keep her emotions contained – and that meant that someone might get hurt.

"Hey, beautiful."

"Hey," she replied.

"Are you okay? You look pale."

"I think I'm coming down with something. I feel tired and I ache all over."

"Oh no, is there anything I can do?"

"Nah, I'm sure I'll be fine. It's just been a hectic week. I probably just need a couple days of downtime. Luckily the weekend is almost here, and I can relax and enjoy the festival."

"Yeah, that makes sense. Plus, you will be in the new house tomorrow so that will be a weight off."

"I'm really looking forward to being in there properly. Just in time for the New Moon and Imbolc." She smiled.

"Perfect timing," he said.

"So, what can I get you? Coffee? Doughnuts?"

"Nothing, I came to let you know my family has arrived. I know you don't feel well, but I was wondering if you wanted to pop over after work and meet them?"

"I would love to. I may not be the best company though, and I can't stay long. I really need to try and sleep this off for tomorrow, but I would like nothing more than to come over." She gave him a smile.

"Brilliant. And yes, you need your rest so I will make sure they don't talk your head off for hours on end."

"I'll just pop home first and freshen up then I'll be straight over."

"Alright, I'll see you later."

Valorian kissed her and then left. Freya sat on the stool, lips tingling.

Freya closed the café and tidied up, rushing home to get changed. Pulling out her small make-up bag she looked in the mirror. She had dark rings under her eyes and her bronze skin looked dull and paler than usual. She applied just a touch of make-up, brightening her cheeks and lips and applied some concealer under her eyes. Taking her hair out of its ponytail she gave it a shake and checked how she looked. It would do. There was no escaping how tired she looked but at least she wouldn't be mistaken for a zombie.

As she walked over to the bookshop, she felt the nerves in her stomach. Meeting Valorian's family felt like a big step in their relationship, and she hoped they would like her as much as she liked their son. The bookshop was closed, so Freya hit the bell next to the door. Valorian was there in seconds welcoming her with a warm embrace.

"You look a little better now," he said giving her a look over.

"That's the power of cosmetics." She smiled.

"Are you nervous?"

"Maybe a little."

"I can hear your heart beating like it is trying to escape."

"Oh, yeah. I just hope they like me."

"They will love you, just...not as much as I do."

"I love you too," she said, grabbing hold of his hand.

She followed him upstairs. Valorian's family stood in the dining room, awaiting her arrival. Valorian pushed open the door and Freya was met with a bunch of curious stares and smiles.

Valorian squeezed her hand as his father moved forwards towards her.

"Hello, Freya, I'm Maykn. It's a pleasure to meet you," he said, holding out his hand.

"It's a pleasure to meet you too," she said, shaking it.

Valorian's mother walked over and hugged Freya.

"I'm Emeline, and this is Eli and Phoenix - Valorian's brother and sister - and Ezra, Phoenix's partner," she said, pointing each person out in turn as she named them.

Freya looked around and smiled.

"Hey, it's lovely to meet you all."

"Valorian speaks very highly of you," Maykn said.

"You mean he does nothing but talk about her," Phoenix said, laughing.

They all sat around the dinner table. Valorian had put out a selection of food for them. Freya started to relax as she slipped into a conversation with Phoenix about how much they both loved Crestwood. Next to her, Valorian sat with his arm wrapped loosely around her back, resting against the chair. It comforted her to know that he was not keeping his distance while his parents were there.

The night had grown long, and she stifled a yawn.

"Maybe it's time we got you home," he whispered.

"I think you might be right," she replied. They got up.

"I'm sorry but I need to leave. I am shattered after being at work," she apologised.

"Don't worry about it. We Vampires never grow tired and sometimes we forget what it can be like. We can have a catch up tomorrow," Emeline said, giving Freya a hug.

They all said their goodbyes, and Freya took Valorian's hand as they walked to her flat.

Even the cool night air wasn't enough to rouse Freya from her tiredness. *There's no way I'm going to be able to pack any boxes tonight.* Pausing only to kiss Valorian goodnight, she headed into the apartment and locked the door behind her. She set her alarm for early in the morning, so that she would have time to finish packing, then she climbed straight into bed, pulling the duvet tight around her. Her body eased into the mattress and the aches slowly faded away as her heavy eyelids closed and she fell into a deep sleep.

Freya woke to the sound of her alarm. The room was bright with the morning sun, and she was surprised to find that after a good night's sleep she felt much better than she had the previous night. Rising, she looked over at the mountains. This would be her last time admiring this view from here. Tomorrow she would wake and have the forest to look at, the mountains would peek up above the row of shops in front of the new window, but she would miss this view first thing.

At the new apartment, the first thing Freya noticed were several large boxes that Valorian had sent on ahead. She left them for a moment to speak to Poppy, who was already unpacking and arranging them onto the shelves in the living room.

"I put the box with your bedding in your room, I figured you might want that ready straight away," Poppy said.

"Brilliant, thanks. I'll go do that now, then I want to open all these parcels Valorian sent." She gestured towards the stack of large, sealed boxes.

"Okay, I'll finish putting these books away. I am dying to see what's in those." Poppy said.

Freya went through to the bedroom; this was by far her favourite room. The dark wood furniture against the pale paintwork and delicate floral wallpaper looked amazing together. Valorian had already hung the butterfly cage from the ceiling near the window for Mael. He fluttered down and as he landed on her shoulder, she heard his voice in her head.

I'm glad I'm around to see an Evermore return.

"It feels good to be here, Mael. I'm looking forward to spending more time with you."

As am I, the voice echoed before he flew back to the cage.

Freya made the bed. When she had finished, she stood with her hands on her hips, smiling as she looked around. It was perfect. She returned to the main room, where Poppy was sitting on the sofa waiting. She grabbed the box opener off the table and went over to the large pile waiting for her. Poppy jumped up to join her. Freya carefully ran the knife along the tape and opened the first box. Inside was a large, black cast iron lamp that was ridiculously heavy. It took both her and Poppy to pull it from the box. The iron had intricately carved roses along its stem.

"This is beautiful," Freya said.

"It really is. It would look fantastic in the bedroom next to your bed."

"Oh, yes! Let's go put it in there now and see."

The pair went to the bedroom and placed the lamp. It stood out against the wall and fit the floral decor perfectly.

"Let's go see what else is there," Poppy said, running out. Freya giggled and ran after her.

The remaining boxes were full of various house items: a beautiful handmade rug, some new Egyptian cotton towels, a new kitchenware set, with pans, plates and cutlery. Valorian had bought her everything she was missing to fill the home.

"This was really sweet of Valorian," Poppy said.

"Yeah, it was. He didn't need to do any of this. He has pretty much nailed my style too," Freya replied.

"That man sure knows his Freya," Poppy said.

"Talking of men. How are things with you and Anderson?"

"Great, like.... sooooo.... good."

Freya chuckled with her friend.

"We should have a double date one night. Maybe as an apartment warming dinner?"

"Oh yes! What a good idea. Valorian and Anderson get on really well so that would work."

The girls sprawled on the sofa and chair.

"Thanks for helping today, Poppy. I couldn't have done it without you."

"You are more than welcome. I know you've been run off your feet lately helping with everything and doing the apartment up."

"Yeah, and I felt unwell yesterday. So weak. I thought I was perhaps coming down with something, but I feel much better today."

"Probably just needed a good night's sleep. Tonight's your last night at work for a few days, isn't it?"

"It is. It's going to be such a good long weekend as well. Valorian's parents are here, the New Moon is tomorrow and then there's the three-day festival for Imbolc."

"Valorian's family are lovely. Phoenix is a riot. Crestwood was never quiet with her around." Poppy laughed.

After Poppy left, Freya wandered into the kitchen and put on the kettle, as she thought about the upcoming new moon. Sometimes I miss my magic. Celebrating the lunar cycles is okay as a human experience but it's nothing compared to the release I would get if I still used my magic. That connection was powerful and freeing - it felt as if her entire body was made of electricity and fire when she connected to the lunar energies. She had always considered herself a lunar Witch. Before she had moved to Crestwood, back when her parents had still been alive, and her friends had been a part of her Coven, she had lived her days based on the phases of the moon. She still tried to keep up her old habits, but without accessing her magic, it all felt unfulfilling - and it left a pit in her stomach that never seemed to go away. She sat on the bench at the kitchen table with a cup of herbal tea and a couple of biscuits. I wish I could turn my brain off sometimes. Thinking about what used to be is never a good thing. I'm supposed to be moving forward - and that won't happen if I keep looking to the past. Freya stood up, brushed the biscuit crumbs into her hand, and tipped them into the bin. It was time to get ready for work.

CHAPTER SEVENTEEN

Freya arrived at Marly’s just in time to see Jackson leaving.

She smiled as he passed her, and he bowed his head in response. *I wonder if something is going on between Marly and Jackson. They seem to be spending a lot of time together recently.* It made her smile; she could imagine the two of them together.

“Hey, Marly,’" Freya said, walking around the counter to go and hang her coat in the office.

“Evening. How did the move go? All settled?”

“It went great thanks. Poppy helped a lot, we even managed to get everything unpacked and set up.”

“That’s good. You look much better today. I take it whatever was wrong yesterday has cleared up?”

“Seems to. I must have just needed a good night's sleep. I feel much better today. I was dreading being ill and missing out on the festival.”

“I’m glad to hear it. You could always ask Poppy for a little healing if you ever need it. She isn’t a doctor, but she does specialise in healing magic. We do also have a fabulous town doctor who can treat you non-magically too.”

“Thanks, I’ll keep that in mind. Hopefully that’s it now. Since we have the extended long weekend off work, and the flat is done, everything should go back to normal."

"Plenty of time to rest and recuperate."

"Exactly," Freya replied.

The evening was filled with customers talking about the upcoming festival. A buzz permeated the atmosphere and left Freya feeling excited at the days ahead. Crestwood really did take their festivals seriously, and it felt like every single person that lived here would be out to celebrate. It took a while for the last customers to leave so that she could close and go home. With Valorian's family in town she had no idea whether she would see him tonight, and with no firm plans, she had decided to go home to a hot bubble bath and an early night. The new moon tomorrow was bound to bring with it some restless energy as it always did, so she wanted to make the most of the calm period beforehand. Freya went to say goodbye to Marly, but she was on the phone, so she gave her a wave and mimed the word 'goodbye'.

The night air was fresh and still held the last winter's chill in its grasp, but it felt good on her skin after being in the warm cafe all evening. The breeze carried a hint of the scent of newly budding spring flowers and Freya smiled to herself. *Spring is such a wonderful time. All the fresh growth of the plants, the trees regrowing their leaves, eggs hatching, and animals being born. It always feels like it's mother nature's promise, a promise of better things to come. Whatever was, has been and whatever is, will come.* Freya longed for the warmer weather to arrive so that she could lie in the meadow with the wildflowers, basking in the feeling of the warm sun against her skin.

As she entered through the shop, she could see a light coming from the stairs. Sure she had turned it off before leaving, she quietly made her way through and up the stairs. Halfway there the smell of roast beef hit her, and her stomach instinctively rumbled. She entered the living room, to find the lamp was on, and as she walked into the kitchen, she found Valorian standing over the stove wearing an apron.

"Surprise!" he said, turning around.

"It is. It looks fantastic." she said, her mouth watering, as she stared at the meal and the fresh flowers he had placed on the table.

"I thought after the last few days you could use a treat and a decent meal, and it gave me an excuse to come and see you since my family are here."

"Well, I appreciate it, I am starving, and I did want to see you. Thank you."

"Let's tuck in. I just finished putting it out so it will all still be nice and hot."

They both sat and started eating, talking casually about how Freya's job had been going, and about what Valorian had been doing with his family. Mael fluttered in, landing on the flowers in the centre of the table and listening to the conversation. When they had finished, Freya looked at the dishes with a sigh.

"I'll sort those in the morning." She indicated them.

"Nope, I will do them now. It won't take me long."

"It's cheating when you have the ability to go super speed," Freya said.

"I think it's using my gifts to make life easier for the woman of my dreams."

"Oh yeah, woman of your dreams? Who is she? Am I going to have to fight her for you?" she said with a smile.

"I don't want you to hurt yourself." Valorian gave her a beaming smile and Freya chuckled.

"You go sit down and rest. I've got this," he said.

Freya went into the living room and sat on the sofa with her knees pulled up under her. She could hear Valorian humming a tune while she cleaned up, and she wondered what it would be like to live with him, if he was always this happy and this helpful. Within a few minutes Valorian came and sat next to her.

"Finished already?"

"I told you, super speed." He winked. He placed his hand on Freya's leg and rubbed it with his thumb.

Heat spread up through her body like a bush fire. She coughed and shifted positions.

"So, what are the plans with your family for tonight?" she asked, trying to distract him.

"Night hiking up the mountains. We need to hunt some food; they prefer theirs fresher than I do."

"I see," Freya replied. She knew that Vampires lived on blood, of course, and she knew that Valorian's family fed on animals rather than on human blood, but it was something that had never really come up in conversation before and she wasn't sure how to respond.

"What are your plans for tomorrow evening?" he asked. If he had noticed her discomfort, he didn't show it.

"It's the new moon so I have planned a ritual, but other than that I have nothing else going on."

"Would you like to come over for dinner? Around eight o'clock?"

"I would love to. It will be nice to get to know your family better before they have to leave again."

"They have been bugging me to get you over, especially Phoenix. She seems to have taken a particular shine to you - and my father really wants to ask you about your family. He was very close to your ancestors."

"Great, it's a date then," she replied.

"I can't wait," he said, kissing her hand. "Right, I'm going to head back over and let you get some sleep while I rescue the shop from Eli."

"Okay. I'm going to have a bath then head to bed."

Freya saw Valorian down to the door and kissed him long and hard before letting him leave. She watched him walk over to the shop and wished she could still be in his arms. *I have to get a handle on my emotions. This is ridiculous; I can't keep avoiding close contact with him.* Worry etched her face. *What if he goes off me because he thinks I'm playing games with him? I could lose him - and that isn't something I'm prepared to let happen.* Tomorrow, she decided, she would ring Poppy and ask for her advice. *Maybe she knows a spell that could help me?*

Freya woke early, forgetting for a brief second that she was in her new apartment. The sun hadn't yet risen but she felt rejuvenated. Mael was asleep in his cage, so she quietly crept out of bed, placing her feet into the fluffy slippers beside her bed. She opened the curtains as she walked through the rooms towards the kitchen. A thought entered her head: *How wonderful would it be to make a flask of tea and go watch the sunrise from the meadow up across the mountains.* The idea filled Freya with a sense of calm, so she got herself dressed and ready, grabbed a blanket and made a flask of tea. The increasing light of the day made everything feel like it was waiting in a sense of anticipation. There were no people around, but she could see the lights of the Spellbound Café were on, as they prepared to open their doors to the world.

The birds chirped and called to each other as she passed, and the approaching spring felt strong today. She walked through the freshly growing grass and found a spot where she could see the mountains, the faint yellow glow of the sunrise showing softly behind them. She took out the blanket and gave it a shake, placing it on the ground and sitting. It was still cold outside, but she felt warm wrapped in her coat with the warm flask in her hands. If this was any other place, she might have looked odd, sitting in the middle of the field before sunrise, but here in Crestwood she knew no-one would bat an eye. She looked over towards the forest. The never-changing evergreen trees stood tall and proud, resilient against the winter. They were like watchers, standing their ground in all seasons to protect the town from whatever lay beyond them. The forest kept the town enclosed and offered a boundary between them and the harsh, snow-capped mountains. As the sun began to rise above the peaks, her thoughts turned to Valorian, and she felt that familiar stirring starting in her stomach. She really would have to speak to Poppy and see what advice she could get about the situation. She had spent almost two months not using magic (despite finding it difficult) and it didn't seem fair that it could just show itself like that when she wasn't focused. Of course it would be the magic that could potentially ruin things between her and Valorian. They had got so close, and she longed for that feeling again. She craved his touch, his love, but it felt so far away now. She didn't want to tell him about her fears. She knew he would be ok with how things were - that the magic didn't bother him - but it scared her. She couldn't bear the thought of losing anyone else she loved or cared for - even if Valorian was almost impossible to damage. She sipped the tea in the flask, and she felt its warmth spread out through her body, easing her feelings of dread. Freya lay back as she watched the sky above her turn from a dark blue to a bright blue. Clouds floated past and she gazed up at them trying to make out shapes in their form. She got up and put the empty flask and blanket in her bag and headed home, sending Poppy a quick text to ask whether she would be free later.

Freya was immersed in reading when her phone bleeped, alerting her to a message she had received. It was from Poppy, saying she was free for a couple of hours that afternoon and would pop over as she had some exciting news to share with her. Freya smiled and put the phone down, wondering what Poppy had to share. It was great having Poppy as a friend; she had never had this sort of genuine friendship before. Crestwood was turning out to be a place full of surprises, and it seemed they were all good ones.

The morning passed slowly and, for the first time in what felt like weeks, Freya could just enjoy the peace and serenity of being at home without having anything to do. The sunrise walk had left her sated and feeling content within herself and she couldn't remember the last time she had felt this way - if she ever had at all. Mael had made himself comfortable, perching on the back of the sofa.

"You aren't a cat, you know," Freya said, stroking his small furry body.

Which I am glad about, Mael replied, his voice in her head.

The doorbell rang and she ran excitedly down the stairs and swung open the door.

"Hey," She greeted Poppy.

"Hey," Poppy said.

They went upstairs, Freya made them both a drink and they sat together on the sofa.

"So, what's the big news?" Freya asked excitedly.

"Well...I stayed over at Anderson's last night," Poppy said.

"Oh, did you now." She winked at her friend.

"Nothing happened though. Not because I didn't want to, but his mum was around, so it was a bit weird, you know?"

"I get it. Still, it's a great step forward in your relationship though."

"He was so sweet, Freya, he made me breakfast in bed and held me all night. It was so difficult not to give in and ravage him," she said, almost growling.

Freya laughed. "Yeah, I bet it was. I wanted to talk to you about something similar actually."

"Oh yeah? You and Valorian having some bedroom issues?" Poppy said wiggling her eyebrows.

"Actually, yes." Freya blushed.

"Ah crap, I'm sorry. I didn't know."

"It's okay. Anyway, well. When we were about to… for the first time, I somehow let my magic lose. I didn't mean to, but whenever my emotions are heightened, I lose control. I almost set his flat on fire."

"Oh my, that's not good at all!" Poppy exclaimed

"Do you know of any spell or something that could help? I feel awful trying to avoid more intimate times with him, but I don't trust myself."

"Yeah, it would be an issue for me too. Don't worry, I totally get what you mean. What does Valorian think?"

"I haven't spoken to him about it. He just shrugged off the incident as nothing. But I know he's going to notice that I'm avoiding being alone with him. And besides - I don't want to avoid being alone with him! I want to be close to him."

"Hmm, I can't think of anything that can help off the top of my head, but I can have a look through our Grimoires and see if there is something. Did you look through yours?"

"I did. There wasn't anything in mine, and I'm still not even a quarter of the way through transcribing my ancestors' Grimoire."

"You want a magic suppressor. I can ask about it as well if I can't find anything. I'm sure there must be something we can do that would help."

"Thanks, Poppy. Oh, and another thing. Do you know any Herbalists? I'd like to stock up on some medicinal tinctures and salves. I left all mine in the city, but I hate using tablets and such for remedies."

"There's a good herbalist in Hawthorne Hollow, but if you want to write me a list I could get you some ingredients if you wanted to make your own?"

"I could but I won't be able to add any magic to them, so they won't be as potent. I'll pop over to Hawthorne next week and get some. Cheers for that."

"No problem at all, that's what friends are for." Poppy grinned.

"Do you have time off work for the festival?" Freya asked, changing the subject.

"Yeah, barely any of the shops will be open during it. Since the festival is during the night, most people sleep during the day."

"That makes sense. I've never been good at sleeping through the day, but a few hours should be possible. I'm really looking forward to it."

"The town goes all out on the sabbat festivals. Everyone can come out and celebrate without fear or judgement. Many of the town's Shifters will even change form and come as their animal counterparts. Witches will be performing magic for all the children. It's great."

"Wow, it sounds amazing. Do you have any plans for tonight's new moon?"

"My Coven is gathering at midnight to do a ritual. What about you?"

"I'm just going to do a ritual once I get back from a meal with Valorian and his family. Since I stopped using my magic it's been harder to connect to the energy in the same way. I can feel it, like a hum under the skin, but I can't quite catch it. I didn't realise how little humans feel the natural energy around us. No wonder they all think we only exist in fairytales."

"It must be hard, going from using all that power to not using it at all."

"The first couple of weeks were difficult. Just using my hands and body for things my magic would normally do was difficult. I also never realised how heavy things were, or how exhausting it is doing day to day chores like washing dishes or doing laundry."

"I don't think I could do it. I use magic without thinking."

"I was the same. If anything, it's been a lesson to appreciate humans more than I had before. They live like this and will never experience what magic can be like. But that also means they won't experience the devastation it brings either."

"I'm not sure about that. I mean humans still feel it when they lose someone they love, the same as we do, and if that loss had a magical cause, they're left with so many unanswered questions."

"I never thought of it that way. That must be terrible. Imagine losing a loved one to magic and no-one having a clue what happened. You would never get closure."

The girls sat deep in thought for a few minutes.

Freya broke the silence. "Anyway, enough doom and gloom. What are you going to do about the Anderson situation?"

"Urgh, I don't know. One of our parents always seems to be around and we can't get any alone time. I'm sure that my car or his is not going to be a place for our first time either."

"I'll have a think, maybe I can help find a solution, before you combust." Freya laughed.

"Right, I best get going. I have loads to prepare for tonight's ritual. They left me in charge of gathering all the correspondences this month," Poppy said, rolling her eyes.

"Okay, thanks for coming over. It was good to chat this through with you."

"Anytime. See you tomorrow," Poppy said, skipping down the stairs.

CHAPTER EIGHTEEN

Knowing that it would be late when she returned from Valorian's, Freya made a start on preparing for the new moon ritual. She took out a silver and white candle, placing them both on the slate tile next to each other, taking some sage and cloves, along with calendula from the jars of herbs, which Poppy had placed on the bookshelf for her. She placed a tablespoon of each in a small silver bowl and mixed them together before sprinkling them around the candles ready for later. She then made up the same mixture, adding bergamot and pink salt and took them to the bathroom to use in her ritual bath. Picking up the velvet tarot bag she placed it along with her tarot journal on the table next to the sofa. Everything was ready and it brought her a sense of peace and calm. Taking a deep breath, she released it with her eyes closed. Normally she would be feeling the heightened energy by now - the new moon energy used to make her feel so powerful - but now she just felt it murmur quietly, skipping the edges of consciousness, but never quite reaching out to touch her. She sighed. *I really miss that feeling, and without it I do feel somewhat like an outsider. But it's my cross to bear, and I'm sure that eventually it won't feel as bad as it does now. Or at least I hope it'll get easier.*

With a few hours still to go before she was due at Valorian's,

Freya decided to go out for a walk and visit Mystique's Boutique, to buy herself something nice to wear for the evening.

The street was quiet as Freya walked down it, and a light rain was starting to fall. Grey clouds dominated the skyline, and in the distance, she could see they were even darker over the mountains. She hoped that whatever downpour was due to come would do so before tomorrow's festival. Hurrying into the boutique, Freya was immediately drawn to a floral dress. It was perfect. The material was soft and floaty, and the floral pattern was feminine and perfect for spring. She picked it up and checked the price. It was a little more than she would normally pay but since there was no rent for her to pay for anymore, she treated herself. She picked out a pair of stylish shoes to pair with it, and a small yellow shoulder bag which matched the colours in the dress. Just as she was about to go pay, she caught sight of a pair of beautiful flower detailed white sandals. *Screw it*, she said to herself and picked them up, taking them to the counter along with the other items. As she left the store, the heavens opened on her, and she decided against going for a coffee and instead made her way back home.

Freya hung the dress up and decided that she was going to have a pamper session. Her bathroom cupboard held an array of facemasks, which she had bought on a whim from Bert's the previous week. She had a quick shower to wash her hair, then she lay across the sofa with her hair in a towel while she smoothed on the facemask, leaving it for several minutes to settle into her skin before she washed it off. She stroked her cheek; the skin there felt soft and rejuvenated. She had styled her hair into soft waves which fell down her back and applied just enough makeup that it enhanced her features while remaining natural. She decided to wear the heels; it felt like a good occasion to dress up and she wanted to look good for Valorian, even if she suspected that he didn't care what she wore. Looking out of the window, she could see the rain bouncing off the road outside, and she hoped that she wouldn't get too wet on the short walk from her place to Valorian's, especially since she couldn't find her umbrella anywhere.

Darkness had fallen and with it the thunder and lightning had arrived. Freya grabbed her jacket and held it over her head, hoping it would be enough to keep the rain from ruining her hair. She ran across the road to the Moonlight Emporium, where Valorian was already waiting with the door open. He took her jacket and hung it on one of the hooks just behind the counter.

"You look amazing," he said, eyeing her appreciatively.

"Thank you." Freya blushed.

Valorian took her in his arms, kissed her lips, and sighed.

"I've missed this," he said, running his thumb along her bottom lip.

"Me too." She nestled into him. "Let's go up, I don't want to keep them all waiting," she said after a moment, although she would have much preferred to spend her time alone with Valorian.

She could hear them all chatting away as she made her way up the staircase, and as she opened the door, Phoenix let out a squeal.

"She's here!"

"Hey," Freya said, she couldn't help but smile.

Phoenix came over and gave her a hug. Everyone was sitting around the table, which was laid with the most beautiful china plates and crockery.

"This looks beautiful," Freya said, taking a seat next to Valorian's chair.

"It is an old family dining set we don't often have the opportunity to break out," Emeline replied.

"It's so delicate and the detailing on that gilded pattern is stunning," Freya said.

Valorian brought over the last of the food - a giant roast beef joint – before sitting down beside her.

"Feel free to dig in now, everyone," he said and gave her a wink.

Everyone filled their plates with beef, potatoes, veg and gravy and they talked between themselves.

Maykn sat at the other side of Freya. "How are you enjoying your time in Crestwood so far, Freya?" he asked.

"I love it. I can't believe I didn't know about this place until I ended up here. It's truly one of a kind."

"Yes, it really is. I would love to come and live back here, but unfortunately work keeps me away."

"That's a shame, maybe in the future you will end up back here."

"I'd like to think so. Your ancestors loved it here. It was hard when they left. It must have been harder for them though given their situation."

"Yeah, I can imagine it must have been. I can only imagine that they felt they had no other choice."

"I think you're right. They would never willingly have left otherwise. I do wish they had come to us all with the problem. We could have helped."

"They probably felt that the best option was just to get as far away from the Emerys as possible. From what I've heard they were not nice people to be involved with."

"No, they weren't. Their involvement in dark magic impaired their judgement about many things. They saw it as a shortcut to gaining what they wanted. It backfired on them, and they paid the price heavily."

"Oh, how so?" Freya asked, intrigued.

"When everyone found out Everlyn and her family left, we were all devastated. But not the Emerys, oh no they were angry. Carrington, however, did not direct his anger at anyone other than his family. He blamed them for the fact that he had lost the love of his life, and his child. He left not long after that, but not before casting some dark magic of his own, preventing any of his family from having children."

"Wow," she said quietly.

"His remaining family tried everything to lift the curse, but it was impossible, and that was the end of their family line. Carrington never returned and we had no idea if he had found Everlyn or if the curse had also affected him."

"This is such a sad story. There were no winners here. Everlyn and Carrington lost each other, an entire bloodline was wiped out and a town was left without one of its founders."

"Exactly. Crestwood went into a state of mourning for

months when they left. It took us a long time to recover. Their absence was felt by everyone. No one could find them; they made a good job of hiding their location."

"I wonder what happened with Carrington. I had never heard his name until I moved here so I don't think he found his way to Everlyn."

"I often wonder too. He was a nice boy, never much like his family but I can understand why your family left. The baby would have stood no chance with his family around."

Valorian put his hand on her leg.

"Everything okay?" he whispered.

"Absolutely. This meal is delicious," she replied, putting a forkful of potato in her mouth.

"I hope my father isn't boring you, regaling tales of the past?"

"No, not at all. It's actually very interesting hearing it all from someone who lived it first-hand. It's like having pieces of them given back to me."

"Good, but if he starts going on, just tap my leg and I will be your knight in shining armour."

"Okay, I'll be sure to do that," Freya said with a laugh.

The conversation flowed as easily as the wine in the relaxed atmosphere and Freya felt as if she had known everyone for her entire life. She had never felt so comfortable with anyone other than her parents, but despite how much she was enjoying herself, she was beginning to feel tired. She turned to Valorian and squeezed his leg.

"I am really enjoying this, but I am going to have to leave soon," she said, pouting slightly.

"I thought you would have left an hour ago. I didn't say anything because I don't want you to go." He kissed her cheek.

"I'm off for five days now, so I am all yours."

"My parents are leaving on the last day of the festival so we will get a couple of days together before you have to go back to work. Maybe we could plan something nice to do, if you want to, of course?"

"I would really like that," she replied.

Freya hugged Phoenix and Emeline and said goodbye to the others.

Valorian walked her back down to the door and put her coat over her shoulders.

"I'll walk you over," he said.

"There's no need, it's only across the way. No point in you getting wet too," she said, indicating the pouring rain.

"It's just a little rain, I would feel much better if you let me." He put out his bottom lip and gave her puppy dog eyes.

Freya laughed. "Okay then, as long as you promise to never do that again," she said.

Freya shut the door behind her, shrugged off her wet jacket and hung it on the peg at the bottom of the stairs, and grabbed a basket of logs from the workshop. Upstairs was chilly, the rain had brought in a cold front, so she flicked on the heating and lit the fire in the main room. The cosy warm light from the lamps and the crackling fire made Freya feel sleepy, so she went into the kitchen to make a coffee. Usually, she wouldn't have drunk coffee so late at night, but she had to stay up longer tonight for the New Moon ritual and so that she would be awake for the festival the following night. Coffee in hand, Freya sat on the fluffy rug near the fire and started her ritual by lighting the candle she had prepared earlier and saying out loud her intentions and wishes for this moon. Once that was done, she shuffled her tarot deck and drew the cards. She looked at them carefully, analysing each one in turn, and sighed. *Not the most positive of spreads.* Her reading showed a potential trouble on the horizon if she didn't learn to move forward with some issue in her life. Freya assumed this was due to the magic and Valorian thing, she didn't need the cards to tell her there would be issues if she didn't fix herself soon. An idea popped into her head, and she felt stupid for not thinking of it sooner. *Holden! He's the oldest Witch I know; he would probably know exactly how to help me solve this issue. I'll visit him tomorrow, before the festival starts, and see whether he can help.*
Giving herself a mental pat on the back, she picked up her book and relaxed as she started to turn the pages.

Freya looked at the clock, it was almost four in the morning, and she couldn't keep her eyes open any longer. Placing the book on

the table she took her cup into the kitchen, made sure the fire was out and went to the bathroom to get ready for bed. She yawned loudly as she made her way into the bedroom and Mael fluttered his wings, clearly unimpressed with being woken by her. "Sorry," she muttered under her breath.
She pulled back the covers and climbed in. Almost as soon as her head hit the pillow, she fell into a deep slumber.

Freya awoke to a loud knocking on the front door. She could hear the rain coming down hard and had no idea what time it was. A grey, dull light emanated from the windows as she went quickly through the rooms and down the stairs. She unlocked the door and opened it. A woman stood outside, clad in a black cloak, her hood up and a large black umbrella in her hand.

"Hello, Freya," she said.

"Urm. Hi," Freya responded, confused.

"My name is Beatrice La Rue. I am the Elder for the local Coven, and I was wondering if I could come in for a quick chat?"

"Sure, of course. It's very wet out there," she replied, opening the door wider for Beatrice to come through.

Beatrice folded her umbrella and left it standing to the side as she walked up the stairs. Something about the graceful way she walked made Freya dislike her.

When they reached the top of the stairs, Beatrice peered out of the living room window.

"Quite a view from here, it is rather splendid."

"It is. Though I thought you would have a better view of the mountains from home, being so close to them in Hawthorne Hollow."

"We do, but sometimes we are too close to see the mist sitting across the peaks as you can here."

"Can I get you a drink or something. Tea perhaps?" Freya asked, unsure why Beatrice was here, in her living room.

"No, thank you. What I have come to say won't take long," she said as she walked over to sit on the sofa.

"And what is it you have come to say?" Freya remained standing.

"I want to invite you to take your rightful place in The Coven of the Great Stag, like your ancestors before you," Beatrice said, looking Freya in the eye.

"I see. Thank you for the offer but I would like to decline. I no longer practice magic," Freya replied.

"Yes, Poppy had mentioned that to me, but I cannot understand why a Witch, especially one of such pedigree would give up her magic, and how she could contain it?"

"I have my reasons, none of which I need to explain to you." Freya said, folding her arms.

"Perhaps, but you can't run from your magic, Freya. It's in your blood, in your DNA. You might think you can put it in a box, but you can't. I'm sure, if your ancestors were here, they would say the same thing."

"My ancestors would understand, and this doesn't concern you. I am not a member of your Coven."

"That is where you are wrong. Every Witch living here or in Hawthorne Hallow is my concern, especially those who might prove to be unstable."

"I am not unstable. I just refuse to use my magic, and I am much happier without it. I'm sorry you wasted your time coming here in the rain," Freya retorted, defiance in her voice.

"As am I. The offer is there, should you come to your senses," Beatrice said, getting up and making her way down the stairs.

Freya followed.

"My senses are just fine, thank you."

Beatrice opened the door and shook out her umbrella, popping it up above her head and stalking off into the rain without a glance back.

Freya sighed as she closed the door, hoping that it would be the last time she saw Beatrice La Rue.

CHAPTER NINETEEN

Freya woke in the early afternoon. She opened her eyes, groaning as she thought about Beatrice's visit earlier that day. Her head felt heavy and fuzzy, and she was determined to put the Coven and Beatrice's visit to the back of her mind. She got out of bed, walking through the living room and into the kitchen, pouring herself a glass of cold water. She drank it down at once, hoping it would bring her some instant relief, but it didn't. She decided that she needed a coffee to wake her up, so she filled the kettle and plugged it in, flicking down the blue button on the side. The kettle sparked, and the electricity went off - reminding Freya of sparklers on Guy Fawkes night. She quickly looked around and saw that none of the other appliances were working. *Just what I needed, the electricity to trip. I hope it's not going to be one of those days where everything goes wrong.* She sighed, setting off downstairs to find the fuse box.

The downstairs workshop was cold, and she wished she had put her bathrobe on. The fuse box sat at the back of the room, and she quickly reset everything and went back to the warmth of the apartment. Deciding against making coffee, she got dressed. *I'll pick up a coffee from Spellbound when I get some cake for Holden.*

Hoping that the fresh air and walk would clear the strange

feeling in her head, Freya stepped outside and stood, open mouthed, on the doorstep. People must have worked hard while she had slept, because the town had been transformed for the festival. Green and yellow ribbons were wrapped around all the lampposts, fresh flowers adorned the back of benches and sat in pots down the street. Shop windows showed displays of corn dolls, Brigid crosses and snow drops. It was all bright and perfect for Imbolc. She walked over to Spellbound, admiring all the work that had been put into decorating the street. Lanterns hung from ropes across the buildings. Her little shop stood out like a sore thumb; it was the only one not decorated, and she vowed to change that when she got home.

Spellbound was quiet and she got served straight away. Anderson was on the phone, but he gave her a wave. She put the cake in her bag, grabbed the cup of coffee, and set off to Holden's house.

As always, his house was alive with fresh flowers and the faint buzz of bees. She wondered what it looked like on stormy days. *It must really stand out against the dark and moody mountains.* She knocked on the door and it creaked open. From inside Holden shouted for her to come in and take a seat. She shut the door behind her before sitting at the table, carefully taking the cake out of the bag for him. A few minutes later he walked through and smiled at her - and she realised it was the first time she had ever seen him smile.

"I brought you some cake," she said.

"Thank you. Is something troubling you? Or have you drunk too much of that?" he said, nodding towards the coffee she was jiggling against her leg.

"I was wondering… is there a way to hinder your magic, to suppress it?"

Holden looked at her for a moment, deep concern etched on his brow.

"I'm sure there is but it would be dangerous. Magic isn't supposed to be suppressed; it can't be pushed aside. It's part of our very fabric, and it would make the suppressor very ill. It could end very badly should it ever be freed. I have only ever known people suppress the magic of those who wished to harm others."

"What do you mean it can make you sick?" she asked.

"Magic is in our DNA, if we don't use it, it can build up, destroying our cells from the inside out. It can become unruly and uncontrollable. Even if it isn't felt, it can affect things around us."

"I see," she said, thoughtfully.

"Why do you ask?"

"I'm struggling to keep a hold of mine when I get emotional. It's like I forget to keep it tightly bound and it just comes out unexpectedly."

"It wants to be free. I would advise against using any form of spell to keep it supressed, Freya. It is extremely dangerous."

"I guess I will just have to avoid getting emotional then." She sighed.

"Are you experiencing any other symptoms? Headaches, electrical faults, weakness, tiredness?" he asked.

"No," she said too quickly. "I mean I have been a little run down, but it was just because I had a lot on. I feel better now though."

"Well, if you're sure that is all it was. Just be careful though, if you find yourself feeling run down more often, it would be wise to release some of that magic, so it doesn't overwhelm you."

"Thank you for your help, Holden, but I won't be using my magic. I'll figure it out somehow."

A look of disappointment crossed his face, but he didn't continue to push it, much to Freya's relief.

"Are you going to the festival tonight?" he asked, changing the subject.

"Yes, I am really looking forward to it." She smiled.

"I haven't been for many years, but it was always a highlight of my year," he said, taking a seat opposite her.

"Why don't you go now? I'm sure everyone would love to see you."

"That's kind of you to say, but I have had my time. I am too old and frail now, and I don't particularly like the company of others, so I am sure it wouldn't be as much fun as it was when I was younger," he said wistfully.

"If you decide to change your mind, I would love to see you

there and I know Valorian would as well. Anyway, I better get going. I am meeting Valorian's sister in Jackson's before the festival starts, so I should really go get ready."

"Enjoy the evening," Holden replied.

Freya left and started walking home. Her thoughts turned to what Holden had said about the magic. She had told herself that it was just being run down that had made her feel ill, but deep down she was beginning to question whether her magic might be involved. Shaking her head, clearing away the paranoia that had started to edge in, Freya sped up, wanting to get home to get ready – and to distract herself from her thoughts.

Freya stood in front of the full-length mirror that hung on the bathroom wall. Her hair was tied up in a tall ponytail, she had applied subtle smoky make-up to her eyes, and she wore a long knitted black jumper with leggings and boots. *Comfy and classy.* She was pleased with her look, and she made her way to Jackson's already looking forward to getting to spend more time with Phoenix.

Jacksons was busy, with people crowded around the bar and tables, and there was a buzz in the air - everyone seemed happy and excited for the festival.

Freya felt a warm gaze on her, she turned and locked eyes with Valorian. He gave her a subtle, sexy smile, and she blushed, looking down at the ground before making her way over to him. Valorian wrapped his arms around her and kissed her. Freya felt her legs wobble beneath her as she melted into his arms.

"Put her down, will you," Phoenix said, a drink in her hand.

Valorian released his grip, and Freya turned to Phoenix, who was sitting at the table with Ezra. A selection of empty shot glasses were scattered around them. "Hey," she said.

"What do you want to drink? I was just about to go to the bar," Valorian asked her.

"Pink gin and lemonade please," she said, taking a seat next to Phoenix.

"Okay, back in a minute."

As they chatted, Freya heard a familiar voice behind her.

"Freya!" Poppy pushed through the crowd, with Anderson

following closely behind, holding her hand.

"Poppy! Anderson!" Freya stood up and hugged her friend.

"I'm so glad you are here. We popped over to the apartment before coming here but you weren't in. I thought you'd either be here or at Valorian's. Hey, Fi, Ezra." Poppy smiled at Phoenix and Ezra.

"I do wish you wouldn't call me Fi," Phoenix said, rolling her eyes.

"I only do it because I know you hate it." Poppy gave her a big grin.

"Careful, Witch, I will drink you dry," Phoenix replied licking her lips.

"Promises, promises." Poppy winked. They both laughed and hugged each other.

Valorian returned with the drinks, and the six friends sat together, enjoying the merriment of the night. Freya loved how well they all got on and how easily she fit into the group considering she was still new to the area. They had welcomed her with open arms, and it made her feel as if she had always been there. Valorian sat next to her, their legs touching, and his hand on her knee. She was struggling to focus on anything but the electricity that seemed to spread from his fingers to her skin. *I'll have to slow down the drinking otherwise I might not be able to control myself with him.* She hated having to stop herself from being how she wanted to be around him.

"You okay?" Valorian whispered in her ear.

"Oh, yeah, sorry. I was in a world of my own then," she said looking up at him.

"The festival starts soon. Are you tired?"

"I didn't get up until this afternoon, so I am feeling pretty good now. Though I should really stop drinking. I'm such a lightweight. I don't drink often so it goes straight to my head." She laughed.

"Don't worry. I'll look after you." He winked.

"Ah, well then I am in perfectly safe hands," she said, giving him a kiss on the nose.

The group finished their drinks and made their way outside ready for the start of the festival. Thankfully, the night was clear, stars twinkled in the sky above them and the streetlights reflected a hazy glow on the wet floor as they walked to where the entrance had been set up.

A large group of people stood on the road near the meadow, where wood had been piled up, ready for the bonfire. The main street looked amazing now it was dark. All the lanterns were lit, and the shop window displays had been lit up by gold and green twinkling lights.

Freya could see various fairground games and entertainers along the street, waiting for the main event to kick off the three-day festival. She smiled and squeezed Valorian's arm tighter.

"This is fantastic," she said, her eyes bright.

Valorian looked at her and he stroked her cheek.

"You have no idea how adorable you are right now."

"Adorable?" she scoffed.

"Yes, adorable," he said leaning close, and taking her lip between his teeth.

Freya groaned.

"Behave yourself." She bit her lip and then smiled at him.

"Okay, but I make no promises for later." He smirked.

More people joined the gathering crowd and Freya looked around. She had never seen so many people out together here; it was nice to see new and familiar faces. Everyone was happy and smiling.

Maykn stepped onto the small, makeshift stage. "Goodnight, Ladies and Gentlemen. I have been given the honour of opening tonight's festival by lighting the Imbolc Bonfire. For those who would like to make a wish, there is a table set up over there with pens and paper," he said, pointing to a table situated near the bonfire. "Please feel free to throw them into the fire and may the Goddess Brighid bless us all. Without further ado, I declare the festival open," he said, making his way to the bonfire and lighting it with a torch from a nearby stand.

The fire went up hot and fast, glowing red, purple, blue and green and Freya felt her stomach do a flip. It was so magical.

"Impressive isn't it," Phoenix said beside her.

"It's beautiful," Freya replied.

"Like you." Valorian winked.

Freya snorted and rolled her eyes towards Phoenix, who laughed at her.

The group made their way to the table, and they each wrote a small wish on a piece of paper. Together they stood around the bonfire and on the count of three, threw their wishes into the flames. They walked back towards the main street. Music played from a live band who had set up at the side of the street and the atmosphere was one of excitement, hope and joy. Freya smiled as she watched the stilt walkers, jugglers and fire breathers entertaining young children. Every sort of species could be found - human, Shifter, Vampire and Witch all enjoying their time together - and Freya felt pride burst within her, she was part of this community, and she loved it.

Valorian grabbed them both some food and a drink from one of the food stalls.

Freya bit into the hotdog. "This is so good." She closed her eyes and licked her lips.

"There is nothing nicer than the food they prepare on the sabbats. I'm sure they use magic to enhance the flavour," Valorian said, tucking into his own mustard-covered hotdog.

"They can keep doing it if it is all going to taste this good," Freya said, licking tomato sauce from her lips.

Phoenix dragged Ezra to the Ferris wheel and Freya giggled as she watched them. The expression on Ezra's face said he clearly didn't want to go, but he was not going to say no to an excited Phoenix.

Poppy and Anderson walked hand in hand just in front of Freya and Valorian. Freya smiled at her friend - she looked so happy to be beside Anderson, and he couldn't seem to take his eyes off Poppy. Freya wondered whether she and Valorian looked at each other with the same doe-eyed expression. She didn't think so, but most of the time when she looked at Valorian, the rest of the world seemed to have melted away, and she felt like she was floating.

Valorian stopped at a Hook-A-Duck stall and gave the man some change.

"I am a hook-a-duck champion, you'll see." He winked at Freya.

"I'm sure you are," she said with an easy laugh.

Concentration was etched on his face; his brows came down together and his tongue slipped out.

She was so busy watching his face she missed him catching the duck, and only knew he had won when his expression changed to one of pure delight and he turned to smile at her.

"Well done," she said, with a laugh.

"Why thank you, kind lady," he said, taking a bow. Valorian picked a bear holding a heart as his prize, and passed it to Freya.

"This is for you, my love."

Freya took the bear and smiled. "Thank you," she said, reaching up on her toes and planting a kiss on his lips.

"I may have to go win more often if this is the response I get," he said, wrapping his arm around her.

"I don't need an excuse to kiss you," she replied.

The rest of the night was filled with fairground rides, game stalls and glorious food. Freya found herself growing more tired as the hours ticked by.

"Can we sit for a minute?" she said.

"Sure," Valorian said, as they perched on the bench closest to them. "Getting tired?" he asked, brushing aside a strand of hair that had fallen lose from her ponytail.

"Yup, definitely feeling it now," she said, looking at her watch. It was just after 4:30 a.m. and she had lasted longer than she thought she would.

"It's been a great night. I'm looking forward to seeing who the special guest is tomorrow," Valorian said.

"There is a special guest?" Freya looked at him curiously.

"On the second night of the festival they always have a special guest come and perform."

"Oh, that sounds intriguing," she said, yawning again.

"We should get you home."

"I don't want to leave, but I think I will have to agree. I was fine ten minutes ago but now I feel like I've been hit by a truck," she said.

They stood to leave, when Freya felt that same strange

sensation of somebody watching her. She glanced around, but she couldn't see anyone.

"What's up?" Valorian asked.

"Ah, nothing. I think being tired is making me paranoid. I could have sworn I felt someone watching me."

Valorian had a quick look around. "There doesn't seem to be anyone here."

"I am just overtired, it'll be nothing."

Valorian walked Freya back to the apartment.

"Thank you for another lovely night," he said pulling her close.

"Thank you for inviting me to come with you," she replied snuggling closer.

"I wish I didn't have to leave you." He kissed her forehead.

"I know. I miss you even though you are only over the road," she said.

"I miss you too. It's hard sometimes not to come over here when I know you are sleeping."

"You can always wake me."

"I know, but I don't like to disturb you."

"You're never a disturbance to me, Valorian," she said, looking him in the eyes.

He bowed his head to kiss her; she wrapped her arms around the back of his neck and pulled him closer.

"I love you," she said.

"Not as much as I love you," he replied. He stepped back, and Freya opened the door.

"See you tomorrow," she said.

"Definitely," he replied. He turned and walked back towards the festival, as Freya locked the door behind her and made her way up to the apartment. She walked around closing all the curtains and then went straight to the bathroom to get ready for bed.

As she laid her head on her pillow, she could still smell Valorian's scent. She closed her eyes, smiling to herself as she drifted off to sleep.

CHAPTER TWENTY

Freya carried the bucket of soapy water into the front of the shop. Today was officially Imbolc, and she felt restless. Looking at the street, with all its décor and beautifully decorated shop windows, made her feel as if her shop stood out for all the wrong reasons. She cleaned down all the shelves, emptying all the jars of things that had long since gone out of date - or looked very suspicious - before filling each jar with a little bleach, washing up liquid, and hot water. Once all the surfaces were clean, she grabbed the sweeping brush and swept the floor, before finally cleaning the windows. Proud of her efforts she made a start on the back rooms, cleaning out all the rubbish. *I wonder how many of my family worked from this cauldron. Generations of Evermores would have used it for their spells as well as for the shop. It's crazy to think that I'm here after everything,* she thought as she worked.

Her stomach rumbled, and she realised how hungry she was. Making her way back upstairs, she took leftover pasta from the fridge, turning it out onto a plate, and sitting down at the kitchen table to eat it. *I'm going to need a shower before I see Valorian tonight, there's no way I want to turn up looking this sweaty and gross after all the cleaning I've done.*

Mael fluttered in, taking a place on the table beside her. *"Are you enjoying the festival?"* he asked.

Freya swallowed her mouthful of pasta.

"It was wonderful. I'm really looking forward to tonight. It was quite something to see everyone out together like that. Do you ever fly down there?"

"I used to, a long time ago, but I haven't since your ancestors left."

"That's a long time to have spent here alone. Don't you want to go?"

"I would like to, but I have not been given permission yet."

"Permission for what?"

"To leave this place. I was ordered to keep a watchful eye on it until someone from the family returned and gave me permission to leave."

"Is that something I can do?"

"You can do it. It doesn't require magic, just words."

"I am so sorry. I had no idea. In that case, please feel free to leave here. Fly freely. You've served this family for long enough."

"I shall always serve you, but it would be nice to spread my wings outside of these walls. Thank you."

"Mael, I really do appreciate what you have done for my family."

"I have served the Evermores since my creation, and I shall serve them until I cease to exist - whenever that time may come."

"Thank you. Now go, enjoy your freedom." She smiled at the butterfly.

"As you wish," Mael whispered as he took off and fluttered through an open window.

Freya sighed. *I had no idea Mael was trapped here. I wonder why he didn't tell me before.*

Freya had just finished showering and dressing, when the doorbell rang. She ran down the stairs to find Valorian on the other side of the door.

"Hey," she said.

"I thought I would come and spend some time with you before we go over to Jackson's," he said.

"I just need to sort my hair out and then I'll be ready to go," she said, indicating the towel wrapped around her wet hair.

Valorian made himself comfortable on her bed while she sat

at the dresser putting the finishing touches to her hair and makeup. She could see him watching her, and she felt that familiar heat rising through her body. He looked good - very good - and she could only try to distract herself from her thoughts, from how badly she wanted to go and lie down next to him, how badly she wanted to be close with him. He smirked at her in the mirror, and she had the strange feeling that he knew what she was thinking – and he was enjoying every moment of it. Freya coughed, shifting slightly in her seat and focused her gaze on her hair. When she was finished, she got up and grabbed her boots from the wardrobe and pulled them on.

"I'm ready," she said.

"Best get your jacket, it's chilly outside tonight."

"Okay," she said, pulling on an aubergine-coloured jacket.

Jackson's was quieter than it had been the previous evening, much to Freya's relief. She spotted Phoenix, Ezra, Eli, Poppy, Anderson, and Marly sitting at a long table next to the back window and she gave them a wave, heading towards the bar with Valorian.

"If you want to go sit with the others, I'll bring the drinks over."

"You sure? I don't mind waiting with you."

"Nah, it's fine, go have fun," he said, kissing her cheek.

Freya joined the others.

"Hey, everyone," she said, draping her jacket on the back of the chair.

They all said hello, and she sat down next to Poppy.

"I walked past your place earlier, and I noticed the windows had all been cleaned downstairs. Been busy?" Poppy asked.

"Yeah, I thought it was the perfect day to start cleaning up the shop area. I managed to get it all clean ready to paint tomorrow."

"Oh, nice. What colour did you pick this time?"

"Just white. Thought I'd better keep it simple."

"It will make that wood pop for sure," Poppy replied.

"Did you have a good night?" Freya asked her friend.

"Brilliant. I stayed at Anderson's; his mum and dad were out all night at the festival, so it was nice to get some alone time."

She winked.

"Oh, I see." Freya winked back.

"We're going to need to have a catch up," Poppy said.

"Absolutely."

"I can come over tomorrow, if you aren't busy in the afternoon?"

"Other than painting, I have zero plans, just pop over whenever you're ready. I probably won't be up until about two-ish though."

"I will be the same, it's probably going to be about four. I'll bring some food over too, and a bottle of wine."

"That sounds fantastic. I'm looking forward to it."

"Room for another?" Phoenix asked across the table.

"Of course," replied Poppy.

"What about me?" said Ezra.

"Girls only, I'm afraid," replied Phoenix with a smirk.

Ezra folded his arms, feigning a sulk, and the others laughed.

Valorian appeared with a tray of drinks for everyone.

"I got everyone a top up," he said as Eli cleared the table.

Everyone thanked Valorian and grabbed a drink from the tray. He took a seat next to Freya.

"Thanks," she said, taking a sip of her gin.

"Anything for you, my love," he replied causing a blush to spread across her cheeks.

Freya enjoyed the evening with her friends - it was easy to forget about the world when she was in such good company. Grabbing their jackets, they all made their way to the festival to enjoy the night's entertainment. The drizzle must have started when they were in the pub, it had left a fine sheen of moisture across the road and benches. Thankfully the stalls were hidden under canopies, and it hadn't dampened the mood. At the end of the street, where the road had been blocked off, a stage had been erected, but there was no sign yet of who the special guest might be.

Freya and Poppy decided to ride the Ferris wheel together. Freya had never seen the town from this height. The woodland stretched around the small town, denser than she had realised, while the mountains stood tall in the background, snow still covering their peaks despite the approaching spring. Freya's legs felt a little wobbly as she stepped down from the ride, and she followed Poppy as the two of them looked for their friends. They found Valorian trying to beat Anderson's whack-a-mole score without breaking the gameboard. Freya wrapped her arm around Valorian's waist, and in the background, she heard a crackle as a microphone came to life.

"Goodnight to the people of Crestwood Falls and tourists. Tonight, we have a special treat in store for you all. The weather might not have worked in our favour, but the sun will always shine on this community. It is with great pleasure that I announce tonight's special guests. The one and only Nocturne!"

The crowd cheered loudly.

"Nocturne are a popular band who had success with many songs. While it had never been confirmed, the rumour was that they were a group of Shifters who left their packs to form a band and strike out on their own," Valorian whispered to Freya.

Poppy squealed loudly. "Oh My God! I love Nocturne! I can't believe they're here. I need to get closer," she said, pushing her way to the front of the crowd.

"I guess that's me not getting my girlfriend back for a couple of hours," Anderson said, as he followed her.

Freya giggled.

"Don't you want to join Poppy?" Valorian asked.

"Nah, I'm good. Truth be told, I'm not really a big fan anyway. Just don't tell Poppy that, she may disown me as her friend."

"Your secret is safe with me." He winked.

Freya and Valorian left the others dancing to Nocturne as they made their way around the craft stalls. Freya bought a new hand sewn bag decorated with tiny, stitched daisies, while Valorian got himself a new black leather bracelet. They made their way to the food stalls and bought some chips, taking a seat on a bench hiding under the awning to eat them. They were mid-conversation when Freya felt an icy chill down her spine, and she became aware of that strange feeling that someone was watching her. She stopped talking and scanned the crowd around them, finally finding the source of her discomfort. She locked eyes with the stranger who had spoken to her at the outdoor movie, and shifted uncomfortably in her seat.

"What's the matter?" Valorian asked.

"That guy from the movie, the one asking about the shop. He's walking towards us."

Valorian turned around, anger flashing across his face.

The stranger looked at him and smirked. "Hello again," he said.

"Look, she isn't interested in selling the shop to you. She's told you already."

"That's not why I am here, and my conversation is with her, not you." The stranger looked Valorian in the eye. If he felt any fear about the fact that he was arguing with a Vampire, he gave no sign of it as he spoke.

"What do you want then?" Freya asked.

"I want to introduce myself. I should have done it the first time I met you, but I was too nervous."

"Why would you be nervous?" Valorian asked.

The stranger ignored Valorian, continuing to look at Freya. She felt a mix of caution and curiosity as he spoke.

"My name is Carrington Emery Junior, and I am a relative of yours."

Freya's blood turned to ice and panic swept across her face. She looked at Valorian, fear in her eyes.

"I'm leaving," she said to him, as she got up and briskly walked away.

Valorian looked at Carrington.

"Please," Carrington said, grabbing Valorian's arm, "I am just trying to get to know my family. I heard what happened to her parents. I am all she has," he said, removing his hand from Valorian, who was now glaring at it as if he wanted to rip it from its socket.

"Perhaps after everything she knows about your family, she doesn't want to know you."

"I know, but I am not like them. None of us have been. Not since what happened with Freya's ancestors. Here, take my number, please give it to her. If she wants to talk to me, she can call me any time. I won't approach her again, I promise. I just wanted her to know I existed. I lost all my family too. I know how lonely it can be."

Valorian's defences were on edge, his eyes grew darker, and his face changed into something more menacing.

"I will take this and pass it on, but it really would be wise to keep your distance. Freya isn't lonely, she's moving forward, and she doesn't need you dragging her backwards."

"Thank you, I appreciate it," Carrington said before walking away.

Valorian closed his eyes and with his heightened senses, he picked up on Freya's scent and rushed straight to her.

"Are you okay?" he asked.

"I don't know. I mean, yes, I'm fine, but shocked, you know? I didn't even know he existed, or that they would know who I am."

"He has probably been watching the shop waiting to see if it was ever claimed. It can't be a coincidence that he turned up right after you moved in."

"You're probably right. I don't know what to do with this information. Everything I know about that side of the family terrifies me - what they have done in the past, who they are. It scares me."

"He gave me this," Valorian said, passing the piece of paper to Freya. "He said he just wants to get to know you, as you are his only living relative. You can contact him any time if you want to talk. He won't approach you again though."

Freya took the piece of paper and looked at it, Carrington's number was written in perfect scripted handwriting.

"I need to think about this before I do anything else," she said.

"That's probably the best decision. Give yourself time to really think it through."

"Yeah, maybe. What would you do, if you were in my situation?"

"I don't really know. Given everything you've been told about that family, I would probably avoid them, but I'm not you, and I have never had to deal with a situation like this."

Freya sighed heavily.

"Can we just forget about it for now and enjoy the rest of the night?" she asked.

"Of course. I'm here if you want to talk. For now, though…" He laughed. "I have an idea," he said, grabbing hold of Freya's hand and pulling her towards another stall.

Freya rushed to keep up with Valorian. *I'll try to put Carrington to the back of my mind, at least for the next couple of days.*

Valorian stopped at a stall that Freya hadn't noticed before. In front of her, Silas sat on a stool, while on the floor all around him was what looked like broken pastry and soft whipping cream.

"Pie throwing?" Freya sniggered.

"Yup. What's better than throwing cream pies at a friend, while he has to just sit there and take it?" Valorian said innocently.

"Why did he sign up for this? It doesn't look as fun from his perspective," she asked.

"Raising money for the Mountain Rescue Team. They want to put up new fencing and signs to warn hikers of some of the dangers in the mountains. There have been a few people hurt in avalanches over the last couple of years."

"That's awful. If it's for charity, then we better get some pies thrown," Freya said with a mischievous smile.

Valorian passed the stall holder some coins and they both picked up a pie each.

"Ready?" Valorian asked.

"Ready." Freya nodded. Together they launched their pies through the air. Valorian's pie hit Silas on the side of his shoulder. Freya's pie got him square on the nose.

"Good shot!" Valorian said. Silas wiped his face with a towel and glared at them both. So, they picked up another pie each and did it again.

"That was fun," Freya said as they walked off towards the candy stall where she picked up a lolly the size of her head. It was round and multicoloured and tasted delicious.

"Should you be having that much sugar before you go to bed?" Phoenix asked as she appeared behind them.

"I'm sure I'll be fine," Freya said, taking a big lick of the lolly.

"How was the band? Valorian asked.

"Great. I think Poppy is totally fangirling though. She hasn't taken her eyes off them, much to Anderson's dismay," Phoenix replied.

"Oh no, poor Anderson." Freya giggled.

Phoenix, Ezra and Eli made their way back to the Moonlight Emporium while Valorian stayed with Freya to make sure she got home safely.

"I had a great night with you," he said, leaning against the doorway of her shop.

"Me too, thank you for the distraction," she said.

"Anytime. Remember, if you want to talk it through or whatever, I'm here. Just text me and I can come straight over."

"Thank you." She smiled.

"My family is going home tomorrow evening. We can have some proper time alone then, I've missed it."

"I'll be sorry to see them leave, but I've missed spending time with you as well."

"Text me later?"

"Of course, don't I always? she said.

"Yes, you do. Goodnight." He kissed her softly and walked towards his shop.

Freya shivered as she walked up the stairs to the living room. The drizzle had made the air cold and damp and, despite the early morning hours, she piled the fire with wood and lit it. She made a hot cocoa and then curled up on the sofa with a blanket. She pulled out the piece of paper Valorian had given her with Carrington's number, and she placed it on the table in front of her. She had no idea what to do with it. She was curious about him and - based on what Holden had said - Freya knew that Carrington senior had left the rest of his family and dark magic behind. He was her only living relative - but at the same time she didn't know if she really needed to get to know him. He had never been part of her life, and she wasn't sure what might be dragged up from their ancestor's history. She didn't want to anger any of her familial spirits when they had given up so much to get away from them. She was torn, torn between what she knew from her past and what might have changed in the future. *Perhaps*

I should speak to the ancestral spirits in the mausoleum and see what they think about Carrington Junior and his request to speak to me. Her brain hurt trying to figure it out and she was too tired to give it any serious thought. She lay down and picked up her book, deciding that getting lost in its pages would be a welcome escape from her racing thoughts.

CHAPTER TWENTY-ONE

Freya stretched, almost falling off the sofa. She hadn't meant to fall asleep there, but the warmth of the fire had lulled her into closing her eyes for a brief second, and she had woken to find that hours had passed instead. The sun shone brightly through the window, illuminating the room. It was much earlier than she would have liked, but despite sleeping on the sofa, she was surprised at how good she felt. She sat up and yawned, caught sight of the piece of paper on the table, and she groaned. She stood up and crept into the bedroom to find her slippers, noticing that Mael had returned and was sleeping in his cage. She decided she would wait until he was awake to talk to him, she wanted his opinion on what to do about Carrington.

Since she was awake earlier than expected, Freya decided to take a walk to the mausoleum. She needed guidance about this whole situation and between Mael and her ancestors she couldn't think of anyone better to speak to.

Besides, she had been so caught up with renovations, work, and the festival, that she hadn't been to see them as much as she had wanted, and she was eager to talk with them again.

The air was fresh, and the sun warmed her skin as she walked around, careful not to step in the cold shade that was very much still held in winter's icy grip. The spring flowers had started to show themselves in the meadow. Yellow daffodils, purple crocuses, and white snowdrops were scattered throughout the dead grass in bunches. The colours were even brighter, as if the petals called to the beaming orange sun, basking in its rays. Freya smiled to herself. This time of year always felt new and fresh, the prospect of better things to come, of hope seemed to weave itself through the very fabric of life. Inside, the mausoleum was cold. Freya lit all the candle sconces and spoke to the empty air.

"I'm sorry I haven't been back sooner. This last week has been so very busy, and I have barely had a moment," she apologised, unsure whether any of the spirits were listening. She could feel their presence but that didn't mean they would pay her any mind.

"It's fine, dear, you have a life to lead. Tell us, what has been happening?"

Freya quickly told them about the shop and the Imbolc festival.

"Sounds like you have been busy. What about that handsome Vampire of yours. Are things still going well with you both, are you courting still?"

"Things are going well with that, and yes we are." She blushed. "I do have something I would like to get your thoughts on though," she said, sitting on the cold stone bench.

"If we can offer any assistance, then we will."

"I was approached by someone a week ago who wanted to buy the shop. I politely said no, of course. He approached me again last night. He said he is called Carrington Emery Junior. I didn't speak to him, but he gave his number to Valorian for me to contact him if I wish to do so. He says that he also has no remaining family other than me, and he thought it would be good if the two of us got to know each other. I am torn about it, knowing what his family were, and what they caused mine to do, but then Holden did say that Carrington removed himself from his family, and cursed them for their actions."

"I see. This is a complicated situation. What happened with Carrington and Everlyn was after our time, but the Emery family had been around as long as we were, and they were always troubled. They were not always a family that enjoyed the pull of the dark power, but all it takes is one bad apple to spoil the crop, and once they started to practice dark magic, the lure became too much. They lost a lot of friends choosing to behave as they did."

"That's what I have been told too. Holden told me Carrington was different; he hated his family, especially after Everlyn was forced to leave. There is that chance that he passed on his morals to Carrington Junior."

"I think that perhaps you should give this man a chance to at least talk things over. Get a feel for him, see what your intuition tells you about him. Use your abilities."

"I can't, and I won't do that, but my intuition is something I can't ignore. When I first met him, he left me with an icy chill, something that told me to be wary."

"That could have been your senses picking up on the fact that he wasn't all he seemed. It does not necessarily mean he is untrustworthy."

"That is true. I just don't want to get hurt. I don't think I could bear it right now."

"It may hurt you more to know that you have family out there which you have chosen to ignore."

Freya sighed. *I know the ancestors are right, but I don't know if I can open my heart again. Especially not to a part of the family who had at one point been intent on using such destructive dark magic - and even more so knowing that Carrington is probably a Witch with active powers. That could open a whole other can of worms. So much for an uncomplicated fresh start!*

"I will give it some more thought, but I really do appreciate what you have said, and I know it makes sense. I just don't know how I feel about it right now."

"You have gone through a lot, and you will still be processing what happened with your parents. Give it time if you must, but I'd be hesitant to just ignore it entirely."

"I won't, I promise," she replied.

By the time Freya returned home, Mael was awake. She found him sitting on the windowsill, looking out into the street.

"I need some advice," she said.

"I'm listening," he replied.

She told him about Carrington and what her ancestors had said.

"So, what do you think? she asked.

"It is not my job to offer my opinion on such things, but since you have asked, I would err on the side of caution. The Emerys were very dark and dangerous people, and they caused a lot of problems for others. We don't know whether Carrington Junior has had any contact with any of them, or where he draws the line on the use of such magic."

"That's what I'm concerned about. Part of me thinks that I am happy going along as I am - after all, I didn't know about him so why should it be an issue to be without him now? The other part of me wants to know him, wants that family back in my life."

"I'm sure you will find the right path, just let your intuition guide you. It has never done wrong by you yet. Without it you would not be here now."

"I think that's all I can do really, isn't it? Just wait and see."

"Sometimes the hardest thing to do is trust yourself."

Freya slumped onto the bed; her thoughts turning back to Carrington. She wondered what he was like, how his life had been while growing up. Whether his family had kept their turbulent past secret from him, or whether they had told him the truth. *I really don't want anything to upset the status quo, things are so good right now. I just need to find a way to learn to suppress my magic in a healthy way, and then I can really settle into my new life and forget about the old one.*

Freya's phone lit up with a message. It was Poppy apologising for not coming over, and explaining that she and Anderson were spending time alone while they had the house to themselves. Freya replied letting her know she would see her later that night.

Darkness had settled and outside the rain was pouring. She wondered what might happen with the festival, she couldn't foresee many wanting to stand around in this - it was torrential. Her phone pinged and she reached for it, finding a text from Valorian telling her that his family had just left, and asking if he could come over. She fired a quick message back to tell him that she couldn't wait to see him before sliding the phone into the back pocket of her jeans. She jumped up, cleared away the few cups she had scattered around the room and then straightened the blankets on the sofa. Mentally she scolded herself. *Why am I so nervous? We've been alone together many times before, but he still affects me the way he did on that very first day.* She picked up a new log to put onto the fire, and the heat flowed into the room. The doorbell rang and she ran downstairs. Valorian stood outside, smiling.

She ushered him in out of the rain.

"It's awful out there," he said.

"It's been doing that most of this afternoon. What will they do about the festival?"

"They will no doubt have Poppy and her Coven place a spell over it so that the rain doesn't fall over the main street."

"Oh, yeah, of course," she replied, feeling a little silly that the thought had not occurred to her.

Upstairs, Valorian made himself comfortable on the sofa while Freya made them both a hot tea.

"I really do like it in here, it's so cosy and has a great relaxing vibe to it," he said, looking around.

"Me too. It feels more like home than home has ever felt to me before. It's hard to believe I only recently moved in because it feels like I have always been here."

"It's in your blood."

"I went to the mausoleum today to speak to my ancestors about this whole Carrington thing."

"And what did they say?"

"They think I should probably hear him out, give him a chance. Mael, on the other hand, thinks I should be cautious."

"I see, and what are your thoughts now?"

"I still have no idea. Mael said I should trust my intuition and follow that as a guide. I just don't know yet what my intuition is telling me, which is where the problem lies."

"It will come to you."

"I do feel that perhaps I should hear him out. If nothing else, I'm curious about him."

"Well, if you do decide to speak to him, I am always here if you want me to come with you."

"I appreciate that, thank you, but I feel like this is probably something I should do alone."

Valorian tensed and Freya tilted her head.

"You disagree?"

"I think you should do what you feel is best, but these people have a history with your family, and you don't know him. It could be a trap. He could hurt you."

"I don't see what he would have to gain from that, but I can look after myself," Freya replied.

"Can you? Without having your magic to help you?"

Freya stiffened; she didn't like where this conversation was going.

"People have defended themselves for centuries without the help of magic."

"Yes, they have, but they often don't fare well against those with magic, and we both know he is likely to possess it."

"We don't know that for certain. Who knows what Carrington Senior did when he left. But I don't feel like he wants to hurt me, my intuition is telling me that."

"Okay, okay, I'm just concerned that's all. I know you are a strong woman, and I know you can look after yourself but as your boyfriend, I'm allowed to worry about you." He looked at her, a smile playing on his lips.

Freya's shoulders loosened.

"I know you are. I'm sorry. I didn't mean to get defensive."

"It's okay, I asked for it."

Freya sat down next to him and cuddled into him, laying a kiss on his cheek.

"Now this is something I really like," he purred into her ear.

Freya shivered as his touch burned against her. She moved her lips to his and pulled him closer to her. She knew she should stop before they took it further, but she desperately wanted him. He moved his hand up to the nape of her neck and into her hair, clenching it softly.

She gasped slightly as he turned to face her, without breaking the connection of their lips.

"I'm sorry," she said, breaking their connection. "I just need time to figure out everything first."

"It's okay, Freya, there is no rush. I'm going to be here forever, and this is all I need," Valorian replied.

Freya lay down on the sofa, wrapped in Valorian's arms. A tear trickled down her cheek.

"Don't cry. It's okay, really," Valorian said, wiping away the tear.

"I know, and I believe you. It's just that everything feels so messed up right now and I don't know what I'm doing half of the time." Freya sniffled.

"Things will work out, they always do, and I am right here by your side for whatever you need," Valorian replied.

"I just didn't want anything to come between us. This is all so new and wonderful. I didn't want you to be put off because I couldn't manage my magic."

"There's nothing you can do that would put me off you. When I said I loved you, I meant it and I have not loved anyone in over a hundred years."

"You haven't?"

"No. There have been girlfriends and such, of course, but someone I would give my heart to? There has only been you."

"Only me? In your entire lifetime?"

"As a Vampire, yes. When I was human, I was engaged to be married but my wife-to-be was murdered before we wed. I have never loved since then. It's easy as a Vampire, just to turn it all off, to not feel it and I did for a long time. I had no care for human life, for love. But you cannot escape love even when you try. Grief and love, they come for us all eventually."

"I had no idea. I'm sorry for your loss. It must have been devastating for you to go through that. I can understand why you would want to switch it all off," she said, sadness in her eyes, as her heart broke for Valorian.

"It was a long time ago and anyway, I have you now," he said, pulling her closer.

"Yes, you do." She smiled up at him.

The rain fell heavily against the window as they lay under a blanket on the sofa, wrapped in each other's arms with the fire gently crackling in the background.

"It's almost midnight, we should probably get ready if you want to make the final night of the festival," Valorian said, breaking the silence and tucking some hair behind her ear.

"Okay." She sighed, reluctantly removing herself from his arms and standing up.

She felt happiness in every part of her, lighting her up from her core. *I don't want life to go back to normal, I want to stay right here with Valorian in this bubble forever.* It meant a lot to her that despite his many years on this earth, she was his first real love since he was turned. *A man like Valorian would attract many women, but he didn't want them - only me.* She scooped up their clothes and went through to the bedroom.

CHAPTER TWENTY-TWO

Valorian had been right, the Witches had cast a spell over the festival. The rain abruptly stopped as they stepped onto the main road. The night closed with a beautiful fireworks display in colours of white, yellow and green, and Freya enjoyed them with Valorian by her side.

They were just about to leave when Freya spotted Poppy. She jogged over to her.

"Hey! I've been looking for you."

"Hey, yeah, we were a bit late. Anderson had a few things to take care of before we could leave. What's up? Poppy replied.

"I was wondering if you were busy tomorrow. I was thinking we could have a catch up at mine. Watch a movie or something if you fancied?"

"That would be great. I'm free all day and a movie sounds good. What time shall I come over?"

"Around one p.m. okay with you?"

"Yeah, sounds good. I'll will bring some lunch over with me."

"Awesome, we are just heading back to mine now. I'll see you tomorrow."

"Alright, have fun," she said with a wink.

"You too," Freya replied.

Freya and Valorian walked the short distance to her apartment. Relieved to get inside out of the rain, Freya put on the log fire and got changed into something more comfortable while Valorian made them both a hot drink.

"Fancy a game of monopoly?" he said.

"Sure," Freya replied. "You know I am a pro at this game," she added, cockily, as she plucked the box from the shelf.

"Oh yeah? Well, I have had a lot longer than you to dominate so bring it on," Valorian said, rolling up his sleeves.

They sat on the floor enjoying the game and each other's company.

Valorian sat back, leaning against the sofa and folded his arms smirking at Freya.

"I did warn you that I am impossible to beat," he said.

"Yeah, yeah, you did." Freya rolled her eyes as she started to clear up.

"That was fun, we should play games more often," he said.

"It was. It was just the evening I needed. I'd be up for this again."

"It's getting pretty late now, want me to stay over until you fall asleep, or would you prefer me to leave now?"

"What sort of daft question is that?" She grinned up at him.

"Well, it's polite to ask. Who knows, maybe me climbing into your bed uninvited could have caused you to throw me out in my underpants."

Freya sniggered. "Like that would ever happen. I'd much rather keep you chained in my basement."

Valorian burst into laughter, "I didn't realise you were into that sort of stuff," he said, raising his eyebrows.

"Do not get any ideas." She glared back.

Valorian put the game away, and they made their way to the bedroom. Mael fluttered out, wishing Freya a good night, giving them both their privacy.

"I'm just going to freshen up," she said, walking to the bathroom.

When she returned, she found Valorian already in bed waiting for her. Her face flushed and heat surged through her. *I will never tire of this feeling.* She undressed, placed all her clothes in the laundry basket and got under the covers. Valorian wrapped his arms around her, and the feeling of his skin against hers set her alight; she felt fire run through her veins. She had never felt such passion or desire as she did when she was with him, when he touched her body. She ran her hand through his hair, pulled him towards her and kissed him hard.

"I love you, Freya." He pulled back to look into her eyes

"I love you too," she said, closing her eyes and giving in to sleep.

Freya woke with a start. There was a voice ringing in her ears - her mother's voice. Nausea swirled in her stomach as she jumped out of bed running for the bathroom. She just made it in time before vomiting into the toilet. She sat on the cold tiled floor, her hands shaking, struggling to find her breath. Tears streamed down her cheeks and an overwhelming feeling of loss flooded her. Her heart felt heavy, and her limbs ached. She sobbed loudly, letting all the pain she felt spill out. This was the first time she had let the loss of her parents really hit home and it hurt.

Mael fluttered in. He didn't say a word, just perched himself on her shoulder, letting her know he was there for her.

She cried until she couldn't cry anymore and then she slowly stood up. Her legs felt weak, and her throat was dry. She made her way slowly into the kitchen, grabbed some water from the fridge and drank it greedily. She was shocked at her reaction; her mother's voice had stirred so many emotions, but one among them was clearer than others. Guilt. Hearing her mother's voice had reminded her how important family was, and now she felt guilty for dismissing Carrington so easily. She decided to take the dream as a sign that she needed to contact him.

Mael had followed her through to the kitchen, and he sat on the table, his presence bringing Freya some small comfort.

"Thank you for being here," she said, shakily.

"I wouldn't want to be anywhere else. Are you going to be okay?"

"I think so. I just had a dream that my mother was calling to me. It hurt so much."

"You miss her, it wasn't so long ago that you lost her, things will feel raw for a while. It's okay to have moments where the loss of her overwhelms you."

"I need to meet Carrington. He is family and I've lost so much already. I can't risk losing him too without ever trying to get to know him."

"I understand, and I will be there with you through it all. You must do what you feel is right."

Freya picked up the piece of paper that Carrington had left with Valorian, typed his number into her phone, and sent him a text message asking if he would like to meet for coffee at Spellbound Café sometime. She tried to remain casual despite the pounding of her heart in her chest and her clammy hands. This was a big step for her, and she was nervous and excited at what the outcome would be. Deep in her soul she wished that Carrington would be someone who she could trust and have as part of her life. *Even though his original family weren't good people, Carrington Senior tried his best to remove himself from them. I can only hope that Carrington Junior is like his father.* The phone beeped and Freya picked it up, finding that she was suddenly nervous. *What if he's changed his mind about wanting to get to know me?* She opened the message and breathed a sigh of relief. Carrington's reply was to the point; he thanked her for getting in touch and said he would be free tomorrow around eleven a.m. to meet for coffee, if that would work for her. She sent a quick reply to let him know she would see him then. For the first time in the days since she had found out who he was, she felt at ease with herself. *Even if this goes nowhere, I owe it to both of us to at least try. From the sounds of it, Carrington longs for family just as much as I do.* Freya decided to have a quick visit to the mausoleum and let her ancestors know the outcome of her decision regarding Carrington, as she had promised to keep them updated.

"Would you mind if I accompany you?" Mael's voice floated softly through her mind.

"Of course not, you are more than welcome," Freya replied.

The weak spring sunshine felt uplifting and despite her exhaustion she felt it rejuvenate her. Mael fluttered around her as she walked down past the meadow and over to the churchyard.

"There is a stream in the woods which has a small waterfall, that's how Crestwood Falls got its name," Mael whispered.

"Oh, I would love to see that," Freya replied enthusiastically.

"When the ground has dried, I can show you if you would like?" Mael offered.

"I would love that, Mael, thank you," Freya replied. Deciding that she would love to go on a hike up the mountains as well, she made a mental note to ask Valorian about it when she saw him next. Hiking up there was something he did often with Silas and Eric.

Freya opened the large heavy door, and the light poured into the damp and musty mausoleum. She left it open, allowing the fresh air to circulate the room and the spirits cooed with pleasure.

"I have news!" she said happily.

"Do tell us, child," one of the voices replied.

"I contacted Carrington this morning and have arranged to meet him for coffee tomorrow. I figure I owe it to us both to at least try to get to know him before I dismiss the idea of having any sort of relationship with him."

"Ah, child. I knew you would come to the right decision. It may not work out, but you have nothing to lose by trying."

"Exactly, and…" Freya hesitated. "I had a dream about my mum last night. She told me how important family is. I can't help feeling that it was a sign to pursue a relationship with him."

"Our mind often finds ways to tell us what we need to hear when we aren't paying attention to anything else."

"I wish it had found another way. I haven't heard her voice for months and I miss it so badly."

"Perhaps you would not have listened to anyone else's voice, and that's why it needed to be hers. Though it must have been hard for you."

"I didn't realise how much I still miss them until this morning. I thought by moving and changing things that I was starting to move forward, that the grief had passed, but now I feel as if I haven't even touched the edges."

"Unfortunately, you can't escape it. Even moving away, starting a new job, living a life without magic will not stop your grief from coming for you. You need to allow yourself to feel it, otherwise these moments of total overwhelm will consume you."

"If I let it in, it will consume me anyway." Freya looked down.

"Maybe it will, but it is the only way you will ever truly move past this and find happiness. Otherwise, your grief will continue to haunt you."

"I just need to get this stuff out of the way with Carrington. Perhaps we can help each other."

"I hope so."

"Why can't I hear my parents here, with you? I hear everyone else, why not them?" Freya asked, frustrated.

"You won't be able to communicate with them here, child. In time, when you are ready, you may be able to communicate with them in the place that they were buried."

"They weren't buried. The Coven had them cremated and their ashes sit in special pots within the Chamber of Swallows and Stars under their headquarters."

"I see. Then without a body to tie them to this plane it is unlikely they will be able to return in spirit form. It is unusual that a Coven would cremate its Witches, but I know times are changing."

"I wish I had thought about things more carefully at the time, I was just so in shock and trying to deal with everything on my own. It was suggested by members of the Coven that they should be cremated and I never thought to question it, but you are right, it isn't what usually happens."

"Perhaps when you are ready, you can go back to the Chamber and make your peace with the choices you made. You cannot be blamed for decisions made when you were vulnerable, hurt and upset."

"I know, I just… I wish I hadn't had to do any of it." Freya said, as a tear slipped down her cheek.

"Time heals all things, Freya. Allow yourself that," the voices responded.

"I will, thank you. I should get home now," Freya replied, wiping the tears from her face.

"Farewell, child." The voice quietened.

Freya walked home with Mael on her shoulder. Neither of

them spoke for a long time.

"Mael, I can sense you thinking," Freya said at last, breaking the silence.

"Ah, yes, sorry. I just, well, something feels off about the whole cremation thing. When you feel up to it, would you allow me to explore what happened with you?"

"I would like that. I'm sure a second pair of eyes would help a lot."

Poppy arrived that afternoon, bringing a bottle of wine with her. The girls sat together, and Freya filled Poppy in on her day.

"Are you working tomorrow?" Freya asked.

"I am, I start at ten. Why?"

"I have decided to meet a long lost relative of mine at Spellbound tomorrow at eleven. He approached me at the festival. I am nervous about it. Valorian doesn't think I should meet him, as his family had ties to dark magic in the past, but I need to try. I have already lost so much."

"Well, I will be on shift so I can keep an eye on things. I think it's a good idea to at least try and figure things out."

"Thanks, Poppy, it means a lot."

CHAPTER TWENTY-THREE

The bell tinkled, announcing her arrival in the shop, just as Valorian appeared from the back room carrying a large box.

"Hey, beautiful," he said as he saw her.

"Hey." She offered a smile in return.

"I've got a few boxes to unload today. I didn't bother doing anything when my family was here, and now I'm having to play catch up."

"That's okay, I can give you a hand."

Freya and Valorian brought through all the boxes, and she started to arrange all the new books on the shelves, while he explained which books should go where. There was a variety of different genres of books scattered throughout the shop, from true crime to high fantasy, but Freya's favourite was the section on mythology and legends. There she could find books on everything to do with Witchcraft, herbalism, sigils as well as Norse and Greek mythology. *I always felt drawn to these subjects, knowing that the possibility that these gods and creatures really exist makes me curious.* Today she was putting out Folklore books for Northern Ireland, something she had read little about and decided to get herself a copy while she was there.

"Fancy a cuppa?" Valorian shouted.

"Yes please," she said, arranging the last of the books on the shelf and making her way to the counter area.

Valorian brought over two mugs of tea, and they sat and drank them together

Freya took a deep breath. "I had a really strange dream about my mum. She was talking to me about the importance of family, so I've taken it as a sign and decided to arrange to meet Carrington for a coffee tomorrow." She waited for his reaction.

"Oh," Valorian said, putting his cup down. "Are you sure that's wise?"

"I don't think I have anything to lose in trying to get to know him. I'm more likely to regret it if I just ignore it."

"Please be careful, there is something about him that doesn't sit right with me. Will you have anyone with you tomorrow?"

"I will. I'm going to Spellbound to meet him. Poppy will be working at the same time. I felt for our first meeting I wanted it somewhere I felt more secure."

"Good. That is a wise choice."

"I'm not daft you know. I can look after myself," Freya responded, her brow drawn together.

"I know, and I don't think you're daft, but this guy turns up out of nowhere, just after you inherit the shop and apartment and announces he is long lost family. Why had he never bothered looking for you before? Why did he come to you under the pretence of buying the shop? Something isn't right."

"These are all things I have thought of myself, and I'm planning on asking him. It could just be that he didn't know I existed until I got the apartment. After all, the family was hiding. And he might not have had the confidence to approach me without the story about the shop. I want to give him the benefit of the doubt."

"Okay, but you will let me know if he does something untoward though, won't you?"

"Of course I will. You'd be the first person I would speak to. You know that."

"Good," he said, offering her a small smile.

"Anyway, enough of that. I have a question for you."

"Okay, shoot."

"How would you feel about taking me on a hike up the mountains? I would love to go up there," she said.

"How would I feel about it? I'd feel great about it! Me and Eric have a hike planned for the weekend after next if you want to join us? He won't mind at all."

"Oh wow, that soon. I need to get some supplies and new boots etc, but I'd love to join you. Check with him first though. I don't want to cramp your style," she said with a giggle.

"Well, that's something you won't do. I have some spare equipment I can lend you, and I'll have a look after I close the shop tonight and text you a list of anything else you'll need to get."

"Thanks, I'd appreciate it. I've never been hiking before, especially not up mountains like those."

"I think you'll love it. Just wait until you see the view from where we usually camp."

"I'm really looking forward to it," she replied.

They spent the rest of the evening tidying away the remaining stock, while Valorian chatted happily about his favourite hikes. By the time Freya left to go home, her mind was abuzz with energy and excitement for the upcoming hike - and for tomorrow's meeting with Carrington.

Freya rose early the next morning. She could feel the nerves setting in as she thought about talking to Carrington, and a wave of doubt washed over her.

Mael gave her some comforting reassurance and told her he would perch himself on the flower basket near the cafe window in case she needed some more moral support.

I wonder if Carrington is as nervous as me. It must have taken some courage to approach me, and I didn't respond in the best way. I wonder what his father told him about his family, about our history? She was curious to hear what he had been told about everything. She couldn't face eating anything, so she made a cup of tea and tried to distract herself until it was time to leave. She wanted to arrive early and get a window seat where she could calm herself before he arrived.

The café was empty when she got there. Poppy made her a tea

and got on with preparing for the lunchtime crowd. Freya sat down and watched as Mael hopped from flower to flower in the arranged spring basket just outside of the window. She heard the door open and looked up. Carrington walked through and looked at her, offering a cautious smile.

"Hello, Freya," he said, taking a seat opposite her.

"Hi," she replied. She looked at him, trying to find the familial similarities. His jet-black hair and chocolate brown eyes matched those of her mother. His nose turned up slightly at the end like hers. She smiled.

"Do you want another drink?" he asked, nodding down at Freya's empty cup.

"Yes please. Black coffee would be great. Thank you."

Carrington came back carrying two cups, and placing them on the table. "Thank you for meeting with me. I know it must have been a shock when I introduced myself the other night. The timing wasn't great, but my courage had failed me on the previous two occasions."

"I'm sorry I ran away. It was a shock. I genuinely had no idea that you existed. I didn't even know about your family until I moved here."

"My father told me about Everlyn, and when he passed away last year, I vowed to see if there were any more family members. I'd had no luck trying to find anyone but then when I saw you moving into that building, I just knew you and I must be related. It's been standing empty waiting for one of the Evermore family to return."

"I had no idea about that building when I arrived, or about any of my family's history here. When my parents died in December, I just packed up my life and drove. I let intuition guide me and ended up here. It's been one revelation after another since I got here."

"Wow, that is amazing though, how you ended up here without any knowledge of where 'here' was, and its significance for our families."

"I know. I still can't quite believe it if I am honest."

"I moved to Hawthorne Hollow about seven months ago and I love it there. I wanted to see where my grandfather grew up and the place stuck. It must be in our blood."

"What exactly did he tell you about Everlyn?" she asked.

"He told me he was deeply in love with her, and they found out she was expecting their first child together, but her family disappeared one night fearing what that would mean for the baby as my grandfather's family were not good people. He said that he was devastated and that he went looking for her. It took him thirty years before he gave up and settled down with my grandmother. He cursed his family and now the Emerys don't exist."

"That's pretty much the same story I was told as well. I feel for both your grandfather and Everlyn. I wonder what would have been if they had run away together."

"I often wonder that too."

"I wasn't sure if it was true about the Emerys, or at least, I wasn't sure whether they'd found a way around the curse."

"To the best of my knowledge there are no more of them now. Only my grandfather was unaffected by the curse, so we are the last remaining of that family line - and we were brought up very differently."

"It's all rather sad, isn't it?" Freya said, looking down briefly at her cup of tea.

"It is. I couldn't imagine losing my true love - especially if my family were the cause."

"No, me neither. My parents were the total opposite of the Emerys. In fact, they worked for the Coven's Council to expose those who practice the dark side of magic. Ultimately that's what got them killed."

"I'm sorry to hear that. It must have been something they felt strongly about to work in such a high-risk job."

"Indeed," Freya said. She wasn't ready to discuss her parents with Carrington yet.

Carrington must have sensed Freya's reluctance to talk about her parents, because he changed the subject.

"So, Freya, tell me about yourself. What sort of things do you like? Where did you grow up? I want to know everything." He smiled warmly.

She laughed. "Well, there really isn't much to tell. I grew up in the city. I like to read, and I like art. I love walking and forests. I love the beach, but I've only been a handful of times when I was younger. What about you?"

"I also grew up in the city. I was helping run my Dad's veterinary practice when he got too old to manage it, but it wasn't really my calling, so I sold it and bought a small cottage in Hawthorne. I like to read as well, and I play a few instruments. Have you joined the Coven here in Crestwood?"

"I haven't. I haven't practiced magic or used it since my parents died."

"Oh sorry, I didn't know. May I ask why?"

"Everything I have learnt about magic just tells me it causes more harm than good. If my parents had been human, they would be alive now. If the Emerys had been human, then we would probably have been raised here. Nothing good has come from it."

"I can see where you are coming from, it can often feel more like a burden than a blessing."

They settled into easy conversation about their lives. Freya no longer felt that icy unease that she had when she first met him, and she was relieved to find they had a lot in common.

I think this was the right decision. Carrington is someone who I could see myself spending time with regularly. The fact he lives so close by is all the better.

"Unfortunately, I must get going soon. I have an appointment with a real estate agent that I cannot get out of. I'm finally selling the land my dad left me," he said eventually.

"That's no problem. We've been talking for just over three hours. Time has flown by. I would love to do this again," Freya replied.

"I'm free Saturday if you want to meet then? There is a small Inn in Hawthorne which sells the most delicious hot foods, if you fancied it?"

"That sounds great. About the same time as today?"

"Yes, that works. It's really been a pleasure, Freya. Thank you again for agreeing to meet me."

"You're welcome. It really has been nice. I'm looking forward to getting to know you better."

"Me too," he said, getting up and sliding his chair back under the table."

Freya watched Carrington leave, then she picked up their cups and took them over to the counter.

"So how did it go?" Poppy asked, taking the cups and placing them on the tray full of dirty dishes.

"Really well." Freya smiled. "We had a good chat about our families."

"That's really great to hear. What is he like then?"

"He is nice, I felt like we got on. He's much easier to talk to than I thought he would be. I definitely feel like there is a lot of good there, between us. He doesn't seem to be anything like the Emerys. His father brought him up away from all that type of magic."

"Ah, this is great. I'm so happy that it's working out. It is nice that you've found each other given what you both have been through with the rest of your family. I imagine it can be hard sometimes."

"Yeah, it can. I have to admit it would be nice to have some family around."

"I am glad it worked out for you," Poppy replied.

"Anyway, I should let you get on with your work. I am going to convince Mael to take me on a forest walk to see the stream and waterfall since it's a nice day."

"Okay, have fun!" Poppy replied, throwing a rag over her shoulder.

Freya left the cafe and Mael fluttered beside her. She told him about Carrington and asked him to take her to the stream, which he was more than happy to do. She wanted to make the most of her last day off and to enjoy the sunshine while it lasted. The meadow flowers were really starting to bud now, and it was looking even brighter than it had done before - the recent rainfall having boosted the growth. It wouldn't be long before butterflies and bees grazed the flowers. She could hear the birds calling to each other with song, and in the distance the forest already looked fuller.

CHAPTER TWENTY-FOUR

Freya broke through the tree lined boundary. The thick trunks stood tall and proud. Fresh buds of green shot up from the floor beneath her, so she took care to avoid stepping on them as she followed the old muddy trail. She could hear distant grunts and bleats of the deer that now occupied the land. She followed behind Mael, his radiant purple standing out against the brown trees and filtered grey-yellow sunlight.

"Mael, what type of butterfly are you? I have never seen one as beautiful as you."

I am a purple emperor, there are not many of us left when compared to other varieties.

"That explains why I have never seen one like you before."

I have not seen another of my kind for a very long time. There used to be a small group of us here in Crestwood but as the years have gone by there has been a decline.

"That's really sad."

It is. I am only alive by magical means. Butterflies in general don't have a long-life span.

"I'm very lucky then." Freya smiled.

The sound of the stream was growing louder, as Mael lead her through a path which clearly wasn't walked often. Freya found herself having to climb under or over bushes, branches and fallen trees. She could smell the fresh water and as she came from around a large bush, she saw the stream. It was crystal clear, and the water ran fast causing mini rapids downstream. She could see small fish and newts just under the surface. She followed Mael alongside the stream as he followed it up a small hill, and as she reached the top, she was surprised to see three small waterfalls. The largest was about twice Valorian's height, and the smallest was around her height. There was a large boulder in the stream, and she climbed onto it and took a seat. She peeled off her shoes and socks, stuck her feet into the icy cold water and squealed.

"This is wonderful," she said aloud. Lesser celandines, primula and dog's mercury were scattered around her; insects buzzed about. It was as if she had stepped into a midsummer's day. She leaned back resting on her arms and closed her eyes, letting the sun warm her face. The sound of the rushing water, the birds chirping and the sweet scent of the common gorse that sat amongst the trees scented the air. It felt like heaven.

Mael was enjoying it just as much; Freya could sense his happiness as he moved around her.

"This place is amazing," she said.

I've missed it. Considering how long I've been away, nothing has changed.

"I would miss this as well. It's like I have been transported somewhere else and it's so beautiful."

I always wondered if it was bewitched.

"It wouldn't surprise me with a town like this."

Back when your ancestors lived here, this was where all the towns' children would come and play, you could hear their laughter for miles. It was quite something.

"Maybe the children still come and play here."

I find it unlikely; these days are so very different.

"Yeah, I never considered that before. It must be quite something to have seen the world change over the last hundred years."

I only saw it from a window, I didn't get to live it, but this town has seen its fair share of changes come and go.

Freya continued wiggling her feet around in the water, despite the numbness that was starting to creep across them. Clouds floated past her as she lay back on the rock, and the longer she stared at them, the darker they seemed to become.

"I think we may have to leave. I think it's going to rain soon, look at those clouds overhead."

Yes, you are right. I can feel it approaching too.

Freya dried off her feet on her socks and slid her bare feet into her shoes, then stood up and took one last look around before following Mael back out of the forest. They barely made it onto the meadow path before the skies opened on them. The rain fell heavily, bouncing back up in front of them as they hurried back.

Freya glanced up and saw huge black clouds rolling in quickly. Lightning forked across the sky, and she began to run, not wanting to be caught outside in a thunderstorm. Her feet splashed through newly formed puddles, coating her legs in muddy splodges.

She had never been so happy to open her door and get out of the storm. The thunder clapped overhead as she shook herself off, taking off her jacket and shoes before running upstairs and lighting the fire. The dark clouds were now directly above the apartment, making it look more like night than day. Freya went to turn on a light, but the electrics wouldn't work. She noticed as she looked out of the window that none of the other shops or apartments had their lights on either. *The storm must have knocked out the power.* She was thankful that she had a large stash of candles, and she lit some, placing them around the living room and kitchen. She moved the sofa to look out the window, across the mountains and forest, and sat down on it with a blanket. She spent what felt like hours watching the lightning and listening to the thunder, and it was the first time in a long time that she felt completely at peace. She breathed in slowly, releasing each breath with purpose. She had forgotten what it felt like to just be, without any pain, hurt or fear - and she hadn't realised until that moment how much she had missed it.

The thunder passed, sounding more distant with each clap, and she could no longer see the sky light up. The rain still fell heavily, as she closed her eyes and drifted off to sleep.

Freya woke to darkness; the candles had dwindled and there was very little light in the room. She got up and checked her phone, but there was still no signal. She flicked on the light switch and the room lit up. *At least the electricity works now.* She went through to the kitchen, took out a portion of cottage pie from the fridge, and put it in the oven to reheat while she went to get a shower. She had just sat down to eat when the doorbell rang. She answered the door to find Valorian outside, and she invited him in.

He sat at the dining table with her.

"How did it go then?" he asked.

Freya finished the mouthful of food she had just taken and waited a second before answering.

"It went really well. He's a nice guy. We talked a lot about our families, and we've arranged to meet again on Saturday."

"I see. I'm glad it went well. Just make sure you stay on your guard; he might not be as nice as you think he is. You can't trust him yet."

Freya put her fork down, sighing.

"Thanks for your concern, but I'm not an idiot, and I would appreciate it if you stopped treating me like one," she said, more scornfully than she had intended.

"I'm not treating you like an idiot. I just know that sometimes people aren't all they seem to be, and I don't want you to end up hurt or anything," he replied, defensively.

"You are being patronising. I know there may be more to him, in fact I am sure of it. Who lives that long without having some secrets? But going into this automatically being suspicious won't help me build a good relationship with him, will it?"

"I wasn't trying to be patronising. I just think you are going into this without properly considering all the possibilities."

"Okay then, so, how should I approach this exactly?"

"Well, meeting him when I'm present would help, then I can get a feel for him. Ask him the questions that make him uncomfortable, trust your initial reaction if you think he is lying."

"I'm not going to try and get to know someone from my family with you, or anyone else, around. I'm not a child, Valorian, and I do trust my instincts. They're telling me to give him the benefit of the doubt, and I wish you would do the same for me!"

"Look, clearly this has all come out wrong. I care about you, and I worry about you. I'm going to go; I have to open the shop. I love you, Freya." He left.

Freya stayed where she was; she didn't say anything or go after him. She was angry at him. Angry at the way he assumed she couldn't make good judgement calls or trust herself. *He came over here and ruined a perfectly good day by trying to be an alpha male.* She hadn't really known anything about Valorian when she had first met him and agreed to help him redecorate. And he was a Vampire - a predator who was designed to be someone that people would naturally trust, even though they shouldn't – and yet he was the one questioning whether Carrington was trustworthy? No, she wasn't having it. *I'm an independent person and if he doesn't like me making my own decisions then he doesn't know me at all, and we should reconsider this relationship.*

Freya awoke to three messages on her phone. The first was from Poppy asking if she fancied a trip to Hawthorne with her on Sunday morning. The second was from Carrington saying he had enjoyed meeting her and was looking forward to Saturday. And then there was a message from Valorian. She debated opening it, a knot of tension in her stomach. She wasn't sure if he was going to be angry with her or not. Eventually, she clicked 'open'. It was a sweet and simple apology. He said he didn't mean to upset her, it was never his intention to sound patronising, he hoped she could forgive him and that he would see her tonight after work. Her shoulders sagged with relief, and she smiled. She sent replies to everyone, including an apology to Valorian.

Freya noticed how the time had changed in just her few days off; before when she arrived at work the darkness would be creeping in but now it was still light. Summer was coming and she couldn't wait. She wondered how far away the coast was from here; she thought about how she would love to spend some time with the ocean, The familiar tinkle of the bell made her smile as she walked through the café door.

"Hey, Marly," Freya said. Marly was standing on the opposite side of the counter, stocking up the pastries.

"Freya! Hey, how are you?"

"I'm good, how about you? Did you enjoy the festival?"

"I certainly did, what about you? Have some good time off?"

"I really did. I enjoyed the festival a lot and I managed to finish decorating the shop so it's all much neater. Mael took me to the falls as well, which was glorious."

"I haven't been there for such a long time. It is a beautiful place. I'm glad you had a good time. Have you thought of any plans for the shop part yet? Marly asked.

"Not yet, I was thinking of properly sorting access upstairs so I could rent it out, but the longer I'm there the more I hate the idea of someone else being in there."

"Maybe you could open it yourself? You already have the property and it's in a prime location for customers."

"I have no idea what I would even sell."

"You are good with herbs, aren't you? Why not keep it as your family did and open a Herboristerie?"

"I don't know. It would feel strange working with herbs in that way while I'm not using my magic. A lot of the things that would be made need that magical infusion."

"It's something to think about anyway," Marly responded.

The evening passed far too quickly, and it felt to Freya as if her shift was almost over before it had started. She cleaned up and chatted to Marly while she waited for Valorian to arrive. She heard a tap on the window and grabbed her bag.

"Good evening," Valorian said, kissing her forehead.

"Evening," she replied, looping her arm through his.

"How was it being back at work?"

"Good. My shift went quickly tonight but it was a pleasant night, and it was nice to see all the regulars again."

"I'm glad to hear it. I hope you are hungry because I've cooked up a good meal."

"I'm famished actually," she replied, her stomach rumbling as if in agreement.

Valorian hadn't been joking; his dining table was full of the most delicious looking foods. A roast chicken sat in the centre, surrounded by roast potatoes, various vegetables, Yorkshire puddings the size of dinner plates and a jug full of gravy.

Freya licked her lips; this was very much needed. She didn't cook for herself often and never anything like this - her speciality was anything quick and easy.

"This looks scrumptious," she said, putting her bag on the hook.

"Scrumptious." Valorian giggled, "Yes, it does, doesn't it?"

"Are you mocking me?" she said, smiling.

"Maybe a little." He smiled back.

Freya sat while Valorian opened a bottle of white wine and poured them each a glass.

"This is my way of saying sorry for being a massive douchebag," he said, putting the bottle down and picking up the knife to carve the chicken.

Picking up her glass of wine she took a sip. "If this is your way of saying sorry, I may have to argue with you more often."

"I would cook for you anytime. That way we can avoid the arguing."

"I like that idea better."

With her plate full of food, Freya tucked into the meal, rolling her eyes in pleasure at the delicious flavours.

The next few days went past quickly. Freya spent her days working and reading - and then her nights with Valorian. Saturday morning arrived and Freya woke excited to see Carrington again. She drove herself over to Hawthorne Hollow, using her car for the first time in weeks. The Inn was small but a cosy and friendly place. Carrington was already inside waiting for her.

"Hey," she said, approaching the table.

Carrington was deep in a book, and he hadn't seen her arrive. "Oh, hey, sorry. I was way too involved in this story."

"I get it, I do the same." She smiled, and took a seat.

"How are you? It's good to see you again," Carrington said.

"I'm doing good. Work is keeping me busy, but it is nice to be back after having those days off. What about you, everything okay?"

"Yeah, same as usual. I've been spending a lot of time in the forest these last few days. Researching the foragables that grow there."

"That sounds exciting. Did you find anything interesting?"

"Not yet, just the usual sort of stuff. But now everything is starting to grow back I am hoping that - given the location of the forest and magic dwellers that live so close by - there are some unusual plants around."

"I would think so too. You'll have to keep me updated."

"I would love to get up on the mountains for the same reason, but I don't really fancy hiking solo up there."

"I get that. Valorian and his friends are going up next weekend and he is letting me tag along with him. I will keep an eye out and see if I spot anything."

"That would be great, thank you."

Freya and Carrington browsed the menu and ordered soup and fresh bread for their lunch. Freya enjoyed the food as much as she was enjoying her conversations with Carrington. They spent time talking about their favourite books, movies and music and the embarrassing things that had happened to them growing up. Freya was so relaxed around him, and she was sure he felt the same. She decided she would ask Valorian if Carrington could join them on their hike and - if he said yes - surprise Carrington with the invitation. She really liked the idea of them both getting to know each other, it would help her convince Valorian that Carrington wasn't a bad guy, and they might even become friends. The thought made her heart happy.

Freya hadn't realised how long she had been sitting talking in the Inn with Carrington, until she noticed it starting to get dark through one of the windows.

"Wow, it's getting dark already. Feels like I have only been here for a couple of hours."

Carrington looked at his watch. "More like almost six hours."

Freya laughed. "Oops. I have had a great time, but I should really head back before it gets too dark. I still don't know these roads too well and it isn't the sort of place you want to get lost in at night."

"No, it isn't. I'll see you to your car. I've had a great time as well."

"I'm hiking next weekend but how would you feel about meeting up the weekend after?"

"Sure, do you have anywhere in mind?"

"Jacksons, over in Crestwood? Or here again. I don't mind."

"Let's do Jacksons, we can keep alternating each time."

"Best of both worlds," she replied with a smile.

Carrington walked her to her car, and she waved at him as she drove off. She was feeling happy, her heart felt fuller, and she felt good about having Carrington around. Now she just needed to go home and convince Valorian to let him come on the hike - and that was going to be difficult.

CHAPTER TWENTY-FIVE

Freya arrived back home just before she received a message from Valorian letting her know he would be over in an hour. He wanted to see her before he opened the Emporium. She was nervous to ask him about Carrington and the hike - she didn't want to end up in another argument with Valorian - but he had promised he would make an effort with Carrington, and this would be good for the three of them, she could feel it in her bones. She left the front door unlocked so that Valorian could come straight in, and she set about preparing a cheesy pasta bake for them to have for dinner. She had the radio on low and felt the vibration of the door close downstairs. She rinsed her hands and walked towards the stairs. Valorian appeared beside her with a huge grin on his face. She sometimes forgot he could move so swiftly, and it gave her a shock but before she had time to react, he scooped her up and kissed her hard before releasing her.

"I missed you."

It took Freya a moment to find her voice, "I would never have guessed," she chuckled. "I missed you too."

"Smells good in here, what are you cooking?"

"Just cheesy pasta bake, nothing special."

"I highly doubt that. Everything about you is special."

"You are a charmer," she replied grinning up at him.

"How did today go with Carrington?" he said, taking a seat at the kitchen table.

"It was really good. I ended up staying there much longer than I intended, but we just clicked and talked about everything, and I didn't realise how late it was getting."

"I'm glad you had a good time. Do you have plans to meet him again? I would like to meet him, if possible, sometime. If he is important to you then it's important to me."

"Well, it's funny you should say that because I did have a favour I wanted to ask you. I have arranged to meet him the weekend after our hike, but how would you feel about asking him to join us? He mentioned today he would love to go hiking in the mountains, but he doesn't know anyone he could go with, and he doesn't think it's a good idea to go up alone."

"He would be right there, that place is not somewhere to go on your own. If you want him to come with us, then I'm okay with it."

"I thought it would be a good opportunity for you and him to get to know each other as well. In the long run it would make life so much better if you both got on."

"You're right it would, and I haven't been fair to him about my thoughts and feelings. I am willing to give it a go, if he wants to."

"I'll message him now." She smiled, walking around to give him a kiss on the cheek as she excitedly picked up her phone and sent a message to Carrington.

Valorian helped get everything ready to eat and Freya's phone bleeped back a message.

"Is that Carrington?"

"Yeah, he said he would love to come, and do we know what he will need as he has no equipment."

"Just forward him this message." Valorian got out his phone and sent a message to Freya. "I was supposed to send it last night, but I forgot. It's everything you'll need for the hike. He will need the same stuff."

"Brilliant, thank you," she said, forwarding the message. "This works out quite well because I am going to Hawthorne Hollow with Poppy tomorrow to get some stuff so I can visit the shop there and get what I need."

"They have a good range of things there. It's usually where we all get ours too so it should do you well."

"That's a relief, I was dreading having to order something to arrive in time."

They both sat at the table and ate while Valorian told her about some interesting stock he had managed to get hold of for the shop.

"These items are from the sale of an old property. It is rumoured the lady who resided there before her death was a 700-year-old Witch," Valorian explained.

"Wow, that's really cool. If it is true, there must be all sorts of wonderful magic items," Freya replied.

"I know, I thought the same."

"Would you mind if I help you with it all?"

"No, I would love it actually. I will wait until you finish work tomorrow and we can make a start."

"That's great, thank you," Freya replied.

Valorian stayed long enough to watch the first half of a movie before he had to leave to open the Emporium. Freya decided to have a nice bath and get an early night, ready for meeting Poppy early in the morning.

Poppy's car horn beeped, as Freya frantically searched for her keys, suddenly remembering that she had left them on the stairs when she had come home the previous night. She ran down and grabbed a jacket and picked them up off the stairs. It was misty outside; the sun was still burning its way through, and she didn't want to be caught out without a coat if it rained.

She got into the car.

"Hey, morning. Sorry about that. I couldn't find my keys."

"No problem, it's not like you kept me waiting for an hour like Anderson did yesterday," Poppy said, rolling her eyes as she pulled off down the road.

"Oh no, what did he do?"

"He was supposed to come over to mine while we had the house to ourselves, but he got caught up playing some video game with Silas and was an hour late."

"Ouch, I hope he apologised at least?"

"Oh, he did, and brought me flowers but still, he missed out on alone time."

"I guess that is punishment enough." Freya laughed.

"For me too though!" Poppy said, her high-pitched voice making Freya laugh more.

It didn't take them long to arrive in Hawthorne Hollow. Poppy disappeared to collect the supplies in from the bakery and Freya went to the hiking shop. She managed to get everything she needed and scouted out a few extras just in case. She wanted to be as prepared as possible. It was okay for the others, they all had experience (apart from Carrington), but she didn't know what to expect. She trudged her way back to Poppy's car and put all her bags in the boot then sat in the car waiting for Poppy to get back.

The car door opened, and Poppy passed a tray of warm baked pastries and cakes over to Freya then slid into her seat.

"Fancy going to Jackson's for lunch once we've dropped all this stuff off?"

"Yeah, sounds good," Freya replied.

The drive back was quick, and Freya went to put all her bags in her apartment while Poppy took the tray and dropped it off at the café.

Jacksons was fairly quiet, as it was just before lunch. Anderson, Eric and Rusha were sitting at the table close to the window.

"Hey, guys," Poppy said as she caught sight of them.

"Hey," they all replied.

"We were just about to order food and drinks, you two want anything?" Anderson asked.

"I'll have cheesy chips and a coke please," replied Poppy.

"Urm, cheese and onion toastie for me, with a coke as well please, Anderson," Freya replied.

"Okay, back in a minute."

"Nice to see you out and about, Rusha. I was starting to think you'd forgotten about us," Poppy said, smiling.

"Work and doing this university course aren't leaving much

time for anything at the moment."

"I bet. How is the course going? Surely you don't have much longer left?"

"About eight months, then I am done."

"What are you studying?" Freya asked.

"Veterinary medicine. I want to open a vet once I am qualified."

"Oh wow, that's great. Here in Crestwood?"

"Yeah. I want to move over from Hawthorne. For now, it's better living with my parents while I finish my studies, but with work being here and there being an empty shop which - fingers crossed - doesn't get rented out, it would be great to set myself up here."

"And you'd be closer to all your friends," Poppy said enthusiastically.

"Exactly," Rusha replied.

Anderson came back to the table with a tray of drinks for everyone. Freya thanked him and took a sip of her drink. The group talked about the upcoming hike and plans that they had for the summer. Poppy and Anderson were hoping to go abroad for a week somewhere hot, and Eric had decided to stay local this year so he could save for a snowboarding holiday later in the year. Freya hadn't given any thought as to summer - or beyond next weekend. She wondered whether Valorian had any plans to go away this year, and she thought that perhaps they could go away together. Though she didn't like the thought of leaving Mael, even if he was capable of looking after himself.

Deep in thought, Freya hadn't seen Beatrice approach the table. She shifted uncomfortably while Beatrice spoke to Poppy in hushed tones. Freya picked up her glass as Beatrice turned towards her.

"I suppose Poppy hasn't managed to convince you to join us?" She looked directly into Freya's eyes.

Poppy's eyes widened as Freya looked from Beatrice to her and back again, composing herself.

"No, she hasn't. Poppy is a great friend, and we don't discuss it, as she respects my boundaries," Freya said, heatedly.

"Yes, I am sure she does. Your boundaries just happen to be

ridiculous, which is the problem." Beatrice said, with a touch of venom.

"Look, Beatrice. As I have told you once already, I am not interested in joining you. I don't particularly care what you think of me, or my reasons for living *my* life the way I see fit. Personally, I find your harassment is becoming a bit of a problem and I would appreciate it if you would refrain from speaking to me or about me again," Freya said loudly, emphasising her words.

The electric lights flickered as Freya struggled to contain her emotions.

"Fine. I won't ask you again but don't come crying to me when you sort yourself out. The Coven wouldn't want Witches who negate their magic," Beatrice replied, her face slightly flushed. She turned and strode out of the café.

Poppy let out her breath.

"Wowsers, that was a bit heated. I've never seen anyone shout at Beatrice before. I thought her head was going to explode."

"I'm sorry, I just wish she would give it a rest. It's nothing to do with her."

"I know. She's a hardcore, old-time Witch. She doesn't understand a lot of things, though she is brilliant with magic."

"I'm sure she is. Can we just forget about this and enjoy our drinks?"

"Absolutely," replied Poppy as she took a big swig from her glass."

As time ticked by, Jacksons filled with more people. Freya found her eyes wandering to her phone more frequently to see if Valorian had messaged her yet as he always did when he woke up. It was dark out now and she knew it wouldn't be long before she heard from him. Rusha had left to go home, and Eric followed not long after. Freya was starting to feel like a third wheel as Anderson and Poppy were whispering and giggling to each other in the corner. She saw her phone light up with a notification. Finally, Valorian was awake. She sent him a reply saying she would be right over and said goodbye to the lovebirds.

The door was locked when she arrived at the Emporium, but the lights were on. She knocked quietly on the door and Valorian popped his head up from behind the counter and came over to let her in.

"You got over here quickly," he said, opening the door for her.

"I just really wanted to see you, that's all. Plus, I was getting a bit bored while Poppy and Anderson flirted with each other at Jacksons, and everyone else had already left."

"Ah I see, did it make you want to come over and flirt with me?" He winked.

Freya scoffed. "Ha, yeah, sure it did," she said, wrapping her arms around him and squeezing his bum.

"You are a terrible flirt, Freya Lockchild."

"Evermore. Freya Evermore."

Valorian cocked his head, questioning. "Oh, you decided to go back to using Evermore?"

"I have. I should never have stopped using it. I'm ready now though. It's my family name and I should wear it with pride."

"I like it, Freya Evermore," he said, kissing her lips.

"And I like that," she said, her eyes closed and a dreamy expression on her face.

"Well, don't get too used to it just yet, we have many boxes to unpack, and I am dying to see what's in them."

"Come on then," she said, walking towards the back room.

Valorian locked the door and followed her.

There were two large boxes on the back-room table, they each took one and started to open them. Freya was telling Valorian about her day as she stripped bubble wrap from various items. She picked up a smaller bubble wrap packet and slid out a black velvet box. She jumped up onto the counter, crossing her legs as she looked at it. There was something about it that drew her in, as she carefully opened the box. Inside lay a delicate gold chain bracelet with a small amethyst in the centre of a gold flower setting. She took it out of the box and immediately a sense of calm washed over her as peace settled through her core, through her bones. She knew it was bewitched; she could feel the magic in the item.

"Valorian, come here a sec please."

He put down the lamp he was holding and walked over to her.

"What's up?" he asked.

"How much are you going to sell this for? I want to buy it."

"You can't buy that."

"Why not?"

"If you want it, keep it. I haven't priced anything up yet and that would look amazing on you."

"Are you sure?" she asked.

"Positive, it's really pretty."

"Hold it, tell me if you can feel what I feel."

Valorian took the bracelet in his hand and closed his eyes.

"Serenity," he replied.

"Yes, I felt it too. Inner calm, balance, peace. I love it. It must be bewitched, but it would help me control my magic, if I am calm, I can't react too emotionally."

"Are you sure that's wise though, didn't Holden tell you not to suppress your magic?"

"He did, but he didn't say I couldn't suppress my emotions."

"Hmmm, I'm not sure."

"What if I take it for him to look over, see what he says? Will that make you happier?"

"It would."

"Okay, I will do that in the morning," she said, taking it back and putting it in the box and slipping it into her bag.

The rest of the boxes didn't hold anything else as interesting, just random figurines, statues, books and random furniture pieces.

The next morning arrived bright and sunny. Freya sat eating breakfast in the kitchen with the box next to her, she opened it clumsily with one hand and ran her finger around the chain. Again, the sense of peace flowed through her. She planned to leave early, and head over to see Holden, popping into Spellbound for some of his favourite cake on the way. This bracelet could help solve her problems, especially where magic was concerned, and it would be nice to not have to worry about being intimate with Valorian all the time. If there was one thing she was certain of, it was that this could change everything.

CHAPTER TWENTY-SIX

The street was unusually busy as Freya made her way to Spellbound café. Her bracelet was stowed safely in her bag, and she was in a good mood, smiling at everyone she saw along the way. It was the first time she had ever seen a queue in Spellbound, and Poppy looked flustered.

"Everything okay?" Freya asked, reaching the counter.

"Yeah, all good. Just busy. It's not usually like this but everyone seems to be out and about today. What can I get you?"

"Slice of cake, boxed please, I'm on my way to see Holden so I'm taking a bribe with me."

Poppy laughed. "Probably for the best." She passed Freya a paper bag with the boxed cake in.

Freya paid and told Poppy she would catch up with her later.

The walk to Holden's was relaxing, and Freya enjoyed seeing all the signs of spring on her way. The flowers had started to bloom and there were fresh green shoots everywhere. Holden's house stood out less against this backdrop, compared to the first time she had seen it in the winter.

The door opened as she walked up the path - Holden must have seen her coming. She took a step inside the dark kitchen, the one small window barely let any light in with its windowsill full of plants. Holden sat at the table.

"Hello, Freya," he said, not looking up from whatever he was reading.

"Good morning," she said, putting the bag on the table for him.

"You sound happy, things must be going well, I assume?"

"Things are good, yes."

"How did things go with Carrington?" he asked, finally looking up at her.

Freya took a seat, "Things are going really well. We get on very well and he is interesting. I'm so glad I gave him a chance."

"That's good to hear, I am glad that it is working out for you. So how can I help today?"

"Me and Valorian were unpacking some new stock for his shop, it came from an old lady who was rumoured to be a Witch. I came across a bracelet, and I think it is bewitched to make the wearer feel calm. Valorian gave me it and I promised him I would have you check it over before I wear it. I thought it might help with my impulse control when it comes to emotions and my magic."

"I see. You've brought it with you?"

"I have," she said, plucking the black box from her bag and pushing it on the table towards him.

Holden took out his monocle and opened the box, carefully not touching the bracelet while he looked over it.

"There doesn't seem to be anything extraordinary about it, do you mind if I take it out of the box and get a feel for the magic?"

"Feel free, do what you need to."

Holden took the bracelet out of the box carefully and held it in his palm. He placed the other hand above it and a violet mist formed between his hands. Freya watched, and as she did so, something within her tugged and she realised she was envious. It was the first time she had watched magic being performed since her parents' deaths - and she wished she was using hers. She pushed the feeling down and focused on Holden. His eyes were closed, and he was utterly silent. The mist faded and he opened his eyes, placing the bracelet back in the box.

"Well, it is perfectly safe. You are right, it is bewitched but with a simple serenity spell."

"That's good then. So, it won't cause any issues for me to wear it? Valorian was concerned after the warning about suppressing my magic."

"No, you will be fine wearing this. All it does is feed your inner calm. Your magic can still be used, this will just help tame those extreme feelings."

"Thanks Holden, I really appreciate it."

"It's not a problem, though it was an easy enough thing for me to do and you could have done it yourself if you would just allow yourself to use the magic within you."

"If I used the magic within me, Holden, I wouldn't need to wear the bracelet, would I? But as I've said, that isn't going to happen."

"As you keep saying but you will have to face it one day. You can't hide from it, it lives inside you."

"I can try though, for as long as I possibly can."

"So be it, just remember, I am here if you want to talk about things."

"Thanks, if I ever do, I will let you know."

"Is that cake in that bag?" Holden said, changing the subject.

"Of course. You didn't think I would come out here and not bring you some, did you?"

"I'd like to think not." He gave her a crooked smile. "Would you like to stay for a cup of tea?"

"Yes please, that would be lovely." As Freya replied, she wondered whether Holden was lonely. The fact he had asked her to stay for a drink made her think that maybe he didn't want her to leave just yet.

Freya enjoyed Holden's company. They talked about her family as they had their tea, and she felt closer to them just hearing his stories. The way he spoke about Everlyn made his face light up, and Freya felt such sadness for him. He had never married, and once Everlyn had left, he had started keeping to himself more and more as time went on.

She hoped that she would have this sort of love, one that

endures throughout time. She loved Valorian, but it was still early days yet and she didn't want to get ahead of herself. He was, after all, a Vampire and she would never live as long as he would. She hated the feeling of being apart from him, knowing one day she would pass to the other realm, and he would remain here on earth.

The sound of her phone ringing pulled her from her thoughts.

Holden stopped talking and looked at her, waiting for her to answer the phone.

She picked it up and saw Carrington's name on the screen.

"Hello," she answered.

"Hi, it's just me. I wanted to check something with you quickly. I'm in the shop buying supplies for the weekend and it occurred to me I will probably need food, should I grab some of these MRE food portions for you as well, or are you okay?"

"Hmm, I totally forgot about that. Could you get me a couple too then please?"

"Of course."

"Thanks, Carrington, I don't know what I would have done if you hadn't thought of it."

"It's not a problem, I almost left without thinking about it. Thankfully the lady was putting them over near the door, so they caught my eye as I was about to leave."

"She probably knows people forget," Freya said with a giggle.

"Probably." He laughed back. "Anyway, I must get going. See you at the weekend."

"Okay, see you then, and thanks again," she said, pressing the end call button. "Sorry about that," she said to Holden, putting the phone back in her bag.

"It's fine," Holden said, wiping cake crumbs from his shirt.

"Me and Carrington are going hiking with Valorian and some others at the weekend. Neither of us have been before and we almost forgot to take some food with us. Luckily Carrington remembered and grabbed some for us both."

"The lovely dry stuff the army use, how delicious," he said sarcastically.

"My thoughts exactly. Better than starving though."

"Barely." He chuckled.

Freya smiled, she had never heard Holden really laugh before and it was a lovely sound that tinkled through the air. "I should really get back now, I have work later and have some shopping to do beforehand," she said.

"It was lovely to see you and thank you for the cake. I could get used to your visits if you keep this up."

"You are more than welcome. Thank you for checking the bracelet for me. It will put Valorian's mind at rest."

"Anytime."

Freya left, shutting the door behind her. As she walked back, she made a mental note of all the things she needed from the shop; she had neglected going for a while and was almost out of food and toiletries. The town was still busier than usual, a group of tourists were taking photos of the old buildings with the backdrop of the mountains. It was rare that she saw out-of-towners here and they looked out of place. She hurried past them with her shopping bags and quickly unlocked her door. Tourists often had a habit of trying to stop people and talk a lot and she didn't want to end up in an hour-long discussion about how beautiful the mountains looked.

She unpacked the shopping and then sat with a cup of tea at the kitchen table. She took out the bracelet from her bag and slid it onto her arm. Now she knew it was safe to wear, she didn't really want to be without it. The delicate gold glinted in the stream of sunlight coming in through the window. It was so pretty; the owner must have really liked it for it to still look this pristine. She let the peace flow through her as she made a late lunch, picked up her book and relaxed on the sofa before she had to get ready for work.

The week dragged on, despite work being busier than usual. Freya had invited Carrington to come and have dinner at her place on Friday evening. They would be setting off for the hike as soon as darkness fell. She wanted to make sure they had eaten well beforehand and had bought everything for a roast dinner. Valorian was going to be coming over to get to know Carrington before they left and to double check that they had everything that would be needed. The weather hadn't been great, torrential downpours over Wednesday and Thursday had left them unsure if they should go, but the Mountain Rescue team had given them the all-clear as long as they didn't stray from the well-known paths.

Freya took the chicken out of the oven and slid in the tray of Yorkshire pudding batter. The bell rang from downstairs, and she knew it was Carrington. She opened the door, and he stood there kitted out in his hiking gear with a huge backpack on. They went upstairs and he took off his jacket.

"It smells really nice in here. Thanks for inviting me."

"I thought it was best if we had a good meal before leaving."

"Good idea. Here's the packets I got you the other day. There wasn't much choice in flavours, I'm afraid."

"I'm not sure you can tell the difference between them anyway." She laughed. "Thank you."

"You're probably right there."

"Dinner will be about thirty minutes; I've just put the Yorkshires in. Valorian will be joining us, he wanted to check over our gear before we left to make sure we have all the safety stuff set up properly."

"Great, it would be nice to introduce myself properly this time."

"Yeah, rather than me running away like last time." Freya sighed.

"Ah, I can't blame you. I should have been upfront from the start instead of looking like some random stalker determined to buy your shop. I guess neither of us made a great first impression."

She smiled. "Nah, but we got there in the end."

He returned her smile.

"I have something to show you. I found it in one of Everlyn's old photo albums," Freya said as she took out the worn album from the bookshelf and opened it, picking up a photo tucked inside. "It's a photo of her and your grandfather when they were younger. I can't tell if they were together then. I'm not sure who the other people are except for Holden." She pointed towards a man standing next to Everlyn."

"Wow, they were young here, probably no older than fifteen or sixteen I'd say."

"That's what I thought. The black and white is very grainy, so it's hard to see proper detail, but I think this is the only photo of them both together. At least on this side."

"I don't have any either and I didn't find anything like that going through my dad's stuff when he passed away."

"We should get a copy, so we have one each. It's a great reminder of our ancestry."

"I would really like that. I know my dad would have loved to see this. Even though he married my grandmother, I am sure my grandfather went to his grave still in love with Everlyn."

"That's so sad. I can't imagine what it must have been like for them both, or how hard it was for Everlyn to leave him behind and give birth without him."

"Me either," he said, looking at the photo sorrowfully.

Freya heard the door shut downstairs and walked over to the top of the stairs as Valorian came around the corner. He looked up and smiled at her.

"Hey, beautiful, smells like you've cooked up a treat."

"Hey," she said, melting into his arms when he reached the top of the stairs.

They walked into the living room. Carrington stood up and walked over to Valorian, holding his hand out to shake.

"Hey, nice to officially meet you," Carrington said and smiled at Valorian.

Valorian smiled back and offered his hand.

"Nice to meet you properly."

"Thanks for letting me join you on this hike, I'm really looking forward to it."

"It's no problem. Looks like it's going to be good weather for it as well, thankfully," Valorian replied.

"Shall we eat? Then we can go through all our stuff," Freya said.

"I'm ravenous so yes, let's," Valorian replied.

The three of them made their way into the kitchen. Freya started plating up all the food and set the plates on the table.

Valorian took a seat next to where she would sit while Carrington took a seat opposite. Freya put the jug of gravy on the table and sat down.

They made small talk as they ate their meal. Carrington asked Valorian about life as a Vampire and Valorian asked Carrington about where he had grown up. Freya smiled to herself, they seemed to be getting on well, both making an effort to get to know more about the other and she was finding out things about both of them - which was an added bonus. Valorian and Carrington cleared away the pots once they had finished and Freya poured them all a cup of coffee.

"Shall we go through to the living room then and look at all this stuff?"

"Yup," Valorian said.

"What time do we leave?" Carrington asked.

"We are meeting Eric at the forest in about an hour," Valorian replied.

Valorian went through both of their backpacks and checked everything was in order. Freya went to get changed into some thermals and hike appropriate clothing. She tied her hair into a braid and secured it with a hair tie. She laughed at herself as she looked in the mirror.

"Just your regular Lara Croft," she said to herself.

Back in the living room she picked up her small knife and secured it into her special belt.

"I think I am ready," she said.

"Me too. I just need to fill up my water bottles."

"Oh, that reminds me to grab mine from the fridge."

Once they had repacked their bags, Freya checked everything was turned off and they set off, picking up Valorian's stuff from his place on the way past.

CHAPTER TWENTY-SEVEN

They walked towards the mountains and the trees became thicker. Valorian used a torch to light the way ahead of them. After about twenty minutes, they could see Eric waiting in the distance, a torch on his hat giving his position away. They introduced Carrington, then made their way up the side of the smaller mountain in front of them.

"This is the smallest and easiest one to climb. Once we get to the top of here, we will be going around the middle of the next one to climb further from there. In summer we would usually go up this next one but it's too treacherous with the snow, especially after the rain this week," Valorian said, taking his steps next to Freya.

"Okay."

"You'll probably need the walking pole once we get up here, it will help steady you around the side. The drop isn't too sheer but if you lose your footing, it's a long fall."

"How long will it take to get up this one?"

"Usually a couple of hours. Once we are at the top, we will have a drink stop and a short rest. We ideally want to make it around the next mountain and halfway up the next climb before daybreak. There is a ledge we usually camp on, which we are aiming to get to before we set up camp."

"How do you stay safe out of the daylight to sleep?

"I have a custom designed blackout tent, so no light gets in and it has a sensor on the inside, which shows me when it's safe to leave."

"Oh, that's pretty cool," she replied.

"Yeah. Carrington and Eric will stay together in Eric's tent, and you'll be in mine."

"Okay, sounds great," she replied.

They climbed higher. Freya noticed that it got colder the higher they got. The night was clear, and the moon shone brightly, much to her relief. She had been sceptical about hiking during the night, afraid that she would end up putting her foot in the wrong place and falling to her death, but surprisingly, it was quite light, and they all wore torch bands around their heads, which helped. She wasn't used to walking uphill and she was already starting to feel a burning sensation in her thighs. The four of them walked on silently. Valorian and Eric made it look easy, and Freya was glad to have Carrington along as he seemed to be struggling as much as she was. *If it's like this now, I'm dreading seeing how it'll be up the next climb.*

They reached the top and it was time for a small break. Freya put her hands on her knees and gulped in a few deep breaths. The snow was halfway up her calves, and she was thankful that she had opted for the calf-high boots rather than the ankle-high walking boots.

Valorian dusted off a huge boulder for them all to sit on and have a drink while enjoying a much-needed break.

"You see that path just there?" Valorian asked.

"The narrow one that looks dauntingly deadly?" Carrington replied.

Valorian laughed, "Yes, that one. Well, that's what we need to take to go further up. It winds around the side of the mountain"

"Well, that looks fun" Freya said with a grimace.

"I'm going to check it out and see what its like," said Eric.

When he came back, he shook his head at Valorian.

"It's more slippery than usual. I think we could get out the harnesses and ropes and ice-pick around."

"Okay, better to be safe than sorry," Valorian agreed.

"What's happening?" Freya asked Eric nervously.

"The way around is a little more dangerous than we are used to, so we are all going to strap on a harness and be attached to each other with safety rope. I will go first and use the ice-pick to help, and you and Carrington will go in the middle with Valorian at the back. That way if anyone falls, we all have a counterweight to stop them sliding down the hill."

"Are you sure it's safe enough to be going?" Carrington asked.

"Yeah, it will be fine but since you two aren't experienced we want to make sure it's as safe as it can be for you both."

"I think I actually prefer this method, looking at how narrow that is," Freya responded.

They finished their drinks and rested for long enough to start feeling the cold creep back in. Valorian and Eric pulled out the ropes and harnesses and linked everyone together.

"This should take us no more than four hours, if nothing gets in our way, and we don't come across any issues. Once we get to the next part, we will have a small climb to the place where we will sct up camp." Eric said.

Freya followed Valorian and they carefully made their way onto the narrow path. They walked slowly, making sure no-one tugged at the rope between them all. Eric led the way, using the ice-pick to keep him steady. Freya kept her hand against the snowy mountain wall to her left, making sure she watched every step she took. The snow glistened as the light from her headlamp reflected off it. There was what felt like a thin watery layer covering it. She assumed it was a mixture of the rain and the warming sunlight during the day. The side of the mountain was still and silent. All she could hear was the snow crunching under their feet, and their heavy breathing. In some ways she was grateful not to be climbing further up, as this allowed her legs to settle after the initial climb. The magic of the bracelet was working its way through her system; she knew without it she would probably have been a quivering mess at the prospect of doing this for hours.

"You doing okay there, Freya?" she heard Valorian ask.

"Yeah, I'm good. Just concentrating and trying not to die."

"That sounds like a very good idea."

"I wish I was a Vampire, I bet this is nothing to you."

"Well, no it isn't, but I like to make sure my activities are as human as possible. Where would the fun be in just breezing through life?" Valorian replied.

"I guess I can see your point. It would get boring pretty fast."

"And when you live forever, you have to make forever different."

"I never thought of it like that," she replied.

They carried on in silence. The pace of their walking was just enough to keep Freya from feeling the icy chill. The dark sky was full of clouds, and she prayed that it wouldn't suddenly start raining. As they made their way around a corner, Valorian pointed out the ledge on which they would be stopping for the night. From this distance it looked like it was barely big enough to fit one person on - never mind two tents full of four people. She was glad to be nearing the end, her legs felt like they were lead and she was very thirsty. There was only a few more hours of darkness left and soon the sun would start to rise. She couldn't wait to go to sleep - at this rate they would struggle to wake her, and she hadn't even hit the hardest stretch of the mountains yet.

The ledge now sat just to their right. At this point the mountain climbed up higher and was too steep for them to go around the side.

"Right, guys, we will keep on the ropes for this, but I want more length between them. I will go up first and then Carrington. Only one at a time. It will be tough, but it is a fairly quick climb," Eric called back to them.

Eric made his way up to the ledge like a monkey, it took him only fifteen minutes. Carrington was next, his long limbs taking him up quickly. Freya looked up at them both. She closed her eyes and took a deep breath, taking in all the power of the bracelet, and started to make her way up. Her foot slipped and she almost fell. Gripping the uncovered stone jutting out of the rock face, she carried on. Even though she knew Valorian would catch her before anything happened, she still didn't want to fall.

She made it to the top safely and lay across the ledge panting, relieved she was finally able to rest.

"That was tough," Carrington said, sitting beside her.

"It was. My legs are like jelly on fire," she said.

"I feel you, mine are the same. I guess I underestimated how tough it would be."

"Yup, tomorrow will be worse too, climbing to the top of that," she said, pointing to the summit that looked as if it was hundreds of miles away.

"I'm sure it will be worth it."

"Definitely," she replied.

Eric and Valorian set up the camp. They pitched the tents next to the wall rock face and then made a small fire. Eric, Freya and Carrington sat around it trying to warm up while Valorian prepared them some food. They ate in silence.

Freya started to regain feeling in her toes as she stifled a yawn.

"Right, I'm off to go sleep. I'm shattered," Carrington said, getting up and making his way to the tent.

"Me too," said Eric, following Carrington.

Freya climbed into her and Valorian's tent while he doused the fire outside. He had made the inside cosy with an inflatable mattress, sleeping bag and blanket. Once he was inside, she quickly snuggled down into the sleeping bag, wrapping it tightly around her. Valorian wrapped his arm around her to help keep the warmth in. Within minutes she was fast asleep.

Freya felt someone shake her awake. She groaned, sticking her head under the cover.

"It's time to wake up, sleepy head. We need to make a move if we want to make it back here before sunrise."

Freya groaned again. Her entire body was stiff and aching.

"I hurt," was all she managed to say.

"I know you do, but it will hurt less once you get moving, I promise. I've made you some warm porridge and a tea."

"Thank you. Can you pass them here so I can eat in the small amount of warmth I have got?"

"Of course. Do you want the doors open or closed?"

"Hmm, open, otherwise I will see literally nothing in here it's that dark."

"Great, isn't it?"

"It is actually." She smiled.

She ate her breakfast while listening to Eric, Valorian and Carrington talk.

"It will take around three more hours to get to the top," Eric said.

"Okay, that's not too bad. I am looking forward to a longer rest," Carrington replied.

"This part is probably the worst bit. It's rocky terrain but we will take it slowly, and make sure we are all safe as we go," Eric said.

"Okay, I trust you both. I just can't wait to get to the top now."

Freya glanced down at the bracelet on her wrist, grateful for its presence. She got up and got herself sorted. They planned to leave the tents here for the following night, which is where they had decided to stay before heading back. She stood looking around her as she came out of the tent. Below her she could see the snowy mountains reach down to the trees and Crestwood vaguely in the distance, all the streetlights showing where it was. Further round she could see Hawthorne Hollow, dimly lit. From this height they looked much closer together. The views were beautiful. She really wanted to see the sunrise in the morning over this and see what it was like when she had daylight to clear the way.

"Stunning, isn't it?" Carrington said.

"It is. I am going to try and stay awake to watch the sunrise over it."

"Great idea, mind if I join you?"

"Not at all, if we can stay awake after today."

"I have to admit, I am not looking forward to this next climb."

"It'll be fine, but I am not sure how I am ever going to walk again once I get home. I hurt all over."

"Eric said we need ice baths. Apparently, it helps - but I find it very unlikely I will want to sit in ice given that I haven't felt my feet in almost 24 hours." He laughed.

"Yeah, not a chance am I sitting in a bath of ice. I'd be lucky to get out of bed. I should have taken an extra day off work, but I go back in on Tuesday."

"Ouch. Hopefully you will feel better by then. Despite all the pain, this is a great experience, and I can't wait to get to the top."

"Me too. All those views! I bet it is magnificent."

"You two ready?" Eric shouted.

"Yeah," Freya replied. She put on her rucksack, and Valorian secured the safety harness around her waist, and they carefully started making their way up the mountain.

Freya's breath was coming in short bursts, the air getting thinner the higher they climbed. Her hands stung, gripping hold of any rocks she could find, and her feet pulsated with the cold. She kept her head down and carefully watched where she stood, making sure she followed Carrington and Eric's footprints. Valorian followed behind her, occasionally asking if she was okay, to which all she could do was grunt. It felt like they had been climbing forever. The sky had grown darker, and the moon was reaching the highest point in the sky, letting off glowing light. Finally, Freya heard Eric shout.

"We are at the top now guys, just that little push more."

Freya felt excitement course through her, she carried on at the same pace, not wanting to risk speeding up in her excitement. When she took that last step over to the flat uneven ground, she let out a squeal. The air was so thin it made her lightheaded, but it smelt fresher than anything she had ever smelt before. She could see all around her, waiting for clouds to pass below them to get a view of what lay beneath. She felt elated, she hugged Valorian whispering to him,

"Thank you," to which he replied by kissing her lips. She turned around and saw Carrington, a look of awe spread across his face. She walked over to him.

"This is breathtaking," he said as she approached.

"Worth that hike of hell," she replied, grinning at him.

"I can't thank you enough for letting me come with you all."

"No need. I am really glad you are here," she said, touching his arm.

Valorian joined them.

"Thanks, Valorian, this is truly amazing."

"You're welcome. I'm glad you came; it's been nice getting to know you," Valorian replied.

Freya looked up at him and thought her heart was going to burst. This was the best night ever. For the first time since her parents' death, she felt complete. Everything was coming together and having these two getting along was just the most wonderful thing. She grabbed Valorian's hand and squeezed it, and he gave her a wink. They all took seats on the various uncovered rocks and enjoyed a snack and some water while looking out over this glorious view. Freya tried to capture it as much as possible in her memories. She thought about how much she would love to see this during the day, and she decided that she was going to start hiking regularly so she could come up by herself when it was safer.

As they enjoyed the peace, disappointment settled in Freya as Eric told them it was time to make their way back down to the camp. They had to be careful going down as gravity could easily catch them off guard as they worked their way down. Freya took one last look before making her way over to the side and starting the slow descent to base camp. The journey took just under four hours and by the time they reached the bottom they were all cold and hungry. Valorian made up their food packets and passed bowls around and they all ate in silence. Freya's mind was abuzz with the joy of the day - she knew she would be sad to leave the place despite wanting to get home and warm. Her legs still burned, but she felt lighter than she had when they started, and her muscles were starting to get used to the pull of the climb.

Valorian and Eric went to bed while she and Carrington sat watching the sun come up, illuminating the scene below them. They could see much further in the light. The sky turned from black to orange to blue in subtle hues melting into each other.

"I'm glad I stayed awake for this," she said.

"What a day to see all the wonderful things," he said.

"Now this is what I call magical," she said, turning to smile at him.

"It really is."

As the sun started to make its way further up in the sky, Freya and Carrington decided it was time to get some well-earned sleep.

CHAPTER TWENTY-EIGHT

Freya woke, relieved that her aches had now settled a little and her body wasn't so stiff. Valorian was sleeping softly next to her. She opened the tent to see that darkness was starting to fall. Eric was sitting beside the fire, and he offered her a sleepy smile.

"Morning," she said.

"Morning," he replied.

She grabbed the coffee from Valorian's rucksack and put the kettle on the fire to heat.

"Want one?" she asked.

"Go on then," Eric replied, passing her his tin cup.

"It rained while we were sleeping, then the sun came out, so today's journey across the mountain is going to be a tough one, it will be particularly slippy."

"Oh, that's not good. I'm assuming we will be using the rope and harness again then?"

"Yeah, but we would have anyway, I just hope it hasn't loosened the snow too much. I want to get down the mountain but not that way." He laughed.

Freya could sense his apprehension, and she rolled the bracelet through her fingers, allowing its magic to ease her stomach. She was just pouring her coffee when Valorian stuck his head out of the tent, his hair wild and untamed. She giggled.

"Sleep well?" she asked.

"Uh, yeah, I think I did," he said, yawning.

She poured him a coffee as he came to sit beside her. Not long after, Carrington joined them. Eric filled them in on the situation and Valorian offered to go first this time as his immortal abilities would prevent them from falling if the ground was too dangerous to pass. Freya would go behind him; he wanted to make sure she was in reach if the worst happened.

They packed up their belongings and fastened themselves together. With Valorian leading the way they took their first step onto the narrow path. Thankfully this side of the mountain wasn't as bad as they had expected and they didn't have any issues, but once they made their way to the opposite side, which had been in full sunshine all through the day, small channels of water ran down the mountain and over the path. They had to carefully step over them as they walked. Freya gripped the rope tying her to Valorian, taking steady breaths. She took a step over the water and her foot slid from under her. She fell, and the rope pulled both Valorian and Carrington. Carrington shouted her name and, in a flash, Valorian was there heaving her up back onto the path, fear and concern etched across his face. He held onto her tightly, his body shaking. She breathed out deeply, and squeezed him.

"I thought my cold dead heart was going to come out of my mouth then. I've never been so scared," he said into her hair.

"Oh my god, that was terrifying," she replied.

Her heart beat rapidly, the sweat on her skin turning cool under her clothes. Her legs wouldn't move, and goosebumps dappled her skin. Fear. She felt it spread throughout her like poison, her breath turning shallow and her eyes wide. She pulled back from Valorian. She was scared to let go of him but she needed to check. She pulled back her sleeve. The bracelet had gone.

"What's wrong?" Valorian asked.

"The bracelet, it's gone. The one I was using to keep calm, to not worry. It's gone and I can't move from this spot."

"It's going to be fine. I will see if I can find it, but don't panic."

Valorian moved around her, checking the snow for signs of where it had fallen off, but he couldn't see it.

Freya tried not to panic but she could feel it mounting inside her - not just the fear but the magic too. She was scared, her stomach felt like it was doing flips. Her skin prickled.

"Valorian," she said loudly.

He turned to her, the fear on her face making him stop in his tracks.

"What is it, Freya? What's wrong?"

"I can't control it. I can feel it coming. The magic."

"Close your eyes, tame it, control it. You ca—" Carrington said from behind her.

His words were cut short by the unleashing of the magic within her, as bright purple light pulsed from her hands up towards the sky.

CHAPTER TWENTY-NINE

They had never seen anything like it. Purple light shone around them - blocking out everything so that they couldn't even see each other. The air crackled with intense energy so loud in their ears they couldn't hear the rumbling that grew closer. As the light started to dim and the magic was expelled, they finally heard it. Shock registered on their faces.

Freya looked up at the mountain - just in time to see a wave of snow heading straight for them. She dropped her head, locking eyes with Carrington in the moments before she was whisked away. She screamed his name as Valorian appeared out of nowhere, grabbing her and pulling her to safety. The last thing she saw before she was carried around to the safe side of the mountain was the wave of snow washing over Carrington and Eric.

Valorian sat her on the ground, checking her for injuries, running his hands through his hair. She could tell he was scared, and she sobbed, burying her head in her hands. *This is all my fault. I caused the avalanche and now Carrington and Eric are probably dead.*

"I need to go back and see if I can find them," Valorian said, his voice shaky.

Freya said nothing as he sped off in the direction of where she had last seen the others. Her body felt alive, the buzz making her stomach roll. *I can't believe this happened! I'm so stupid, why didn't I listen when Holden told me not to suppress my magic? Why did I think I knew better?*

After what felt like a long time, Valorian reappeared, kneeling in front of her. "I can't see them or hear them under the snow, Freya. I checked the top of the mountain – where the snow came from - and it's stable now."

"What can we do? We need to get help."

"By the time I go get help and get them here, it will be too late. We need to look for them. But I am going to need you to help."

"I'll do whatever I can. This is all my fault. If there is a chance they are alive I want to help."

"I'm going to need you to use your magic. I know how you feel about it, but I can't do this without you."

She stood up, wiping her eyes on her coat sleeve.

"I said I would help; just tell me what you need."

He picked her up and took her to the spot where they had last seen Eric and Carrington.

"I can dig, but I need you to control the snow, so it doesn't cave in on me or cause another avalanche. I need you to protect me with your magic as I go in. Can you do that?"

"Yes, I think so. I can create a magical force field around you, which will hold the snow in place, it should give you enough space to get them both out."

"Are you sure? Do you have the energy? We might be here for a long time, there is no guarantee they weren't pushed further down."

"I can do it, but first let me see if I can sense Carrington. I can try and get my magic to connect to his, then we will know where to look."

"Okay," he said, his face paler than usual.

Freya closed her eyes and took in a deep breath then held her hands out in front of her. Violet smoke snaked out from her fingers and gently caressed the snow in front of them, stretching out in wispy talons before receding back into her palms.

"They are under there. I can feel him faintly. He is still alive, but his energy is dimming."

"What about Eric? Could you sense him?"

"No, I couldn't, but that doesn't mean the worst. He is non-magical so I can't pick up his energy the same way."

"Okay. You ready? I'm going in."

Freya nodded and stretched her arms out again, palms facing the sky as the violet mist spread out encapsulating Valorian. She opened her eyes and nodded at him. She was ready.

Valorian used his bare hands to dig at speed, aiming down to where the path would be.

Freya felt sweat bead down her temples as her magic stretched, rusty from lack of use. She had forgotten how good it felt to let it flow through her willingly, to not fight her very being. She felt strong and powerful. Her body relished the magic's touch. She could feel Carrington's energy getting stronger. *Valorian must be closing in on them now.* She could feel the snow pushing against her, resisting the barrier she had put between it and Valorian. She kept feeding her magic, giving it the energy it needed. She closed her eyes, praying that it would be enough and that Valorian would find them both alive.

A jolt shot through her as she felt Valorian come into contact with Carrington. He had made it. Carefully, Valorian headed back toward Freya, and she saw him exit the tunnel he had dug. Eric lay across his arms, unmoving. It felt as if a rock had dropped into her stomach, and she felt her legs start to buckle.

"He's alive but unconscious. Stay strong, Freya. I need to go back for Carrington."

She breathed out a sigh of relief as he placed Eric down safely before going back in.

Freya could feel her magic waning, and she knew it wouldn't be long before it would give way to the pressure of the snow.

Valorian came back out. Carrington had his arm around Valorian's shoulder, limping.

Once they were both in a safe place, Freya moved backwards, keeping her magic in place. Once she reached them, she stopped fighting, letting the snow cave in on the tunnel. She flopped down on the floor at Eric's side. His pulse was weak.

"You need to take him now," she said to Valorian.

"I know, but what about you two? Can you stay here until I get back?"

"Don't worry about us, leave the bag here and we will figure it out," she replied.

There was a trickle of blood coming from Carrington's nose, but he only nodded at Valorian. Valorian nodded back, picked Eric up and left at speed.

Freya turned to Carrington. "Carrington, I'm so sorry. What can I do to help you, where are you hurt?"

"It couldn't be helped, Freya, you didn't do anything on purpose, please don't blame yourself."

"Eric could die, Carrington; it would be my fault"

"Don't focus on that right now. Can you search the bag for a bandage? I need to find some support for my leg, I think it's broken."

"Sure. I wish Poppy were here, she practices healing magic."

"Have you checked for a signal? Perhaps you could call her."

Freya grabbed her phone from the coat pocket, realising that she hadn't even considered checking the signal. She sighed with disappointment.

"God dammit, no signal," she replied, stuffing the phone back in her jacket.

"We could try linking but it requires magic, and you've just expelled a great deal so it might not work."

"What's linking?" she asked.

"If you can see Poppy's face in your mind, I can try to contact her through you. But you need to open your magic up to link with mine in order to be able to connect to her."

"I've never heard of it, but we can try."

"It's a rare talent, not many Witches have it."

Freya moved closer to Carrington, sitting directly next to him. He took her hands in his and held them.

"Just close your eyes and picture her in your head. You'll feel my magic when I start, okay? Just don't break the connection or get distracted as it will sever the image and break the link."

"I can do this."

"I know you can."

She closed her eyes and thought of Poppy, an image filling her head. The blonde hair and smile bright enough to light the world. She felt Carrington's magic weave its way through her. It filled her head with immense pressure, he was very powerful, but his magic felt familiar. She could feel their familial bond through it, it mingled with her magic, and she shuddered at the feel of it, the power of it. As Carrington withdrew his magic, she felt empty as it receded, her own magic now spent.

"All done. You can open your eyes now," he said.

She blinked and looked at him.

"Did it work?"

"Yes, I told her where we are. She's going to get help and come for us."

"Oh, thank god."

They had managed to shuffle into a slightly wider part of the narrow path while they waited. Freya was exhausted but she tried to keep Carrington awake, worried that he might have concussion or a head injury; she didn't dare let him sleep. The bleeding from his nose had stopped and he said he only felt pain in his leg, but she knew things could sometimes appear to be fine even if they weren't. They huddled together trying to stay warm as the stars glistened overhead. The night seemed to last forever. She knew it would take time for Poppy to get here with the rescue team, but it felt much longer than a few hours. Carrington had fallen asleep, despite her best efforts to keep him awake. She wasn't sure how much longer they could sit here like this. She pulled out the sleeping bag from Valorian's bag and laid it over them to try and keep them as warm as possible. With her magic spent, and Carrington injured, neither of them could muster anything to help. She had just closed her eyes when she heard voices. Her eyes flew open, and she carefully stood, making her way a little further down the path. She had never been more relieved to see Poppy, Anderson, Jackson and Marly walking towards her. She turned around and went to wake Carrington.

"They're here," she said, the relief evident in her voice.

"Thank god, can you help me up?"

"I can, but I think you should stay there for a moment, let's see what the plan is first. This path is already dangerous enough without us risking you slipping down there with your injured leg."

She looked at the mountain side below them.

Jackson and Marly arrived first, leaving just enough room to allow Poppy to get around Freya.

"Are you hurt?" Marly asked, concern written over her face.

"No, no. I'm fine. Carrington is hurt though. I think he has a broken leg and possibly a head injury. He was bleeding from his nose."

She looked over to him. Poppy now knelt by his side, her hands hovering above his body and a pale-yellow light radiating from her palms.

"I can't help him," she said, turning to Freya. "His injuries are too severe, and I am not trained for this level of healing magic yet."

"Okay, Freya, can you go with Poppy and Anderson, they will take you down to the bottom. Me and Jackson can take care of Carrington," Marly said, taking charge.

"I don't want to leave him," Freya replied.

"I know you don't, sweetheart, but this mountain path isn't big enough for all of us and we need to shift to get him down safely. It's best if we just meet you at the bottom."

Freya looked at Carrington.

"It's fine, Freya, I'll see you at the bottom. She's right, it isn't safe up here for us all."

Freya nodded and moved carefully to stand with Poppy, who enveloped her in the biggest hug. It looked like she had been crying. Anderson patted her shoulder.

"What on earth happened?" Poppy asked as they started making their way down the mountain.

Freya told them what had happened. Anderson frantically tried to call Valorian to get an update on Eric, but he wasn't answering. It took them just over two hours to reach the bottom, where they found Marly, Jackson and Carrington already waiting.

"How did you get here before us?" Freya asked.

"Let's just say Jackson is a man of many forms," Marly replied with a small smile.

Freya walked over to Carrington, who looked pale and tired.

"We need to get you to the hospital," she said.

"Already taken care of, I'm going to drive him now, we

thought you would want to come," Jackson said,

"Yes, I do," she replied. "Poppy, if Valorian comes back here looking for me can you tell him where we are? My phone has died."

"Of course. Don't worry, we've got this," she said hugging her friend again.

Freya jumped into the front passenger seat next to Marly, as Jackson got in the driver's side, put his keys in the ignition and started to drive.

CHAPTER THRITY

Freya slumped on her sofa. Exhaustion had hit her like a brick, and she desperately wanted to sleep. It was one-thirty in the afternoon, and she had just got back from the hospital. Carrington had suffered only a broken leg, but he was being kept overnight to rest. She had visited Eric, who was resting in the room next to Carrington, with a serious concussion. They were so lucky to have got away otherwise unscathed, but the guilt that Freya felt gnawed at her soul. *I was so careless. I jeopardised everyone's safety and I'll never forgive myself for it.* Barely managing to pull herself up, she went to the bathroom, splashed water on her face and changed out of the clothes she had been in since starting the hike. Rinsing her body off in the shower she dried off, got changed and took herself to bed.

Sleep didn't come easily, and after an hour of tossing and turning, Freya reluctantly got out of bed. Despite the tiredness that she felt, guilt ate at her, and she was unable to switch off the part of her brain that kept replaying the moment the wave of snow had hit them over and over again - and then fretting over how much worse it could have been.

She knew she would not be able to face anyone in Crestwood today - if ever - and an idea crossed her mind. If she went back to the city, she wouldn't have to face the disapproving stares of the people she had grown to care about. She could deal with this feeling of shame elsewhere. She hadn't even been in Crestwood for six months and she had already caused a near fatal accident by not listening to others and being stupidly stubborn. She couldn't find Mael, so she left the window on the latch for him to come and go. *I've already offered him his freedom, now he can take it.*

Marching into the bedroom she opened her hands as the familiar violet smoke uncurled from her palms. She had missed this feeling, and she quickly moved her hand in the direction of her wardrobe, using the magic to pull out her holdall. She packed up as much as she could fit in there. Grabbing the old grimoire, journal and a few other items she shoved them into a tote bag before picking up her handbag off the sideboard. Freya put her mobile phone down, leaving it behind, and then went down to the shop below. Looking out of the window to make sure no-one was around, she left the property, locking the door behind her and walking quickly to where she had left her old rusty car when she had arrived in Crestwood. Pulling the car keys from her handbag she unlocked the door, throwing her bags onto the back seat, and then sat in the driver's side. She put in the key and turned the engine; it spluttered a few times before giving out entirely. The battery had died. She got out quickly, flipped open the hood of the car and put her hands on the battery, channelling her magic into it. After a few minutes, she jumped back into the seat and tried to turn on the engine again. This time it came to life, purring gently, and she breathed a sigh of relief.

She took the road leading out of Crestwood, sadness filling her heart. I thought I'd found a home here and now I'm leaving it behind, but I just can't face everyone. They said they didn't blame me, but I blame myself - and I know they'll all think differently of me now. Carrington was my family; he had searched for me for years and then I almost got him killed. He deserves better than me and so do the others. She thought about Valorian, and her heart contracted, the pain that she felt leaving him was almost too much to bear. He had become her hero in many ways. Not only saving Eric and Carrington the night before but in saving her from her grief. He had given her hope and focus. She hadn't expected to find love, or friends, when she left the city, she had just wanted to get away from everything that reminded her of her parents. But in spite of herself, she had found them. She loved Valorian more than she had loved anyone before. And then there was Poppy, who had become her best friend, and Marly who had become a solid, caring and wise friend. She would even miss Holden and his grumpy ways. Blinking back the tears, she continued to drive herself back to the city, slowly leaving behind the mountains and trees of Crestwood Falls.

CHAPTER THIRTY-ONE

It was dark by the time Freya arrived back at her old house. The tall three-story building was gloomy and uninviting. A place she had called home her entire life now felt like a stranger. She took her bags from the back seat of her car and found the front door key tucked in the side pocket of her handbag. She opened the door, and a draft of cold, stale air greeted her. Mail scattered around on the floor as she entered, and she shut the door, leaving behind the light from the street. She flicked on the light switch to her left and the hallway illuminated. She put her bags on the floor next to the stairs as she walked past and into the main living room. Using her magic, she lit the fireplace and switched on some lamps. Looking around the room she saw a fine dust had covered all the surfaces. She walked over to the fireplace and picked up a photo of herself and her parents when she was younger and wiped the dust from the glass. She ran her thumb along the face of her mother and tears started to fall unbidden. She sat on the edge of the sofa as she sobbed.

"I have ruined everything, and I miss you so much," she said out loud through her tears.

"I can't do all this without you, I've made mistakes, I need you both. Why did you have to go do this stupid job?" She raised her voice angrily.

She got up and went up the stairs, her parents had always told her never to go into the magic safe they had hidden in their bedroom. Ever since she was a small child, she had wondered what they kept in there, and now she could find out. She knew the magic to unlock it would now rest with her as their next of kin - and this felt like a small act of rebellion.

She stomped her way to the top of the stairs and across the landing to their room, a simmer of anger running like a current under her skin. She pushed open the door. Familiar scenes flickered through her mind, and she felt sadness and grief rush up from her core, smothering the anger she had been feeling seconds ago. The room was exactly how it had been left the morning her parents had gone out. Her mother's bathrobe hung on the hook for the ensuite door, her father's slippers sat at odd angles next to his side of the bed. She felt as if her heart would stop beating if she looked at the room any longer.

She flicked on the light switch, the room illuminated, and she went over to the dressing table and looked in the mirror. Tiredness showed on her face, her skin was pale and her eyes red from crying. She placed her hand under the mirror, palm against the wall and whispered the words of magic she had heard her parents use many times:

"Let me see what is unseen,
Let me open what is locked,
My family, my bond, please let me in."

Before her eyes the mirror disappeared, and a hole started to materialise in the wall. She waited a few minutes while the magic worked. Leaning closer, she looked inside. It was empty except for a manilla folder. Freya's eyebrows pulled together; she was sure her parents kept more in here. She picked up the folder curiously - its edges were worn, and it had something weighty inside it. There was a post-it note attached to the front which read, *To Freya, When the time comes, Love M&D*. She could see it was her mother's handwriting.

She made her way back downstairs and over to the sofa and sat back down. Slowly peeling back the opening, she looked inside and there was a brown folder, which she pulled out. She flicked it open and realised it was one of her parent's case files from when they worked as the Coven's Guardians, only this time it was a file on members from The Coven of the Crescent Moon – their own Coven. She read the pages and realised her parents had been investigating some of the members for using dark magic. And it didn't stop with them, there were links to powerful members of Nebula, the organisation which ruled over all magic and supernatural beings. Her parents had left no instruction or guidance for her but the tiny flicker of doubt she once had about their deaths suddenly felt enormous. *Could this be why they died?* She put the file back in the envelope and thought things over, reliving moments with her parents in the short time before their deaths, trying to seek clues about what they could have been doing - but there was nothing there. They must have been keeping what they were doing close to their chests. As her mind kept going over details of Coven meetings, trying to remember if she had overlooked something obvious, her eyes became heavy, and she slowly fell asleep on the dusty sofa.

The next morning dawned bright and sunny. Freya had spent some time dusting the house and cleaning up after her absence. Feeling fresh after her shower she sat at the kitchen bar with a large cup of coffee and the file from her parents. She had wanted to tidy the house up and get herself sorted before she read it over again more thoroughly. She flicked through the pages, reading her mother and father's handwriting, their scribbles on the pages, and she wished they were there with her. She noticed her dad had written in one of the margins: 'Storms are a good way to clear the air." The sentence felt out of context. Closing the file, Freya went up to her parents' bedroom and started to look around, mulling over the comment her dad had left. She found a photo album on a shelf in her parents' wardrobe, and she started to leaf through it. It was her parents with various friends and other members of the Coven. Deciding that there were no other clues in the room, Freya took the photo album downstairs.

Back at the kitchen bar she began to realise that she was in way over her head with all this information. So many questions were running through her mind about what was going on and whether this file had something to do with her parent's deaths. She realised that she needed help - and that the only people she trusted were back in Crestwood Falls. Picking up the phone off the handset, she dialled Poppy's mobile number, grateful that she had memorised it before Valorian had given her the mobile phone she had left behind in Crestwood.

"Hello." Poppy's cheerful voice sounded down the earpiece.

"Hey, it's Freya."

"Oh my god, Freya, where on earth are you? Everyone was so worried last night when you hadn't been at home. Valorian is going out of his mind."

"I went back home to the city. I just... I couldn't face everyone, Poppy. After what happened. It was all my fault, and I have ruined everything there."

"Oh, Freya, you really haven't. It's not like you did it on purpose, it was an accident, and no one is blaming you, or is angry with you. We're just concerned about you."

"I honestly couldn't have lived with myself if something worse had happened."

"But it didn't happen, did it? Eric is fine and back at home now and other than a broken leg, Carrington is fine. Please come home, Freya, you belong here with us," Poppy pleaded.

"I know I do. I miss you all too. Being here last night felt so lonely."

"Then get back in that rust bucket and head back, you can be here before midnight if you leave soon."

"Okay, I will. I'll pack up some bits here and come back home. Thanks, Poppy."

"You're my best friend, Freya, you don't need to thank me. Shall I let Valorian and Marly know you are heading back?"

"Yes, please. Can you all meet me at mine around one o'clock? I have something I need to speak to you all about."

"That sounds ominous but of course, I'll let the others know. They'll be glad to hear you are safe and well."

"Thanks, Poppy. Right, I best get going so I can make good time on the road. See you tonight."

"See you soon," Poppy said before hanging up.

Freya felt a swell of love in her chest. Going back to

Crestwood was the right thing, she decided. *I'll just have to swallow my pride, face everyone, and apologise – because I can't face never going back there again.* She knew deep down that Crestwood Falls was home.

CHAPTER THRITY-TWO

The car groaned as Freya made her way down the narrow country road. The trees grew thicker and taller as she made her way into Crestwood Falls, and she felt a sense of calm wash over her. She was home. She parked her car in the small car park behind Burt's where it had lived for months previously. She wheeled the huge suitcase down the road behind her, full of items she had picked up from her parent's house - mostly herbal supplies, clothes and the photo albums from her parents' wardrobe. Fishing out her keys, she heard footsteps behind her. Turning, she found herself face-to-face with Valorian.

He looked at her, his face showing echoes of concern, and then his lips tilted upwards. He moved at speed to her, wrapping his arms around her and inhaling the scent of her hair as she let herself be enveloped in his love.

"I've been so worried about you," he said.

"I'm sorry, I just needed to get away. I feel so awful about what happened."

"You've nothing to feel bad about, accidents happen. I couldn't bear it if you never came back."

"I realised that I can't leave this place. This is my home, my family, and I love you, Valorian. Can you forgive me?"

"There is nothing to forgive." He moved, breaking them apart, "Come on, let's get you and this suitcase inside before everyone turns up and we have to have mushy reunions on the street corner." He smiled softly.

They went up the stairs and Freya felt immediate relief to be back in her familial home. She had only been away for a night, but it had felt like much longer. The last few days had exhausted her. She knew that once she had seen the others and had told them what she found out, that she would sleep for a long time.

Valorian put the suitcase in the bedroom for her, while she put the kettle on. She flicked her wrist towards the fire, and it lit instantly.

"Glad to see you are using your magic again."

"It was stupid of me not to, and look what happened."

"Everyone is alive, everyone is safe. What happened, happened and in time you'll have to stop beating yourself up for it."

"I know, and I'm so glad everyone is okay. I realise how stupid I've been though, trying to hide from who I am. And I had forgotten how good it felt to use my powers."

Valorian smiled. "Everyone will be here soon; we are all very curious about what you wanted to tell us."

"That reminds me, I need to grab something from the suitcase. Can you put those mugs on the tray? I thought I'd set up the tea service so we can all have a cuppa while we talk."

"Of course."

Freya opened the suitcase and removed the manilla folder. As she was about to head back, she heard Poppy and Marly's voices downstairs. Valorian must have heard them as well, and by the time Freya returned to the living room he had already let them in.

Poppy grabbed Freya, squeezing her into a hug, and then Marly did the same.

"I want to apologise to you all. I shouldn't have left, and I didn't mean to worry you. I just needed some space. I hurt people - unintentionally or not, it was my fault. I have something important I want to talk to you about if you can forgive me?"

Freya said, tears slipping down her cheeks.

"Of course we forgive you, we care about you, you banana," Poppy said, hugging her hard.

"Exactly what she said," Marly said, patting her arm.

Valorian smiled and winked at her, a sign that all was good between them. They all sat while Freya poured tea.

"My parents kept a magic safe, and while I was at their house, I unlocked it. I thought I should check on it – and also, curiosity got the better of me. I found something that I think I'm going to need help with."

"What was it?" Marly asked.

"This." Freya placed the manilla folder on the table, "It's a file my parents were keeping on the members of our Coven. It looked like they were doing their own investigation into the use of dark magic - and I think this could be why they died."

"Oh shit," Poppy said.

"Can I take a look?" Valorian asked.

"Of course, you all can. I don't know what to do, I have so many questions. I always thought something was off about how my parents died - and if someone from the Coven had suspected they were doing an investigation into them using dark magic then it would definitely have put a target on their back."

"Absolutely, dark magic is forbidden now, it would make them huge targets. This is really bad," Poppy said.

"It looks like they collected quite a lot of evidence, but I don't think they knew who it is that's controlling it all. There are some links to The Witches Council though, so this is much bigger than a local Coven issue," Marly chipped in, as she read through the file

"That is why I can't investigate this alone. I have to find out what happened to my parents. This folder is telling me there is more to their deaths than I thought and this whole thing is much bigger than I could have ever anticipated."

"I'll help," Marly said.

"You don't need to even ask," Valorian added.

"You can count me in," said Poppy. "It might be worth trying to make amends with Beatrice though, I have a feeling she could be very helpful with all this," she added.

"I'll think about that. I do need to tell Carrington though. I'll go see him tomorrow."

"I'll drive you over as I have to go pick up some books from the Witch Book shop near the hospital."

"Great, thank you."

Freya saw everyone out and made her way back upstairs to Valorian.

"I am so tired."

"No offence, but you look it too."

"Thanks," she said, with a hint of sarcasm.

"Let's get you to bed."

"Don't you need to go open the shop?"

"Not tonight, all I need is to lay next to you while you sleep."

She smiled up at him and made her way to the bedroom. It felt good to be back home, among her friends and new-found family. She felt strength in their bond and using her magic again filled her with a sense of pride. She placed her head on Valorian's chest and closed her eyes, enjoying the comfort he brought as she drifted off to sleep.

CHAPTER THIRTY-THREE

The next day Freya visited Carrington in hospital, inviting him over to stay with her while he recovered. She told him about the file she had found at her parents' house, and he agreed to help her uncover the truth. She spent the rest of the day getting the spare room ready to collect him later that night.

The following morning, Freya busied herself in the kitchen, preparing breakfast for them both, as Carrington hobbled into the room.

"Morning," he said.

"Good morning. Bacon and eggs?" she asked.

"Would love some." He grinned, "Thanks," he said, perching on the bench at the kitchen table.

"Marly has given me the rest of the week off, so I don't have to go in later."

"That's nice of her."

"She's a great boss, and friend. I'm lucky to have met the best people since moving here."

"Yeah, trust me when I say that doesn't happen often. When I moved to Hawthorne Hollow, I was met with disdain from most people when they found out who I was."

"That's stupid - it's not like they even knew you."

"I know, but people have long memories. I was actually wondering what your thoughts were on my moving to Crestwood? I noticed there is an apartment to rent above the convenience shop."

"That's my old apartment. I wouldn't have an issue with you moving here. It would be great," she said as she served up breakfast.

"I also had another idea but I'm fairly certain you probably won't be interested in this one."

"Go on," she said, sitting down.

"The shop downstairs."

"You still want to rent it?

"Yes and no. I was thinking that perhaps we could open it together, as a way to keep the memory of our ancestors alive. Obviously, it would be your shop, but I could help you run it."

Freya went quiet as she gave it some thought. She had been avoiding opening the shop herself, as she had known that once it was open it would need to be some sort of magical shop. It had always been with her family and that couldn't change. Not using magic herself had left her feeling that it wasn't something she could do - but now things had changed.

"What sort of shop did you have in mind?"

"Well, my research shows that there isn't a good herboristerie in Crestwood and there's only a small apothecary in Hawthorne Hollow. It would also fit with how it was used previously too."

"Do you think that it would work?"

"I can't see a reason why it wouldn't. With the uniqueness of this town and surrounding villages, we should never be short of customers."

"Hmm. I do enjoy my job, but it would be nice to work for myself."

"Does that mean you will do it?" he said excitedly.

"It means, I will give it some thought," she said.

I think it's a brilliant idea, Mael said as he fluttered down to the table.

"Eavesdropper." Freya smiled as she stroked his furry body.

"See, even Mael agrees with me."

"Men always stick together," she said, taking a mouthful of

eggs.

Freya finished eating, and took her plate into the kitchen, leaving Carrington and Mael deep in conversation about historical events, while she cleaned away the pans from breakfast. She plunged her hands in the hot soapy water, her mind wandering to the idea of running a shop. The more she thought about it the more she liked the idea. Not only because it would give her freedom, but because it felt like a way to honour her ancestors and show the town that the Evermores were back to stay. *I already know that I'm never going to leave Crestwood Falls now, so I might as well utilise what my family left to me. I could forage in the forest for supplies, and we could mix the potions and concoctions in the huge cauldron in the shop. This could be fantastic! And working alongside Carrington could be the icing on the cake. It'd give him a fresh start and show people that his family name doesn't matter, that we can settle any old family differences by coming together.* She knew right there in that moment that her answer was yes.

"I've made a decision," she said, walking into the living room.

Carrington sat up on the seat he was in, Mael on the arm of the chair next to him.

"Well, don't keep me waiting!" he said.

"Let's do it! Let's open the shop and put the past behind us and honour our family."

"Yes! Freya, this is fantastic."

Definitely a wise decision, Mael added.

Carrington and Freya sat for the rest of the day making plans. Deciding what to sell, how to set things up and how to move forward.

Mael went out to the forest to see what type of foragables there were.

They had already made great progress, and Freya couldn't wait to tell Valorian what they had decided.

The next couple of weeks flew by. Freya handed in her notice at the Cafe and Marly - despite losing an employee - was thrilled that she had decided to open the shop. She, along with Poppy, Anderson, Valorian, Silas and the fully recovered Eric helped Freya to set everything up downstairs. Carrington helped where he could, although he was still struggling with his cast on. They had decided to open when his cast had been removed and they planned an opening day celebration involving some of the other local shops. She found that slowly the hole that her parents' deaths had left behind was beginning to feel smaller and less deep, but she also felt closer to them than she had in a long time. They would have been proud of her and how she was moving forward.

She stood in the shop early one morning, looking around her at the well-stocked shelves, the list of potions on the chalkboard, flowers and herbs drying in bunches hanging in the windows, and she felt so full of love it overwhelmed her. Everything had come together, and she felt complete. For the first time in a long time, she felt true freedom, and her grief slowly ebbed away, giving in to the love and friendships she was making. She knew the months ahead would be difficult but the happiness she felt in that moment doused the rising anxiety about what was to come next.

Carrington came down the back stairs, his leg now free from the cast.

"Are you ready?" he asked, standing proudly behind the old fashioned till Eric had fixed up for them.

"I'm more ready than ever," Freya said.

She walked forward and unlocked the door. Outside stood Valorian, Poppy, Marly, Jackson, Silas, Eric and others she had come to know - and much to her surprise - Holden stood towards the back of the group. He lifted his hat and smiled at her as she welcomed everyone into Evermore's Herboristerie for the first time.

ACKNOWLEDGEMENTS

In a little unknown corner of the internet, a small Facebook group called The Fiction Cafe: Writers' Group was where my love for writing was rejuvenated. It was there alongside other members Wendy Clarke and Mooky that a weekly flash fiction challenge inspired me to once again put pen to paper, and for this I will be forever grateful. You sparked within me a light that I thought had dimmed forever.

I would like to thank all the readers and beta readers of Crestwood over the years in which I have worked on it, in its multiple iterations: Katie Wells, Maria Sinclair, Michelle Waite, Sue Shelton, Sarah Price, Michaela Deacon, and Wendy Clarke.

I would like to thank the admin team past and present from the Fiction Cafe Book Club, Wendy Clarke, Emma Louise Bunting, Jennifer Gilmour, Mooky, Pam Devine, Ellie Bell, Melanie Thomas, Sarah Price, Lauren Roberts, Michaela Deacon, and Katy Baldwin, for their support and encouragement and for providing a safe, wonderful bookish environment that continues to inspire and motivate.

My special thanks go to Stuart James, Jim Ody, Katie Wells and Sarah Price, Kirstyanne Ross, Sarra Cannon, Helen Dawson and Carlyann Price for the unwavering support, advice, and for being general superstars. Sometimes this world can be isolating and harsh but with friends like you, the skies are always brighter.

A massive thank you to Amy at Salpe Publishing for taking a chance on a little unknown author and making my dreams come true. You will never know the scope of my gratitude for what you have done.

Finally, to my Witches, Sue, Shell, and Hayley for being the best friends anyone could have. To my family and to my children: Adam, Chloe and Alexis and my partner Chris, and my mum. Without you cheering me on, none of this would be possible. Thank you for believing in me, I love you, always. And to my Gran, though you may not be with me any longer, you have and always were my largest supporter, I miss and love you.

To all those who buy or read Crestwood Falls, thank you for allowing me to share my world of magic.

ABOUT THE AUTHOR

Emma-Louise Smith is an academic, author, and believer in all things supernatural. She lives in the North-East of England with her children and partner.

An avid reader, advocate for disabilities, criminologist, and Autumn enthusiast, she is often found studying in libraries or writing in quiet café corners while drinking copious amounts of tea.

You can find out more at:

Substack: https://authoremmalouise.substack.com
Instagram: @thestationerygeekette
Tiktok: @authoremmalouise

Printed in Great Britain
by Amazon

59695917R00138